PLOUGHING POTTER'S FIELD

HarperCollins*Publishers*

HarperCollins*Publishers*
77–85 Fulham Palace Road, London W6 8JB

The HarperCollins website address is:
www.**fire**and**water**.com

This paperback edition 2000

1 3 5 7 9 10 8 6 4 2

First published in Great Britain by
HarperCollins*Publishers* 1999

A catalogue record for this book
is available from the British Library

ISBN 0 00 651285 2

Set in Meridien and Bodoni

Printed and bound in Great Britain by
Caledonian International Book Manufacturing Ltd, Glasgow

Since those times, it is only rarely that someone has talked to the angels of Heaven, but some have talked with spirits who are not in Heaven. It is with difficulty that these can be elevated. Yet the Lord does elevate them as much as possible, by a turning of love; which is affected by means of truths from the word.

Emanuel Swedenborg
(*Heaven and Hell*)

CLERK OF COURT: All rise. The court is now in session. The Crown versus Francis James Rattigan. Judge Richard Moorland presiding.

JUDGE MOORLAND: Francis James Rattigan, you have been found guilty by this court of the murder of Helen Julianne Lewis, and it is now my duty to pronounce sentence upon you.

Do you have anything to say before I do so?

RATTIGAN: We're all flies.

JUDGE MOORLAND (sighing slightly): Much has been said in this court over the last thirteen days which I'm sure has both distressed and appalled all present. I myself freely admit to being utterly horrified by the nature of your crime upon an innocent, unsuspecting woman. Indeed, I would go further, and add that without wishing to reiterate any of the lurid details of what took place on those three days last September, your crimes are without doubt amongst the most brutal acts of unprovoked violence it has ever been my misfortune to sit in judgement upon.

RATTIGAN (smiling): Bzzzz . . . Bzzzzz . . .

JUDGE MOORLAND (to defence counsel): Mr Sharpe, will you inform your client that another outburst will have him placed in contempt?

SHARPE: Yes, Your Honour.

RATTIGAN (singing): Old Spanish eyes . . . Teardrops are falling from your Spanish eyes . . .

1

JUDGE MOORLAND: I propose to ignore your sorry little diversion, Mr Rattigan. Indeed much has been made by your counsel with regards to your enfeebled mind. I find myself extremely loath to admit that evidence submitted by both independent and the Crown's own criminal psychiatrists forces me to uphold your plea of guilty via diminished responsibility. Though I'm sure, as I feel are many of us here today, that the legal definitions of 'mad' and 'bad' require some urgent reanalysis.

However, it's my job to dispense the law, not examine its workings. I am fully convinced that the graphic nature of your crimes horrifically indicates your permanent danger to society, and although at times like these I wish I had recourse to more traditional measures, I am forced in this instance to sentence you to indefinite detention in one of Her Majesty's secure mental institutions.

Take him down.

(Cheers from the public gallery, hurled insults, sobbing. Rattigan is surrounded by court officials. A scuffle breaks out.)

RATTIGAN (shouting above the din): Bitch done me down! Died too quick! Watched me die a thousand times!

Court Four, Old Bailey, London.
5th March, 1989.

PREFACE

'How d'it start? Christ's sake, stupid or something? Me old man gave me mum one. Nine months later, I dropped out of her cunt. Never done biology?'

The anatomy lesson you've just read was given to me by Francis James Rattigan during one of a series of interviews I conducted with him as a research student in September/October 1997.

Frank Rattigan – the Beast of East 16, intended original subject of my doctorate thesis in forensic psychiatry. Crude, offensive, challenging Frank. Dubbed 'Beast' by the tabloids – their game, not his, a circulation-inspired pseudonym, good for a couple of weeks until the next psycho arrived to darken the blood-red front pages.

Can't remember the name? The crime? Neither could I to begin with. Perhaps cynics might argue that there are too many Frank Rattigans around these days, too many 'beasts' loose on the streets. Today's psycho – tomorrow's chip-paper.

Then I was sent a thick brown file by Dr Neil Allen at Oakwood High Security Mental Hospital, prior to my meetings, stuffed with newspaper clippings, Rattigan's previous criminal record, crime-scene photographs, police interviews and a vast battery of psychiatric reports. After a grim few days spent digesting its often unpalatable contents, ten-year-old memories of an East End slaughterhouse resurfaced, a girl turned to porridge by a man who could offer no motive, save that he did what he did 'for fun'.

On the last page of the dossier was a photograph, the Beast himself, face set in a challenging sneer, eyes seeming to dare me to unlock the depravity which lurked inside. But the longer I looked, the more I became aware of something hiding behind the bravado – a sadness born out of the insanity which led him to his present incarceration. And as I immersed myself deeper into his enigma, I determined that there *were* answers to his crime, had to be, must be. I hardly dared to think that I, a humble student of the criminal mind, might find them; but the bait was down, I'd taken it, and ironically was hooked many years ago by a past which I'd refused to ever really acknowledge.

But what benefits does hindsight ever really bring? Looking back, I see myself as incredibly naive, suddenly excited by the chance of putting textbook theories into practice. I was finally being allowed into the real world, absolutely confident I had the necessary mettle to make it. I, Adrian Rawlings, imminent Doctor of Forensic Psychiatry, would 'solve' Rattigan. I would find the missing motive which had baffled the experts for so long.

Perhaps my desire to succeed was born from the ashes of failure, the ruins of redundancy. Maybe forensic psychiatry became a way of reinventing myself, a chance to analyse others without ever having to look too deeply at myself. But Rattigan changed all that, as surely as holding a mirror to my face.

Parts of this journal take the form of transcribed recordings made with Rattigan over two months during my initial thesis research. I've concentrated on passages which I feel are relevant – to Frank and myself. In reality, over seven hours of taped conversations exist. You may wish to hear them in their entirety. But I doubt it. His voice . . . corrodes.

It's almost impossible to really 'like' a person like Frank. His personality forbids it, couldn't cope with the affection. But perhaps somewhere in the recesses of our lost humanity, there lurks an untapped reservoir of empathy, made stagnant by the greed of the last hundred years. And sometimes, as I found to my cost, the only way to truthfully understand the motives of another, however distasteful, is to look into that dark pool and recognize a little of their madness in ourselves.

We simply have to be honest.

Adrian Rawlings.
December 1997.

1

Disinfectant. Pine Fresh. Dettol maybe

Floor polish, rubber soles squeaking on its brilliant, unyielding surface, heralding my anxious arrival.

And music, piped from God knows where.

I half laughed nervously. 'Sounds like a cheap supermarket.'

Dr Allen frowned. 'To you, perhaps. But to us it's a vital part of the regime. Acts like a clock. Covers of the Hollywood greats from nine till ten. Sounds of the sixties till lunch. Pastoral classical from one till three. Then a bit of New Age synthesizer to simmer things down before supper and medication.'

'The same every day?'

'Its purpose isn't to entertain, Mr Rawlings.' He walked two steps in front, as if keen to be rid of the awkward student following sheepishly behind.

'Dr Allen,' I tried. 'I really would like to say once again how grateful I am that –'

'I know.' He stopped, turned, clearly irritated that his time was wasted talking to a nonentity like me. 'Just don't make too much of it. We've had a lot of research students in Oakwood over the years. It doesn't always work out.'

A scream somewhere close by. I tried to appear casual, unaffected, though sensed Allen saw through the sham, caught the apprehension in my eyes, felt my fear.

'Much of this, of course,' he said, 'depends on Rattigan. Don't think that just because all the papers have been stamped that that's the last of it.'

Another scream. Much louder, closer. A woman? A white-coated orderly ran from one end of the corridor to a door somewhere behind. Then, after a moment – just the Muzak once more.

I tried hard to concentrate on the tall, thin, bespectacled doctor. 'Rattigan decides how far it goes. He doesn't like the look of you – it's off. That simple. Anytime he wants to end it, he can. He deals, Mr Rawlings, you play.' Allen held out a hand. 'We'll be in touch. My staff will inform me of your progress. And give my regards to Dr Clancy at the university, will you?'

He didn't wait for my reply, which was just as well, I had none, throat parched from fear and excitement. I tried my best to steady what fading nerve I had, standing before a stencilled door emblazoned RECREATION SIX. This was recreation? For whom? I felt myself falter, suddenly wanting to be back home, normalized, basking in the silence of an emptied house echoing to the pandemonium of the family breakfast.

But there was no time for second thoughts. This was the moment I'd waited for. Planned for. My meeting with the Beast, the man I'd done little else but read about, speculate over during the previous six weeks, the man who killed for fun.

My legs felt suddenly too light for the weight of my body. What the hell do I do now? Knock? Simply walk in? What would *he* look like in the flesh? What waited to greet me behind the door?

Ever the polite PhD-student-come-to-visit-an-insane-psychopath, I steadied myself, counted to ten silently, then opted to knock. Twice.

A voice answered. His? 'Come in,' it calmly instructed. Couldn't have been Rattigan's voice, surely? A beast would howl, wouldn't it?

The door opened.

'Adrian Rawlings?'

I nodded, watching as the big, bearded orderly waffled efficiently into a walkie-talkie confirming my visitor's-pass details with some unseen agent deep within the hospital. The Muzak changed to the theme from *Lawrence of Arabia*, in any other circumstances an old favourite of mine. Here it seemed tarnished, almost obscene.

He introduced himself as Warder-Orderly Denton. There were stains on his tunic and the black boots he wore smelt strongly of polish. I tried to act as casually as possible, avoiding the urge to peer over his shoulder at the other seated figure beyond.

Finally, the checks were complete. I was ushered inside.

Which is where I met my first surprise. It was just an ordinary sunny room, bland, institutional, innocuous. Not a prison bar nor wall-mounted restraining ring in sight. Just a room, rather like any of the uni.'s study rooms in the humanities building. It didn't seem possible. I wasn't naive enough to expect a medieval dungeon, but I'd imagined something a little more correctional. It seemed incredible that this room also held the Beast.

Next, I found myself taking a ridiculous interest in the grey lino tiling as Denton settled into a plastic bucket seat by the wall. I simply couldn't face looking at *him*, felt I still wasn't ready for an eyeball-to-eyeball encounter. But I knew he was there, caught another glimpse of the figure slumped disinterestedly behind a large table, watching, waiting for me to make the first move.

I gave it as long as I dared, then looked up, met his amused gaze, stared into the blue-grey eyes. And . . . there he was – Frank Rattigan – the Beast of East 16, alive, well. Full-colour flesh-vivid, not a ten-by-eight black-and-white. My second surprise of the morning. Gone was the arrogance I'd imagined to mask some telling sadness, replaced instead by a mid-fifties man, squat, puffy face and lips, balding ginger hair, clean-shaven, waiting for me to sit opposite and begin.

Silence all around. Just the three of us, alone in the room. I sat, making a show of taking items from my briefcase, placing them on the bare tabletop.

He was so close that I caught his breath on my face. Then, the moment came. I could delay no longer. I remembered my tutor Dr Stephen Clancy's advice – stick to the script, be in charge – and I tried to ignore my bone-dry throat and finally begin my first brush with the real world of forensic psychiatry.

'Have you been told why I'm here?'

Rattigan smiled. A normal-looking smile from a normal-looking man. 'Have you been told why I am?'

I nodded, acknowledging the quip. 'My name's Adrian Rawlings. I'm a postgraduate student currently undergoing work on my docorate thesis. My university has connections with this institution. Dr Allen passed a copy of your file to my tutor, Dr Stephen Clancy, for me to read. So yes, I'm well aware why you're here, Mr Rattigan.' I was pleased with the way it was going, but wondered why no one else appeared to hear the beating of my heart as acutely as I did.

Then suddenly, 'You're a pedantic little twat, aren't you? A "yes" or "no" answer would've sufficed.'

I silently counted to three before continuing, hoping the pause would stop me from running from the room. A trickle of sweat ran down my back.

'Good reading, was it?' The Beast goaded.

'Sorry?'

'My file?' Rattigan licked his lips, leant forward, brought himself closer. 'You married, Mr Adrian-fucking-Rawlings? Show it her, did you?' His voice dropped to an obscene whisper. 'Get her going, did it, Frank's naughty behaviour?'

'I'm here to ask you some questions. If you agree . . .'

'I'll get some fags and a few shitty privileges from these tossers.' Rattigan sat back, jerking his head at Denton. The cold eyes quickly resettled on mine. 'I know the fucking score. Been done a dozen times in here. Arrogant little pricks like you come to pick our brains to try and figure us out. Only I'm a little bit smarter than the average defective they've got banged up in here. And the way it's been painted to me, I'm the paymaster. I don't like the look of you and it's over. You have to find yourself another sicko to play with. So you'd better keep Frankie sweet, or I ain't gonna come out and play.'

I looked briefly across to Denton, who offered no support whatsoever. 'You are empowered to terminate the arrangement whenever you chcose. As am I.'

Rattigan smiled again, but this time his bloated lips parted to form a hideously darker, more sinister crack. 'What you got to understand, son,' he said softly. 'Is that I don't get many choices in this shitbin. I'm enjoying this. I could let you dangle for some time, couldn't I? You think we're getting on all right, do you? Going well, is it?'

I cursed myself for having no quick answer, feeling so easily exposed. To my right, Denton suppressed a yawn.

Rattigan sensed my hesitation, leapt on it. 'Never answered my first question. Very rude, that.'

I was hopelessly unprepared for the speed of his attack. 'I'm not sure I . . . ?'

The voice rose. 'I said are you fucking married? Hitched up?'

'I don't see what . . . ?'

'. . . that has to do with anything? Jesus Christ! How old are you?'

'Thirty-nine.'

He paused to laugh. At me. I felt stung by it.

'It was rhetorical, you cunt!' He laughed some more. Then stopped suddenly, milked a heavy silence. 'We have to develop a little trust, Adrian. A little rapport. I know what you want from me. The same shit all the shrinks want from me.' He tapped the side of his fat head. 'What goes on in here, right? What made me do what I did to the fly-girl. Now I ain't going to give that away lightly, am I?' For the second time his voice dropped to an acidic whisper. 'They think I'm low risk. Pump me full of shit to keep me sweet. But they're not there in the middle of the night. That's when my mind begins to wander, Adrian. That's when I want to go over stuff, know what I mean?' A long pause. 'No – I guess you don't. But you want to. That's why you're here.'

I finally found my tongue. 'Maybe. But . . .'

'Maybe – good word that. Like "maybe" I'd like to know more about your missus. Maybe I'd enjoy spending some time imagining all sorts with her.' He sat back suddenly. 'She goes for all that puppy fat, does she?'

'I'm sorry?'

'They've got a gym in here. You look like you could use it. Too soft. Too easy. How much do you weigh?'

'Is it important?'

'Close on thirteen stone: am I right?'

'More or less.' I hadn't bothered weighing myself in years, but I knew he was damn close. Unnervingly close.

'Height? About five-ten, yeah?'

Bang on the money. I attempted an unconcerned smile.

'Know how I know?' Rattigan asked. 'Because it's in me. Takes me about five seconds to suss any fucker, strengths, weaknesses. I look at you now, fat-boy, and I know all I need to know.' He closed both eyes, exhaled, then suddenly blinked them open again. 'Got any kids? Love kids, me.'

Denton moved slightly. 'Less of the pantomime, Frank.'

'Or what? Another month strapped to the fucking trolley?' Rattigan turned quickly back to me. 'A little trust, fat-boy, a little gesture is all I ask.'

'The cigarettes you'll receive,' I replied, struggling to prevent myself from cursing back. 'The privileges, they're the only gestures I can give. You're right. If you don't like me, you can end this, but that privilege is mine, too. You abuse me too often, and I'll inform Dr Allen.'

He aped at pretending to be scared, then instantly switched to concern. 'My life story for a few packs of fags. Bit fucking tacky, ain't it?'

'I don't make the rules.'

'What you here for, then?'

'It's part of my thesis. Work experience, they call it. With your permission, we'll meet once a fortnight when I'll ask you an assigned series of questions before asking some of my own. None of which you are obliged to answer if you don't wish to.' That felt better, building into a rhythm after the early derailing. I almost felt back in charge – for a moment.

'So what's her name, your missus?'

'I'm not allowed to tell you anything about my private life.'

'Yet you want to know everything about mine?'

'I want a doctorate.'

'Fair enough. I'll find it all out anyway.' Another nod towards Denton. 'See that cunt over there? Mr fucking charm himself? Bent as a fucking coathanger, he is. He'll tell me all I need to know. Quick poke around the guv'nor's office, and I'll have the lot.'

I glance at the bored warder-orderly whose eyes remained firmly fixed at his feet.

Rattigan continued. 'Names of your kids, ages, schools they go to, boyfriends, girlfriends, I'll know the bloody lot. Phone numbers an' all. Maybe give you a bell from time to time. Quick chat to the wife while you're fucking around studenting. That's the way it's going to be, Adrian. That's what you're starting with me. I'm going to crawl into your soul and . . .'

'Shut it, Rattigan,' Denton ordered, checking his watch and rising from the chair. 'Playtime's over. Let's get you back to the unit.' He turned to me. 'Mr Rawlings, if you'd like to make your way back to Dr Allen's office now, thank you.'

Dumbly, I complied, beginning to repack my briefcase, eyes doing their best to ignore the grinning, leering face before me.

'So,' Rattigan asked innocently. 'I think that went very well, don't you?'

'As I understand it, the decision's yours.'

'I like you. Gonna tie you in knots.'

'Perhaps. Perhaps not.'

'Listen to the fighting talk, I love all that.' Rattigan stood. 'Go on,' he said. 'Ask me any damn thing you like, and I'll give you the God's honest truth.'

An unprofessional impulse overwhelmed me. The session had apparently ended. Now wasn't the time to pursue anything, except a quick exit. But something in me had to ask, had to start somewhere. 'Why Helen Lewis? Did you know her?'

The Beast waved an admonishing finger. 'We all know Helen Lewis,' he replied slowly. 'Even you, fat-boy. Trouble is, you ain't done for yours. But I have for mine. And that bitch ain't never gonna . . .' He paused, frowned slightly.

'What?'

'Make sure they're Rothmans.'

2

'Jesus,' I said. 'I felt like he was unpicking me.'

'He probably was.'

'Any chance you could open the window?'

Two hours after my first encounter with Rattigan, Dr Stephen 'Fancy' Clancy sat in his college room pulling heavily on a slim panatella cigar. I had the beginnings of a headache, made worse by the exhaled fumes swirling within the confines of the chaotic little boxroom which laughably passed as his office.

I remembered vividly as a psychology undergrad, a mature student, thirty-two, clutching a photocopy of the Essex University humanities building floorplan, walking the humming corridors, searching for his room, buzzing with clichéd expectations of its high ceiling mounted on elegantly windowed walls groaning with dust-laden volumes offering valuable historical insights into the hidden workings of the mind. I expected a pickled brain in a bell jar at least.

But Fancy's 'office' was a toilet, even by his own admission. Blind always down, desklamp permanently burning – his attempt, he explained jovially when we first shook hands, to, 'Tardis my hutch into a tolerable space.'

He'd smiled, and I'd responded. I liked him. Still do. I began a friendship with my tutor that often included him coming over to my place for supper, or Jemimah and I visiting him and his wife Sheila in their Tudor house in Roxwell. In retrospect, I believe that the minimal differences in our ages helped forge the friendship – although at times, his devotion to the long lunch put it under certain strains. He drank – I didn't. Not any more.

'Sounds as if you found the trip out to Oakwood heavy going,' the tall, permanently tanned tutor surmised. 'From what you're saying, Rattigan appears ready to go, and you're the odds-on favourite stalling at the first fence.'

'He frightened me. Really. I felt exposed.'

'Good.'

'Good?'

'Adrian, he's a convicted killer. You aren't up there to become best buddies with the man.'

'I just thought . . .' But I was tired, the words failed me.

'You thought you'd walk in there, and he'd spiritedly comply with your every wish, utterly in awe of your academic prowess.'

'He called me a pedantic little twat. I felt like punching him.'

Fancy suppressed a smile. 'He's simply having some fun with you. Don't get so involved. He wants to see you again, so the job's done. He called you a few names, so what? Christ's sake, Adrian, you're a bloody good student. You have a keen interest in the malfunctioning mind. You wanted to meet him the moment you read the file. Positively salivating at the prospect this time yesterday.'

'That was different,' I wearily protested. 'That was yesterday. I just expected something different. Less challenging. He hates me. I must have spoken to him for no more than ten minutes at the most. Came out shaking like a bloody leaf. God knows how I'm going to get through an hour of it.'

Fancy sighed. 'Look, Adrian. No one's expecting you to unravel the man. It isn't possible. He's a psychopath. You know bloody well he operates beyond the conventional norms of any coded moral behaviour. Just go there, ask your questions, ignore the insults, get out. Business done. And remember, it's an exercise, invaluable work experience.'

He inhaled on the cigar again, a fairly pointless gesture. The tiny dishevelled room was so full of smoke, all he really needed to do was breathe in. I figured he'd unintentionally shared hundreds of cigars with me and countless other psychology students over the years.

'I felt hopelessly unprepared,' I admitted. 'They just more or less left me with him.'

'Like one of his victims?' Fancy stood, turned his back and flipped his fingers through the yellowed Venetian blind, absorbed in the flow of laughing undergraduates passing beneath his window. 'I know what you're thinking, Adrian. How you're out there, dealing with a real case. Your pivotal thesis study-piece. That I wasn't there in the room, that I didn't see the look in his eyes, feel the threat of his rhetoric. But you shouldn't have been there, either. Not Adrian Rawlings. Like I warned you and warned you, you should've left him in Doc Allen's office.' He turned suddenly. 'How is the old sod, anyway?'

'Allen? Sent his best regards. Caustic man, isn't he?'

Fancy smiled. 'Same old Neil Allen. Good, reliable, jaundiced Neil Allen. Which is exactly my point.'

'Oh?'

Fancy sat, and looked for one moment as if he was going to try to put both feet up on the cluttered desk. He opted for leaning back in the swivel chair, hands wrapped around the back of his head. A single plume of dark-blue smoke rose from his cigar, and I momentarily wondered if he might set fire to his hair.

'Neil Allen conforms to all our expectations of him. Slightly bitter, hard-working, reliable, professionally unexceptional, and altogether notionally sane. An all-around good egg. Plays off a seven handicap, you know. Excellent long putter.'

I nodded as if I followed golf.

'Frank Rattigan, on the other hand, has a personality seemingly designed to tease, humiliate and ritually mentally abuse the likes of those sent to gain access to it. But I'm afraid we might be crediting him with powers of which we have no proof. We suspect he revels in some kind of game with you. Whereas the reality is more soundly rooted in the explanation that he's completely insane. Crackers, utterly bonkers. We can't judge him by our standards and suspicions. Remember, it only becomes a game, old friend, if you agree to play it.'

I sighed, rapidly decoding the waffle. Rattigan's nuts – don't make him a clever nutter. 'Maybe.'

'We've all been there, Adrian. He's your chance to prove a hundred little theories you've secretly developed as a BA/MA student. Just don't rely on a loony, that's all.' He smiled, extinguishing the cigar at last.

I was reluctant to admit it, but there was more than a grain of truth in what he said. Rattigan was my chance, I'd felt it as soon as Fancy'd handed me his file. A real-life case study – a mine of horror and chaos waiting for my ordered explanation – my ground-breaking thesis. But we all think like that, don't we? We all want to make some sort of contribution, be the first to spot the obvious, develop it, redefine it, have it historically credited to our good selves. It's called making your mark. It's a base drive. Animal.

'He's bored,' Fancy announced. 'And the more you rise to the bait, the more he'll taunt and tease. Just stick to the script, get the thesis done and forget all about him.'

'What if I can't?'

'Can't?'

'What if he calls my wife when I'm out?'

'He won't. He'll be pulled from the interviewing process and his cigarettes and privileges will be withdrawn. Remember this is probably the most exciting thing that's happened to Rattigan in years. He's going to stretch it out as long as he can. Next time remember you're the one in charge. You can end it just as soon as he can. He'll soon toe the line. The interviews are about the only thing that give him a little bit of temporary status in the hospital.'

'How are they chosen?'

He stifled a yawn. 'Oh it's terribly top secret stuff, dear boy. Committee, proposers, seconders, Home Office types, specialists, the law, a whole plethora of . . .'

'I'm being serious.'

'OK. Basically, once a year, Neil Allen and I try to pair off a PhD student and an inmate.'

'And did you pick Rattigan for me? I mean specifically for me?'

Fancy smiled. 'You flatter yourself, Adrian. You suspect we, the sinister conspiratorial authorities, are at some sort of a loss to unlock the dark secrets of his mind. You see us labouring into the night, shaking our heads in weary defeat. Until . . . until . . . someone mentions Rawlings! Rawlings is the man for the Rattigan job!'

'Piss off,' I laughed, enjoying the energy of Fancy's pantomime. 'I just, you know . . .'

'Neil Allen sends me a few files on selected members of his client group. I sift through them, pass the occasional one on to students I feel would benefit from the experience. It's really that simple. Like I said, just stick to the script.' He stood and squeezed past me to unhook his coat from the back of the door. 'Hopefully you'll get another set of letters after your name, after which you may be some sporadic use sat before a police computer compiling some godawful national nutter database, with which to recognize psychotic characteristics at any number of crime scenes.' His coat was on and buttoned. 'Now,' he said, checking his watch. 'They're open. Buy me a drink and anaesthetize me before my undergrad lecture this afternoon.'

'. . . and during subsequent testing and further detailed psychoanalysis, the subject retained a continuing indifference to the crime of which he is currently accused.

'Indeed, throughout my investigations the subject proved himself an able communicator and was well acquainted with the potential outcome of his present situation. His thoughts and opinions were mostly ordered, and he showed little reticence in mentally revisiting the crime scene.

'However, the prolonged ferocity of the attack itself, the abnormal levels of violence perpetrated on the victim point to a mental psychosis borne out by the subsequent psychological analysis.

'Again and again the subject was confronted with the possibility that his attack was sexually motivated, which he vehemently denied in all instances. His previous encounters with women (if they are to be believed) appear to have taken the pattern of occasional congress with prostitutes.

'The random nature of the crime of which he is accused also points to one of a number of currently understood sociopathic disorders. According to the subject, in no way did he "choose" his victim. Indeed, the very word "victim" seems entirely alien to him. By his own admission:

'"She was there. So I did her. Could've been any fucker."

'Throughout all four interviews with the subject, he repeatedly denied any former involvement with the victim, or that any kind of selection procedure was used.

'A look through his previous criminal record and associated life history reveals . . .'

'So are you going to tell me, or not?'

'Mmm?'

'Adrian!'

'What? Christ! I'm sorry.' Ten before midnight the same day. The bedroom. I turned to my wife. 'You're right. I'm miles away.' I put down Rattigan's file on the linen-fresh duvet.

Jemimah Rawlings opted for tact, starting again. 'I've waited all evening, Adrian. A word or two would be nice. You know, a brief description for the woman who's had to bite her tongue every night for the last God knows how many weeks as you read about the secret freak you finally met today?'

'It's not secret, J. Just want to spare you some of the gorier stuff, that's all.'

'How noble.' She went back to her reading, wearing the slightly-stung-but-indifferent expression which I always found strangely attractive. Her short pointed brown bob perfectly framed the frowning profile doing its best to ignore me. I remembered the first time I'd set eyes on her high cheekbones and deep-set brown eyes. She had the look of an Eastern European, a Hungarian noblewoman, perhaps, smuggled across hazardous borders to escape Communist authorities. A pity to have the romantic illusion shattered, then, when I learnt she'd spent most of her life in Catford.

I rubbed my eyes. 'Want to know what he said?'

'Look, if you don't want to talk about it, that's fine. I can wait for His Master's Voice.'

'He said I didn't look academic enough.'

She put down the book. 'Well, you don't.'

'Thanks.'

'Academics are supposed to look bookish and pale. You look more like a rugby player. Healthier, more well-rounded.'

I was grateful for the compliment.

'Besides,' she added. 'I thought this Rattigan man was insane.'

'Apparently.'

'So it shouldn't bother you what he thinks, then, should it?'

I nodded, conceding the point.

'And what about him, then? What did he look like?'

I thought for a second. 'Sort of normal, I guess. Not a horn sticking out of his head in sight. Which made it worse, I suppose. Knowing what he'd confessed to, and looking like the average Joe.'

'And are you going to see him again?'

'If he agrees.'

'You want to?'

I closed Rattigan's file, placed it on my bedside table. 'I thought I did. It's different, though, in the flesh. I was almost looking forward to it in a way. There's so much about his story that just doesn't make any sense.'

'But that's the point, surely?' Jemimah replied brightly. 'If he's crazy enough to do whatever he did, then surely the motive could be just as crazy?'

'No one really knows what he did. We only have his word for it.'

Another frown crossed her face. 'He killed a woman, didn't he?'

I nodded, slightly uncomfortable with the question. I didn't want Jemimah to go too heavily into the details which had so shocked me.

'So they would have been able to examine the body then? Find out how he killed her?'

I shook my head. 'There wasn't really that much left to examine.'

'Oh.'

'Sorry. But you did ask.'

Eventually, she broke the silence. 'I wish to God I knew what you find so fascinating about evil bastards like him.'

'He's not evil, J.'

'What, you're defending him, now?'

'No. I'm . . .' I sighed heavily. 'Just tired, that's all.'

She relaxed. 'He really upset you, didn't he?'

'He wanted to know all about me, whether I was married, what you were like, did we have kids.'

'And you told him?'

'Didn't have to. He got it out of me. I wasn't concentrating, I suppose.'

I felt her disappointment.

'I'm sorry, J.'

'Look, Adrian, this criminal stuff. It's your choice. Just don't involve me in anything you think I can't handle. Insanity scares me. I get nervous if I see a wino on the street. Jesus, life's mad enough as it is. Just please, don't go telling this man any more about me. He's a killer, Adrian, and I don't want him to know I even exist. Me or the kids.'

She rolled over and I cuddled into the small of her warm back. 'It was a dumb mistake. Like I say, he just got it out of me.'

'Which makes me wonder,' she said quietly, switching out her bedside lamp. 'What else is this man going to get out of you?'

But despite her worries Jemimah was asleep long before I was, leaving me alone with the distant roar of occasional traffic and a wandering mind stuck on the last thing she'd said. When I could stand it no longer, I got up, took the file downstairs, made myself a black coffee and began reading it again. There had to be a clue in there somewhere, a pointer, the beginnings of a possible motive. Even though I'd met the man, felt his open hostility, there was still no way I could simply accept his word that he'd done what he'd done 'for fun'. Insane or otherwise, there was something else he was concealing, I felt sure of it.

And even if that motive made no rhyme or reason to anyone else except Rattigan, I determined that night to get it from him. 'For fun' just wasn't good enough, even for the most sickening demented psychopath. I felt sure it was most probably sexual – he'd spent nearly three days torturing a girl to death, after all – now all I needed was to have the theory confirmed by the Beast himself, then track the psychiatric path which took him there. Which, at three in the morning, sitting in a near silent kitchen, finishing my third coffee, I figured shouldn't take much time at all.

The pointers would be obvious, wouldn't they?

3

Someone once remarked that I had a certain stillness in my eyes. And that no matter how much my face animated itself around them, it was as if they were disconnected from the surrounding expression.

The description unnerved me, partly because I was trying my best to bed the girl in question and now knew she found me to be somewhat strange and disconnected, but also because it was something I'd noticed myself as an adolescent counting spots in front of the mirror.

Another contemporary way back had told me that if you stared hard enough at your reflection, you'd find the devil grinning back. I tried – and found nothing. Just the stillness.

Others too, have sometimes remarked on my eyes. Sad, they've been called, empty, even vacant. I began to study eyes, staring intently with my own duff specimens at others, determined to learn their tricks, syphon some of their vitality. I became expert at eye-widening shock, practised arching my eyebrows for various different studied effects. But however I tried to mask the lifelessness, it remained.

Although to be fair, this optical handicap had its advantages. While some thought I was weird, an equal number were intrigued, or took pity, determined to unlock the secrets behind my flat, staring irises. And to a certain extent, I played along with their games, inventing a variety of instant tragic pasts to gain their sympathy, friendship, sexual favours, or all three. I was in my late teens, insecure, fuelled by hormones, so I can forgive myself for the deception.

But the eyes have stuck. Still as vacant today as when I first perceived them. But now I have knowledge. I know they weren't always this way. They saw something which denied them their vigour. Then spent thirty years colluding with my subconscious to deny me the memory.

And when I began speaking to Rattigan, the lid to Pandora's box began to lift a little. His taunts of 'Fat-boy' were the catalyst, taking me back to my schooldays, when I was frequently bullied over my weight – which I only very recently recognized was another complex psychological mechanism I'd constructed in order to forget.

For me, the term 'hindsight' is the cruellest of puns, but I'm forced to admit it played its part. For the first time in my life, I can really 'see', trace the causes of who I was, who I am now, and what happened in between. I see now what I saw then, and realize why the life drained from my eyes.

To begin at the beginning, I nearly killed my own mother before I'd even drawn breath.

Rawlings family legend has it that on the seventh of March 1958, I caused a twenty-two-hour labour, a badly administered epidural and thirty-seven stitches on the poor woman during my sweating, straining way into the world. Something about my head being too big, her feet too small, though I can't say for certain. Mum and Dad are both dead now, and even though I was present at the birth of both of my own children, I'm still woefully ignorant of the precise biological processes which place a mother's life in danger as she dilates, contracts and finally bears another life.

More of my mother. Gwendoline Sullivan was much younger than my father, theirs being the almost clichéd match between smitten secretary and stoical boss. She was twenty-three when she married George Rawlings – he a handsomely mature forty-two. And from what I remember, it was that most rare of combinations, a marriage which seemed to truly work. That she loved him utterly, I am totally convinced. Many's the time I remember to this day the looks she gave, meals she tenderly prepared, dresses she wore in order to please him.

We lived in Swindon. Dad still worked as boss of a small firm of accountants where he had effortlessly wooed his future wife, while Mum stayed put to look after his son. At the time I felt the almost daily trips to his office to take his sandwiches for lunch were surely just another fine example of my parents' devotion to each other. It was only later that I wondered if Mum was truly happy playing housewife while Dad went to work with his new secretary. Not that anything untoward ever happened, I'm sure. Dad simply wasn't the type, but I think Mum must have had her suspicions.

Unfortunately, I inherited my mother's physical genes. Dad stood well over six foot, Mum barely managing to break the five-foot barrier in high heels. I was chubby, too, having none of Dad's lean wiry physique, and of course, after the birth episode, was destined to be an only child. Sometimes, in the darker moments, I'd lie awake wondering if my loneliness was appropriate punishment for the distress I'd unwittingly caused my mother.

However, any hopes my father had that he'd somehow sired the future heavyweight champion soon withered away as I fell victim to numerous childhood ailments. But, as most fathers do, Dad looked straight through my chubby pallid scrawn, convinced I had the makings of a professional footballer. He'd tried out for Swindon Town as a youngster, and wouldn't accept I hadn't inherited his own magic left foot. Most Saturday afternoons would find us at the local ground, me struggling to see above a sea of heads at the exotic green turf beyond.

They were the best of times, made better when my dad would lift me confidently on to his broad shoulders to catch key moments of the game. I'd sit there, elevated, giving my own childish commentary to the action, hands clinging to his ears and thinning hair, feeling him sway slightly if Town scored, bonded.

Often, he'd carry me aloft as we walked back home, weaving through thousands of jubilant or disgruntled fans, nodding at friends – feeling literally 'on top of the world'.

My bedroom became a temple to the Town, covered in posters, programmes, scarves, away-ticket stubs and league tables. At the age of nine I knew no times-tables, but all of Swindon Town's cup-winning teams by rote. Dad always put me to bed with tales of the 'great' games, vivid descriptions and I clung on to every word.

It was only in later life that my mother's indifference to the Town began to make sense. I think she resented the hold it had on Dad, perhaps even saw me as a rival for his time and affection. But these are suppositions I can only make with hindsight. An attempt to understand why she appeared distant at times. Perhaps I was the son my father always wanted, which my mother dutifully supplied, who then took her place in his heart. Whatever – I'll never know, they're both long gone, and all I'm left with is a frustrating mix of unanswered speculation and distant memories.

I suppose my childhood split itself into two parts. The happy times up till the age of nine or so, then the confusing times after. Dad changed, became withdrawn, older, somehow more fragile. We didn't go to matches any more, I went with friends, while he sat at home, listening to the radio. But it was no gradual slowing down, it simply happened one weekend, almost as if he'd been replaced by an apathetic, stooping doppelgänger during the night.

I continued following the often disastrous footballing antics of the Town for the rest of the season, returning home to give my indifferent dad an increasingly lacklustre match report, but to be honest, without his enthusiasm, my heart was in it even less than his. Down came the scarves, posters and wall-charts, up went Jane Fonda as Barbarella.

And I too, began to change. My weight ballooned, skin stretching under the constant ingestion of crisps and sweets. My eyes took on their now familiar stillness. I went from a slim young boy into a blob, cocooned from a terrible truth I hadn't the will or maturity to deal with. The subconscious took over, remoulding me, distancing me from such things I hadn't the developed intellect to face. And it's only now, all these years later, as the terrible truth emerges blinking into the sunlight of my new reality, that the choices I have made, the things I've done, the hurt I've caused others all fit so hideously elegantly into place.

I didn't eat three Mars Bars every day because I wanted to – it was because I needed to. The promised work, rest and play disguised a deeper, darker need – to forget. And the calories did their job, protecting me from the outside, wrapping me in comforting fat, giving me time to heal before I had the strength to go back and face what had so quickly and violently destroyed both my father's and my own innocence.

But I digress. Back to the potted biography. Next it was eleven-plus, special tutoring and a place at the Boys' Grammar. School caps, long lines of fragile little boys lugging briefcases designed for grown-ups, stuffed with battered text and exercise books. Eng. Lang., Eng. Lit., Geography, Art, French, German, Chemistry, Physics, Biology, Latin, detention, the cane, school reports, fear, and football. I remember my dad extolling my laughably nonexistent sporting virtues at my interview as a huge ape in a Loughborough tracksuit sneered in anticipation of towel-whipping me in the showers. Which he did, many times.

As expected, I was average at just about everything, with the exception of sport. Here, I seemed to excel as an uncoordinated dunderhead, but being one of the widest, if not tallest, boys in my year, I was made substitute goalkeeper in the St Barts third team. I remember Dad would occasionally make a reluctant trip out to the school touchline, joining other rain-sodden parents jeering my efforts as the ball skidded past me into the back of the net. And always after, during the journey home, few words would pass between us, yet I sensed his disappointment. It was a world away from the distant days when he'd lift me on those once broad shoulders, now stooped and rounded by time.

Moving on, past A levels towards 1976, my first job – tea-boy in a provincial advertising agency. The name's irrelevant, so was the job. Amazingly, I lost three stone, my virginity, discovered pot, the music of The Doors, Yes and Genesis. I wore flares and discovered a gift for mimicry and joke-telling which won me many friends my age, but few amongst the management. I had a weekly wage and all the brash confidence of youth. I was impregnable, bolstered by hormones and arrogance.

Then fired for skinning up in the toilets.

London beckoned, and I Dick Wittingtoned to its heady call, winding up as a junior copywriter in a 'mainstream' ad agency on Dean Street.

Jemimah Eliott arrived, full of my imagined Eastern European promise, our brand-new hotshot account handler. I wrote the copy for the ads she presented to the clients. I went to one or two of these presentations, watching her wage a professional charm offensive on our clients in order to bolster the agency's profits. She was good, very good, young, attractive. I fancied her like mad, but thought I had no chance. But we used to laugh a lot together, swapping gossip and tall stories about the guys with their own parking spaces who were for ever offering to take her away for a 'formative think-tank regarding agency strategy for the forthcoming new business pitch' – adspeak for a quickie in a hotel on expenses.

The senior rejected suits had, of course, discovered the source of their failure to bed her. Jemimah Eliott was, in their hugely embittered opinions, obviously a muff-muncher, rabid dyke, prick-teaser. I remember nodding sagely, laughing inside at their broken egos.

Then one day, just another unremarkable Wednesday, she came to brief me on some job or other. At the end she asked me out. As simple as that, just went staight ahead and asked. Unbelievable – but true.

We married in nineteen-eighty – me twenty-two; her twenty-three; two young kids standing at the altar, backs to the world of temptation and drudgery which lay waiting outside the church.

We agreed I would move to another agency, figuring working and living with one another wouldn't necessarily make the ideal platform for a successful relationship. But perhaps we hadn't fully thought it through. Trouble was, we still worked in the same business, only now we were professional rivals. Then disaster – in April 1987, my agency lost a major bit of business to hers. Jemimah was on the pitch team. Word soon got round. I was suspected of leaking details by a paranoid management reeling from the loss of a major blue-chip account. I was history shortly after, summoned by a phone call to a meeting with the smiling executive where a lukewarm pot of coffee, my P45 and a derisory payoff were the only things on the table.

I felt numb, made completely impotent by the decision.

Not that the drop in money affected J and I in the slightest – in a bizarre irony, she'd been promoted to the board of her agency as a result of winning the business I'd been unfairly suspected of losing. We were richer than we'd ever been.

At first we were cool about it, spending the redundancy and planning a heavy freelance career from the ruins of my Filofax. One or two jobs rolled in, charity from old pals, giving Adrian the odd hundred quid here or there. But I grew to hate every minute of it. My heart wasn't in it; I couldn't bear to think of Jemimah leaving for work, while I sat upstairs in the heavy silence, de-roled, emasculated.

Like an idiot, I began to drink heavily, from the moment J left for the station until she returned, often finding me bombed on the sofa, useless. Days, time, dates, all became irrelevant as I woke each day with the sole aim to hit the whisky hard, dull the pain of failure. A never-ending supply of child-minders and nannies looked after Juliet and Guy, our two children, while I set about following a self-indulgent path to oblivion. It was crazy – a very dark and stupid time. I did things of which I'm still not proud, which even now I can't fully explain or understand – but perhaps this is born out of a reluctance to do so.

There are some parts of all of us, I now recognize, which are graphically revealed in a crisis, and need one hell of a lot of honesty to accept. Even now, I have problems with the swiftness of my metamorphosis from happy-go-lucky copywriter to unstable drunk. I shudder at the ease with which I was unravelled.

Then came the move to Essex. Jemimah took charge and issued the ultimatum. She'd had enough. The family was moving from London. I could go with them, or stay and drink myself to death, but without her money or support. I was devastated, and in the selfish way alcoholics have, grew to hate her for making me choose.

Friends began calling less often, nervous of my unpredictable behaviour. Letters from estate agents began arriving. I was sleeping in the spare room when I could be bothered to get off the sofa. I had nothing in my life but alcohol.

One afternoon, Jemimah arrived back to tell me she'd

exchanged on a place near Chelmsford. We had a God Almighty argument. And I hit her.

To this day, I hate myself for that drunken blow. She reeled back, shock and pain writ large on her reddening face. Juliet, our eldest, began to cry. I stormed out, spent two nights with a former colleague who persuaded me to get help. Thank God he did.

The message was stark. I was an alcoholic. Always would be. In less than six months I'd gone from a bloke who could have a couple of pints and leave, to someone who couldn't face the day unless he had three large whiskys to take the edge off it. The only solution was to deny myself the solution. Either that or lose everything.

There were others there, that night. Broken individuals with similar tales, some spanning many years – but always at the heart, I felt, was a reluctance to look inside and face a particular truth which the alcohol blurred. I didn't have the strength to face mine, preferring instead to soak up the group support, start the road to abstinence, persuade Jemimah that I recognized the problem, had taken steps to tackle it, was convinced I would beat it.

God love her – she tentatively agreed to 'take me back'. I began the painful process of working out what I wanted to 'do' with the rest of my life, finally realizing what a privileged position I was in. I could start again, a new life, new friends, new interests, a phoenix rising from the ruins of my own self-destruction. And after a few weeks settling into our new home I was off the sauce, had joined a local gym and, more importantly, had the answer to my new direction.

During the move to Chelmsford, I'd rediscovered an old hoard of crime magazines I'd collected as a youngster, sensational articles offering a tabloid insight into the minds and motives of the evil perpetrators. Rereading them, I found myself fascinated by both the crimes and criminals, wondering what lay at the heart of the human psyche. It seemed incredible to me that humanity, universally acknowledged as an exploratory creature, could put a man on the moon without ever having fully explored his mind.

What shapes the most deviant individuals – brain dysfunction, environmental factors, the past, or perhaps a fatal cocktail of all three? Or is it simply that some of us are born with a terrifying predilection for evil?

The questions fought for space in my mind, as I began to realize I was developing an obsession with human psychology. I began subscribing to modern crime mags, immersing myself in the twisted worlds of current-day serial killers and psychopaths, child-murderers, Satanists and worse. And yet it seemed to me that the more I 'discovered' the less I actually knew. Each publication was merely concerned with sensational grisly details to ensure higher sales. Indeed, sometimes I found myself wondering about the appetite for such bloodthirsty material, speculating that perhaps we hadn't actually evolved all that much since thousands turned up to witness a handful of Christians thrown to hungry lions.

But I too, was hooked. I may have tried to cloak my interest in academic terms, convincing myself I had superior motives for buying the glossy mags and tabloids, but the result was the same, I paid my money – I participated in the voyeuristic merchandising of insanity and pain.

Then one day – a breakthrough. Waiting in Chelmsford Central Library to check out another volume dedicated to the ongoing mystery of Jack the Ripper, I began leafing through a local prospectus. The University of Essex offered a reasonably well-thought-of degree in psychology. Perhaps this was a start then, a move in the right direction. After talking it over with Jemimah, we agreed I should apply. She was still happy enough working at the agency, and provided I really was serious about it, she'd fund my enthusiasm. I was taken on as a mature student the following September.

I worked harder than I'd ever done, couldn't get enough of the subject, eating up theories, devouring vast textbooks, ingesting all that was said in every lecture and tutorial. I was motivated, sober, deliriously happy with my second shot at life.

Former friends visiting the Rawlingses' Essex retreat for dinner would often make the mistake of complimenting me on my willpower, watching as I drank mineral water while they knocked back the hard stuff. I was always quick to correct them. It had nothing to do with willpower – fear was the key. I'd already teetered at the edge of my sanity once, nothing would persuade me to do so again. Or so I thought at the time.

Three years later, the BA (hons) became an MA, with Dr Clancy telling me I had the talent to ride it all the way to PhD in forensic psychiatry if I wanted to.

I dedicated myself to finding a thesis subject. There was so much to choose from, but eventually decided to settle on the media's easy obsession with 'evil', and the damage it caused to proper psychological investigation. I worked hard. Cases like the Wests', Dunblane and numerous others seemed to spring from quiet suburban backwaters almost every month as I toiled away on my researches. And as each horrifying case broke, I found myself ever more on the 'side' of the perpetrators, rationalizing that there had to be some concrete reasons why they'd done whatever they'd been accused of. Concrete beyond the media's constant assertion that they were simply 'evil', anyway.

Next I learnt that the Home Office had agreed to partially fund a series of PhD students through their thesis years if they participated in a national data-gathering exercise for a brand-new law-enforcement initiative identifying behavioural characteristics of incarcerated psychopaths.

Or, as Fancy put it, they'd stump up a few readies if I agreed to ask a nutter some personal questions. The programme had been up and running for a few years, and research gathered had apparently proved invaluable in lobbying the relevant parties for a change in the judicial understanding of random violence.

'Bugger it, Adrian,' Fancy'd said by way of explanation. 'You only have to look at the States to see what a balls-up they're making of it. Defence attorneys are pressing for the admission of "the crime gene" in order to get their psychos out of the death chamber. Like the murdering sods are somehow born to kill, genetically programmed, so it's not their fault. Preposterous!'

'And you say what?' I replied. 'That every lunatic is morally responsible for the actions he commits?'

'We're not that far, Adrian. We need more data. Will you do it? It's bang up your street, nature of evil and all that.'

My thesis, the magnum opus – 'The acceptance of Evil as a resultant supernatural force actively prohibits positive psycho-social studies into the internal and external factors influencing random, unmotivated violence' by Adrian Rawlings (soon to be) PhD.

So I agreed, both trepidacious and excited. Here was a chance to actually step inside a secure mental institution, converse with an inmate, form some kind of temporary relationship, perhaps even finally come to terms with what lured me to the analysis of violence in the first place.

It had been bothering me for some time, silently, something I tried my best to suppress, keep from friends and family. But late at night, while I worked in the gloom of a computer screen, it was always there, a warning keen to be heard and analysed, a fear which had wound its way effortlessly into my psyche, mocking my attempts to reinvent myself over the last ten years.

Maybe longer. The longer I worked at trying to understand the human mind, the more I began to analyse my own. I was finally beginning to have some understanding of my own inadequacies. The reason I had drunk so passionately was a good deal greater than simply hitting my thirties, redundant and shit-scared. No – it was for far simpler, far darker reasons. The more I drank, the less I needed to answer the real questions gently swelling and beginning their way up from deep down inside. Questions I'd buried from childhood and adolescence. Questions which the redundancy had thrown up, and which I feared would never go away.

Fancy duly put my name forward to Dr Neil Allen at HMP Oakwood High Security Mental Hospital, and after a short submission on my part detailing my willingness to compile relevant data regarding antisocial behaviour disorders, I was duly accepted and funded.

'Game on!' Fancy had beamed when telling me the good

news. 'A year from now and I'll be calling the man "Doctor".'

Fancy rang late the following Thursday night.

'He's gone for it, Adrian.'

'Rattigan?' I answered nervously.

'Wants to see you tomorrow afternoon.'

'Shit! So soon?'

'Told you he would. They all do.'

'Jesus. Tomorrow?'

'Don't worry. Pop into the uni. on the way. See me before ten. I'll give you all you need to know. And Adrian?' His voice was deadly serious. 'Remember, you get in, you do this, you get out. You're the boss. It only becomes a game when you agree to play it.'

'But there's so much about him that . . .'

'Shouldn't concern you, Adrian.'

I heard what he said, understood his warning, yet knew following the advice would be difficult, if nigh on impossible.

I was an idealistic mature student with a head full of theories and expectations. Rattigan fascinated me for one reason alone. He claimed to have killed for no other motive than his own self-satisfaction. He'd had 'fun' dispensing slow death.

Why couldn't I heed all the warnings and simply accept this? What drove me to rationalize his monstrous act within my own understanding? Personal ambition? A desire to be recognized as a great forensic psychologist?

Or something else entirely?

It wasn't that Rattigan held the answers, I did. But at the time, I was too scared to face the questions.

To date, neuropsychological studies of offenders have been blighted by small samples, lack of controls and an emphasis on institutionalized populations. However, results from such studies indicate that both poor language skills and impairment of the regulative functions controlled by the frontal lobes are consistent factors in the analysis of sociopathic antibehavioural disorders.

At present, it is almost impossible to gauge whether either factor is the result of developmental damage or neurological failure, and more work needs to be done in order to understand the complex correlation between the two.

However, current thinking suggests that many forms of sociopathic and psychotic behaviours can possibly be explained by the ineffectiveness of the subject's 'inner voice', or learned morality, to temper violent outbursts.

Put simply – they appear to do what they want, to whom they like, as and when mood takes them.

Dr Neil Allen
(*The Roots of Psychopathy*)

4

Three-thirty, Oakwood High Security Mental Hospital, Cambridgeshire, RECREATION SIX.

The same three players, Rattigan, Denton and myself.

I reached into my briefcase, brought out some papers, two packs of Rothmans and a micro-cassette recorder.

Then turned to Rattigan. 'There's one or two things I'm obliged to explain regarding your participation in the programme.'

'Can't wait.' Rattigan was already unwrapping one of the blue and white boxes.

I cleared my throat, anxious to get the script right. 'Now that you've officially consented to my visits, I'll be asking you a series of questions prepared by various agencies in order to gain a greater understanding of antisocial behavioural disorders. In addition to this, I'll also be asking some questions I've formulated myself in order to help with my own studies in the field of forensic psychiatry.'

'Blah, blah, fucking blah.'

I placed the micro-cassette on the middle of the table. 'Are you aware of what this is?'

He looked at the black plastic box for a few seconds. 'It's a penguin, isn't it? A tiny penguin with a lemon up its arse, watching *Pinocchio* in a large block of flats in West Croydon.'

'Each meeting will be recorded for subsequent transcription and analysis on this tape recorder.'

At which point Rattigan lit up. 'Just shows how wrong you can be, eh?'

I switched on the machine, relief flooding over me when

I realized the damn thing was working properly. Next I reached for a green sheet of A4 headed 'Analysis of Institutionalized Offenders – History, Profiling and Sociopathic Behaviour Traits', and began working my way through the answer boxes.

'Name?'

'King of Sweden.'

I put down Francis James Rattigan. 'Age?'

He exhaled violently. 'You've got my details! Go to the fucking governor's office and sort this shit out!'

'Age?' I repeated, unmoved.

'Hundred and seven.'

I put down the pen. 'Frank.'

'Adrian?'

'Refusal to cooperate will be taken as reluctance to comply with the programme.' I was surprisingly cool, amazed the corporate bullshit came so easily. I'd done what Fancy had told me to the last time, left Adrian Rawlings in Dr Allen's office, waiting for collection.

'F602 GPW.'

The combination seemed familiar, but I hadn't asked him for his number yet. 'Age?' I repeated, keeping up the show.

'F602 GPW.' His eyes scanned my face intently. 'Yours, innit? Your motor. Dark-green Vauxhall Cavalier. GB sticker on the back. Go anywhere pleasant?'

The penny dropped. I tried not to appear unnerved. 'I don't see that's relevant, Frank.'

'Bollocks, you're crapping yourself. Can see it, can read faces, fear. Your fucking wheels. I got your wheels. How much longer before I get your phone, fat-boy? How much longer before I'm ringing your missus up while you're hard at work in the nuthouse, eh?'

'Age?'

He smiled, then sighed. 'Fifty-seven. Born twenty-eighth of March, nineteen-forty.'

I filled in the form, inwardly cursing its designers. Rattigan was right, why the bloody hell wasn't this done before the interviews took place? And how in God's name had he got my numberplate? The pen shook slightly. I wanted answers to these ludicrous questions, but knew the cassette was recording my performance as well as his. For some reason I couldn't bear to have Fancy listening to an actual recording of a balls-up. Stick to the script. Stick to the bloody script.

'Offence?'

'Whose?'

'Yours,' I replied, staring at the little box, awaiting his response.

'I chopped up some tart who should've known better.'

'Better?' I'd deviated here, drifted from the protocol, suddenly anxious to press him for more about the murder of Helen Lewis.

'What goes around, comes around, sweetie.'

'Meaning?'

'She deserved it. We all deserve to die. Just got to want it badly enough.'

'So what had she done to deserve it?'

'More a case of what she hadn't done.'

'Which was?'

Rattigan looked deep into my eyes, held it for at least three seconds too long. I felt dissected, invaded, just as much his study as he was mine. When he spoke, the voice was ice-cold, devoid of feeling. Yet he smiled throughout. 'I'd tell you, but I don't reckon you've got the balls for it.'

'Try me.'

'Fighting talk. Like that. Always loved a tear-up. Bit of a pro in my own way.' He paused, squinting slightly, as if the act of conversation was suddenly a leaden effort. 'Know what I learnt from geezers who talked tough?'

I supplied the obvious answer. 'They weren't really all that tough inside?'

Another squint as he struggled to impart whatever ran through his ruined mind. 'I'm mad, right? One of them psycho-whatnots. Done all the fucking tests a million times. Take more drugs in a day than the Rolling fucking Stones in a month. But that's only 'cause I can see through people, like they're fucking transparent or something. Just like I'm looking at you now. Trying to get all chummy with me. Talking like mates. I don't have to tell you fuck-all if I don't want to.'

'So let's just stick to the questions on the form, then, eh?'

But he wasn't through. 'Know why I hate wankers like you?'

'I feel sure you're about to tell me.'

He feigned a slow handclap. 'You're unnatural. Fucking freak. Should be dead.'

I struggled to grasp the concept.

He enlightened me. 'Only the strong survive, fat-boy. Little gits like you have to lock people like me up, 'cause you can't handle us. But you're all fascinated. You poke us about, prod us, ask us shit – always trying to "understand". And you ain't never going to find any answers. We're always going to be out there. Taking what we want. Doing what we want. That's what we're here for. To pass on our genes, or whatever. Fuck ourselves a stronger human race. Science is dead. Drugs won't hold us for ever.'

I wrenched myself from his sneering gaze, turning to Denton, who sat bored by the wall. He'd heard it all before, a thousand times, maybe.

I let a few seconds' silence pass. 'Is that what you were trying to do to Helen Lewis, Frank? Build a stronger human race? Trying to have sex with her?'

He laughed. 'Tinpot theory. Ain't you done no fucking homework? Last thing on earth I wanted to do was fuck the bitch.'

'Yet you stripped her, tortured her?'

'Which turns you on, right? 'Cause that's the only connection your fat little filthy mind can make, isn't it? Just 'cause she was naked, I had sex with her, right? But that's your interpretation, you sick piece of shit.'

'So tell me yours.'

'Fuck off.'

Deadlock. There was little to do but recommence the preset questions. 'Ward?'

And in an instant the demeanour changed. His tone calmed, and we talked like old friends. I didn't know which face frightened me more, the angry Beast, or the good-buddy Frank. 'You see, Adrian,' he grinned and winked at me. A shiver coursed down my spine. 'Reckon they're taking the piss out of both of us. We already know all these answers.'

I found myself apologetic, unravelling in my naivety. Why in God's name wasn't Denton being more assertive, shutting Rattigan up, making him toe the line? 'Dr Allen and the team prepare your questions,' I said. 'I'm just the poor fool designated to ask them. I don't even see them until I arrive. That's how it works.'

'You're crap at this.' A two-beat pause. 'Aren't you?'

'I'm . . .' I shot what must have been an obvious look of desperation at Denton.

'I find it insulting,' Rattigan added threateningly.

'I'm sorry about that . . .'

'It's making me feel demeaned, like some fucking performing seal. And I don't like feeling demeaned, Adrian. I really don't. It just pisses me off, and I do things.'

Suddenly, here it was – a break, a slip, a crack of a chance. I was on it in an instant. 'Like what, Frank?'

He smiled, and I hesitantly returned it, knowing he was drawing me in, but somehow powerless to resist. 'Like with the lady, fat-boy. Now we're getting somewhere, aren't we? Your turn.'

'So you felt demeaned . . . when you . . . ?'

'Oh, I felt lots of stuff.' His fat head nodded slowly. 'Pretty as a picture, she was. Pretty as a fucking picture.'

My throat was bone-dry as I struggled to control the delivery of my next question. 'That demeaned you? Her beauty?'

A slight twitch above his left eyebrow. 'What are you implying?'

'That perhaps you felt threatened by it in some way?'

'That I'm ugly?' He sounded ugly, too. Instantly loud and dense. His eyes narrowed to pig-slits, and his bottom jaw gaped ludicrously.

'I'm not saying anything, I'm . . .'

He turned to Denton, standing and pocketing the cigarettes. 'Take me back to the unit. I don't have to take this shit from an arsehole like him.'

Denton stood, quickly moving between Rattigan and myself. 'Calm down.'

41

'Will I bollocks! This cunt's a wind-up artist!'

Somehow, through my fear came another feeling – stronger, more urgent. Anger. I'd been bloody set up, I was certain of it. I sat seething, staring at the floor and shaking my head. It simply wasn't my fault, none of it was. The whole session had got off to a terrible start with the set questions. But I didn't decide those, Allen and his unseen cronies did. Yet I was the poor mug asking them, getting sworn at and intimidated into the bargain.

I felt Rattigan move past me. 'I'm not a cunt, Frank,' I said quietly.

But he simply left the room, Denton half a pace behind, leaving me with a well of hatred I hadn't felt in years, and a conscience struggling to pull myself from his hostility.

But I also knew full well his anger was born from my delving. Questions I'd asked had rattled the ice-cool facade. His response, his anger at me, was explainable, understandable, logical, rational. Sane, almost. He didn't want me poking, prying. Tough – I was going to upset him a lot more in future.

He felt he'd won – round one to Rattigan. Maybe, but it was going to be a long fight. I'd already beaten the bottle. There was no way Rattigan could be a worse opponent than alcohol.

Could he?

5

'Will I bollocks! This cunt's a wind-up artist!'

Dr Neil Allen switched off the micro-cassette and regarded me cautiously. 'I don't want you to be put off by this, Mr Rawlings. You're doing well. Surprisingly well.'

'It's "Adrian",' I offered wearily, slumped in one of three chairs in his surprisingly spacious office. The distant echo of New Age Muzak did little to calm me.

Allen sat behind the desk, his back towards several large charts denoting duty nursing rosters. It took me a moment to work out what was missing from the room. Windows. Working there would've driven me as crazy as the inmates. 'Coffee?'

'Thanks.'

He poured two cups from a large jug-shaped flask. Institutional black, no sugar. Hideous. 'You're not here to make psychiatric history, Adrian. No one expects anything from you.' He paused. 'Except yourself, maybe.'

He was analysing me. I resented it. 'Oh?'

He stroked his long gaunt face quite slowly, almost caressing the pointed chin. I briefly wondered if his stark looks were in any way connected with the ugly minds under his charge, if perhaps he had started out quite rugged and handsome, then fallen physical victim to their mental neuroses, like certain owners look like the dogs they keep.

'The way you sit there – slumped,' he continued. 'I can tell that it's not turned out as you hoped. I've had words with Dr Clancy. He told me you were pretty shaken from your first meeting with Rattigan.'

'He knew my numberplate, Dr Allen,' I replied. 'I think that gives me the right to be slightly worried.'

43

'About what, exactly?'

'Who told him, of course.'

'You have your own theory?'

I shifted uncomfortably. But I had to voice my concerns. I was worried. 'Rattigan mentioned something about Warder-Orderly Denton perhaps . . .'

Allen allowed my half-mumbled accusation to hang in the air for a toe-curling few seconds. 'And you suspect Dr Millar is in league with Frank Rattigan?'

'Dr Millar?' What in God's name was going on here?

'Your personal assessor and bodyguard, Adrian. Dr Millar holds black belts in three martial arts. Frightfully competent man. As well as being a vital witness on all your sessions, he'll ensure Rattigan's in no position to carry out his threats.'

I was flabbergasted. 'Millar's Denton? So why the sub-terfuge?'

'For Rattigan's benefit. He assumes Millar to be another screw, so he's more likely to open up.'

'But doesn't he already *know* Denton's Millar, or who-ever?'

'Rattigan's kept in the Personality Disorder Unit. It has its own staff. Your sessions are the first time he's set foot outside for years. He sees Dr Millar dressed as a screw and obviously assumes him to be one.'

I was aware I was frowning.

'And as for your numberplate – it's mind-numbingly easy. Rattigan is, in institutional terms a rich man. Cigarettes buy information, Adrian. It wouldn't take much for him to get a message to one of the inmates up on D-Wing. Their cells overlook the visitors' car park.'

'Oh.'

'Shame, isn't it?' Allen sighed, stifling a yawn. 'Like find-ing out an illusionist's best work is done with the humble mirror. Believe me, Dr Millar has only your best interests at heart.'

'Then why didn't he tell me all this?'

'He hasn't had the chance to. Rattigan's always around. Chap doesn't want to blow his cover in the first couple of sessions.'

'Even so,' I pressed. 'I'd quite like to talk to him at some stage. Even if it's just to get his opinion.'

'Maybe. He's a busy man. Anything else that's particularly bothering you? You don't look very relaxed about all this.'

'The questions,' I said carefully. 'They were . . . ridiculous. Stuff that was completely superfluous.'

Allen smiled, holding immaculately manicured hands close to his lips as if about to pray. 'That was precisely the point.'

'Pardon?'

'The questions were designed to antagonize.'

'Deliberately?'

He nodded, allowing it to sink in. 'We need to see how someone like Rattigan interacts with a stranger, Adrian. We're using you, quite blatantly.'

'I'm not really with you,' I mumbled, embarrassed.

'The study,' Allen continued. 'Is as much for the benefit of my staff as it is for the forces of law and order. A spin-off, if you like. We use you in order to get to know much more about Rattigan, his triggers, length of his fuse. Remember how he reacted when he thought he was belittled?'

'Demeaned,' I half-heartedly corrected, determined to score at least one point. 'But you would've known all about that already. Your own counsellors, access to his psychiatric record –'

'Irrelevant,' Allen interrupted. 'Past history. The study of the human mind is in its infancy. We know damn-all about Rattigan, and we've had him here years. The best we can do is adjust his medication to keep him stable. But it's a risky business. Ultimately, our distant aim is to have some insight into the origin of our inmates' various psychoses. Then perhaps we can alter their behaviours therapeutically instead of medicinally. Some at the Home Office think it would be cheaper and probably safer. Certainly, it would be impressive, don't you think? Ground-breaking, even.'

'I'm not sure you're not making fun of me,' I replied, uncomfortable with the way the conversation had turned. I was still quite shocked that my old pal Fancy had betrayed my feelings about Rattigan so quickly. I thought I'd told him in confidence. I began to feel uneasy – again. 'What do you really think?'

He laughed at my naivety. 'The old cliché, Adrian. I'm not paid to think. I'm little more than a dispenser in a suit. They give me drugs, I prescribe them. They come up with some newfangled scheme – I'll run with it.'

It was becoming depressingly clearer. 'So that's all I am – just a budgetary obligation?'

'You get valuable experience, Adrian. A lot more than money can buy.' He sipped loudly at the tepid excuse for coffee. 'And now you think I'm a cynical humbug, don't you?'

'I don't know what to think, really.'

'Let me put it this way. You have an opportunity here to witness institutional life first-hand. Even if that's the sole result of your visits here, it'll have been worthwhile.' He paused, pointing to the micro-cassette. 'You're looking for a motive, aren't you?'

'Sorry?'

'A reason why Rattigan killed the girl.'

'An insight, perhaps.'

'From someone who's certified insane?'

'Too ambitious?'

'Certainly not. Delve away. Though don't pin your hopes on it. He's stuck rigidly to the same story for years.'

'That it was "fun".'

'Perhaps it was. His criminal history is peppered with serious violent assaults.'

'But to simply pick on a random individual and torture, mutilate and kill them? For no reason?'

'For fun, Adrian. Reason enough, perhaps.'

'There has to be more.'

Allen sighed. 'Don't bank on it. You're an intelligent man. Read the papers, they're littered with Rattigans and their victims. But I wish you well. Just don't set your heart on finding some ulterior motive for the murder.' He stood and offered a hand. The meeting was over. He looked me in the eye. 'Perhaps,' he said deliberately. 'It's just as important to understand the reasons why you need to know.'

'You mean my own motives?'

He held my gaze. 'You could be doing anything, Adrian. Yet here you are, hoping to rationalize a ten-year-old murder, unable to accept the killer's own motive. I think perhaps it might prove provident for you to understand your own agenda with Rattigan, don't you?'

I nodded and left the office, glad of the fresh air outside the hospital. I walked quickly to the car without looking back, slapped in some Aretha Franklin and drove away with 'Chain of Fools' assaulting me full-blast.

The trouble was, I knew Allen was right. There was something in me which was desperate to normalize Rattigan's crime. I'd felt it for years, pushed it under with drink, work, life. But the more I tried to uncover its dark beginnings, the less I could pin it down, as if memories had been silenced by time itself.

All I could say for certain was that somewhere within was a knot of fear and shame which was gradually unravelling, day by day, reaching out from my subconscious, readying itself to do battle with my conscience.

And it scared the hell out of me.

6

That night I had the dream again . . .

The ship was listing, spilt diesel oil vaporizing on the salted air as the huge iron hulk began its obscene journey into the foaming black sea.

A lifeboat swung dangerously, tossed by storm-force winds, held by straining steel cables, a puppet boat, dooming its terrified occupants as it crashed into the dark swell below.

But I was safe, a young boy swimming powerfully, away from the sinking liner, making for stiller waters, passing weaker passengers, feeling occasional connections with tired limbs as I crashed by.

Just another thirty yards or so, twenty at the most, then I could turn, tread water, enjoy the dreadful spectacle of the fizzing, popping boat slide into the deep. Safe – beyond the fatal pull of the whirlpool which would condemn so many others to follow its huge turning propellers.

Ten strokes, now.

Nine.

Eight.

Then I heard their voices, coughing, spluttering – Mum and Dad – old, useless, tired.

Mum, hair in thick wet black ropes, struggling to reach me, my point of oceanic calm, calls out.

'Adrian!'

Dad tries too.

But they are too far away.

'Save us!'

How could I? They were as good as dead. To turn back and try and save them would only mean that I would perish alongside them. Lose *my* life. We'd all die. What point would the fatal heroics prove?

'Save us, please!'

But I wanted to live. Let them die. Not me.

Suddenly the whirlpool catches them, and for a second their progress stops. I catch a look of complete disbelief and surprise on their faces, as the huge current begins sweeping them screaming towards the same dark sea the boat once occupied . . .

After, I wandered downstairs to the silent kitchen for a coffee. Jemimah's dream kitchen, elegantly tiled and strewn with cast-iron pots and pans hanging from stainless-steel rails. I sat at the heavy pine table wondering at the laughable irony of the ad business wherein such luxury is achieved by its employees pushing tat on the masses. The result is very often a lifestyle only dreamt of by the unknowing punters.

A sleepy voice from somewhere behind. Jemimah, dressing gown open, yawning. 'Can't sleep?'

I shrugged.

She joined me at the table. 'Bad dreams?'

I nodded.

'You saw Rattigan again today, didn't you?'

'Uhuh.'

'Don't want to talk about it?'

'That's part of the problem, J. I don't know what I want.'

'Middle of the night's a bad time to brood, I know that much.'

'Maybe it's the best time.'

'What's wrong?' she playfully chided. 'Has that nasty man been calling you names again?'

'He's not the problem. I think I am.'

'What are you saying?'

'Something someone said to me today. Saying I should take a long hard look at the reasons why I'm doing this.'

'The PhD?' she replied, then smiled. 'Because you're going to make the best forensic psychologist the ad business ever fired. Because you believe in yourself. Because I do.'

'Thanks, J. It means a lot.'

She reached out for my hand. 'Let me in, Adrian. I can't help if you bottle it all up.'

'Jesus, I'd love to.'

'Then do it.'

'Problem is, I can't even get there myself.'

She half frowned. 'I'm not sure I . . .'

'Remember when I hit you?'

She withdrew her hand, avoided my gaze. 'Adrian, you don't have to . . .'

'But I do,' I persisted. 'It's all tied in.'

'And it's history. Bad history. We've moved on.'

'But I did it. We can't just ignore it.'

'You were pissed. Weren't yourself.'

'But what if . . . ?' I started.

She shook her head, reading my thoughts. 'Don't go down this road, Adrian, please.'

'Maybe I've got to.'

'Why?'

'To face up to it. To me.'

'But it wasn't *you*, don't you understand? It was drink. And now I've got you back. We've moved on. Why the analysis? Why now, for heaven's sake?'

'Because I think I know why I did it.'

She was becoming unsettled, nervous. 'You were bloody drunk. End of story.'

'But I remember the feelings,' I replied. 'And perhaps the booze simply let them slip through. Surface.'

She said nothing, waiting.

'I remember bits of it. I remember you telling me you'd exchanged on the house. Then there was this . . . awful pain . . .'

'Can't we just forget the whole thing?'

But I couldn't. 'It was raw, J. Familiar almost. Like some kind of replay from the past. I felt like I was being abandoned. It was terrifying. It all welled up, sort of roaring, overwhelming. Next thing I remember, I'd hit you. But I don't remember doing it. It had happened. Like I wasn't even there.'

'As I said,' Jemimah quietly replied. 'You weren't yourself.'

'Then who the hell was I? A fucking wife-beater? But I have no memory of it, can't tell you where the rage and the pain came from, except it's there, real. Inside me.'

'You're spending too long on this. It's not good for you. Or us.'

'Listen, J, please. I know enough about the subconscious to realize that those feelings are still there, still have the power to race right up and overwhelm me again.'

'Oh for God's sake, Adrian. We've all got a temper! Right now, you're really beginning to test mine.'

'Sure,' I replied. 'But you wouldn't hit me, would you? Then have no recollection of doing so. This is more than temper, J. This is about something I've buried as neatly as the time when I hit you. Something happened, I'm sure of it, a long time ago. It left me with the anguish I felt when you said you were moving. It's still there, and it frightens the life out of me.'

'So, get help,' Jemimah frostily replied. 'You're a bloody psychiatrist. Get one of your student friends to recommend a good shrink. Hypnotherapy, regression, or whatever the hell you call it.'

'Maybe.'

She stood. 'I'm tired, I'm going back to bed.'

'Sure.'

'You coming?'

'In a moment. I'm sorry.'

She stood by the door. 'What for?'

'Bringing it all up again.'

'Yeah,' she replied, turning. 'So am I.'

'Do you know what really frightens me?'

'I'm not sure I want to.'

'I'm meeting with a man who claims to have killed for fun. It's his sole motive. According to him, he just went ahead and did it, because he wanted to. Yet I find myself wondering what is it about him that obsesses me? And it all comes back to me. He did something, grotesque, irrational, something I can't possibly make any sense out of. Just like I did – when I hit you.'

'Oh, for God's sake, Adrian . . . !'

'I think . . . I fear that in some senses Rattigan and I are possibly the same,' I whispered. 'We've both harmed others without a real motive. Perhaps that's why I'm so hellbent on finding his. Because if I did it'd give me some kind of chance to apply it on myself. I don't know, make me less of a monster than him.'

She'd had enough. 'Christ's sake, Adrian! Listen to yourself. You're not thinking straight. You're not a monster, you haven't killed anyone, and you're putting far too much of you into the whole stupid business. Honestly, it's like comparing a petty shoplifter with the Great Train Robbers. You're talking crap. I'm going upstairs.'

Which she did.

PC KILLER TO HANG

The trial of Joseph Attwood Rattigan concluded yesterday, when Judge Andrew Beaumont Clarke pronounced the death sentence for the silent defendant found guilty of the murder of PC John Scrimshaw, after a late-night brawl during January.

The jury deliberated for less than an hour before returning their unanimous guilty verdict, leaving Judge Clarke with no option but to don the black cap as he passed sentence.

Throughout the nine-day trial, the defendant had refused to take the stand, offering a plea of diminished responsibility and manslaughter, subsequently refused by the court. Upon sentencing, Rattigan silently shook his head, before being taken down.

The guilty verdict comes as no surprise to many who have followed the case. Evidence offered by the Crown during the trial supported its contentions that PC Scrimshaw had been mercilessly attacked while about his duties on the night of January 15th, 1949. Witnesses were able to testify that Rattigan had been seen drinking heavily in a series of public houses found on the Mile End Road, when, stumbling upon PC Scrimshaw about his duties, he proceeded to enter into a drunken verbal exchange with the 22-year-old police officer.

An altercation ensued which rapidly developed into a violent assault on the officer, resulting in Rattigan pushing Scrimshaw through a plate-glass window of a grocery shop. PC Scrimshaw was later identified as dead at the scene of the crime, his throat fatally cut from injuries sustained during his fall through the shop front.

It was only the selfless action of three brave passers-by who managed to manhandle the fleeing Rattigan to the ground as he sought to escape, so bringing the cowardly killer swiftly to justice.

At no point during the trial was Rattigan prepared to offer any motivation for his crime, leaving the jury with little option but to conclude that the defendant's actions were the result of overintoxication due to drink.

In passing sentence, Judge Clarke stated, 'It is the intention of this court that your punishment serve as a warning to all others foolish enough to consider assaulting officers of the law as legitimate sport, following reckless drinking of the sort you were undoubtedly involved in immediately preceding Officer Scrimshaw's untimely demise. Let no one be in any doubt – the law has only one response to perpetrators of this vile, increasing crime. Police officers of any rank will be protected by the law, using its ultimate sanction. And those of us empowered to dispense the righteous justice of retribution will not cower from the responsibilities of our office.'

Solicitors representing Rattigan thought it unlikely he would appeal, as the condemned seemed fully resigned to his fate. At no stage during interviews with arresting officers did Rattigan ever express remorse for his crime, or give solid reasons for his unprovoked attack on PC Scrimshaw.

The Times, Wednesday, 2nd April, 1949.

7

Forty-eight hours later, I found myself back in the smoky, pokey office of Dr Stephen Clancy once more. He had in front of him a thin manilla file entitled HMP Oakwood High Security – Graduate Training Programme. My name had been crudely added to the cover.

I had no idea why he'd asked to see me.

'Come in, sit down,' he gushed. 'Glad you could come.'

'Is there some sort of problem, Steve?' I asked.

'Problem? Good heavens, no. Just thought maybe we should have a little chat.'

'Could've used the phone, surely?'

He shifted a little. 'I wanted to talk face to face, Adrian. Clear the air, perhaps.'

'Go on.'

He chose his words with care. 'I gather from speaking with Neil Allen that you expressed some surprise that I kept him so closely informed of our conversations.'

'I can't remember saying anything at the time.'

Another long draw on the cigar. 'He sensed it. He's a master of body language.'

'Now that you mention it, I was a little taken aback.'

'Don't be. It's perfectly standard. I'm more or less obliged to report back, so to speak. It's nothing personal. Just the form.'

'The form?'

'Procedure, dear chap. Let's just say that one has to exercise great caution when allowing research students to meet with inmates. The experience can prove . . . a little upsetting to those with sensitive dispositions.'

I began putting the pieces together. 'And neither Oakwood

or the university would want any adverse publicity should something go wrong, right?'

He smiled. 'You probably think we're all being dreadfully paranoid, but we have good reason. Very occasionally, exposure to Rattigan and his like can have unforeseen consequences. A similar scheme in Cumbria nearly came unstuck two years ago. The student in question, a woman, I believe, jumped from a tower block midway through her thesis researches.'

'Jesus Christ.'

Fancy held up a hand. 'Now, I'm not saying there was any connection between her death and the work at the hospital, but it could've turned nasty. I mean, for all we know, the woman's love life was probably in a damn mess.'

'You're all heart, aren't you?'

'I'm merely saying it doesn't do to make any assumptions. You only have to cast your mind back to the field day the damn press had with the balls-up at Ashworth to realize the Home Office is rather keen any whiff of scandal emanating from Her Majesty's secure hospitals is kept to an absolute minimum.'

I well remembered Ashworth, the catalogue of damning allegations made by an inmate concerning visits by children to suspected paedophiles. 'You say don't make assumptions, Steve, yet you assume I'm a candidate for the suicide-watch, too?'

He laughed, stubbed out the cigar. 'Good God, no. It's simply that I know you far better than Allen does. And if it looks like the pressure's getting to you, I'm duty-bound to inform the old sod.' He passed the file over. 'This is yours. Inside you'll find a transcript of every interview, together with an assessment of your performance. You can copy all the material inside for use in your thesis should you wish, but you must ensure you return the file for updating at every interview.'

'Right. Thanks.'

'Hope you don't mind, but I've taken a peek. Seems you're still keen Rattigan tells you more about the girl.' He leant forward. 'Just don't pin your hopes on anything.'

'So everyone keeps telling me.'

'With good reason. Besides, what if he tells you something astonishing? Could you ever trust him to tell the truth?'

'He's sitting on something, Steve. I'm sure he is. He keeps letting things slip.'

'Maybe he's doing that deliberately. I suspect you're legitimate sport as far as he's concerned. "Fun", even.' He stood, made for the door, putting on his overcoat. 'You still got that Aretha Franklin tape in the car?'

'Yes?'

'Grand. Shake a leg. We're going for a drive. The good Dr Allen's arranged a little surprise for you and Aretha's just the dame to serenade us on our journey.'

'Bingo!' Fancy exclaimed. 'We're here.'

Twenty minutes later we drew up in front of the Essex Police Headquarters, just five hundred yards from Chelmsford Prison, me still none the wiser as to what the hell we were doing there.

Throughout the journey, Fancy had playfully resisted all my questions, until I grew tired of asking. I contented myself with following his occasional directions, trying desperately to ignore his tuneless warblings.

We parked before a huge complex of grey concrete buildings and playing fields. Stepping from the car, I noticed the tired rows of nearby semidetatched houses, looking as if they clung to the place for the security offered by the Essex home of law enforcement.

A group of young recruits struggled to complete the required number of press-ups barked at them by a muscular intructor, and I found myself cringing at the effects institionalized buildings and their occupants had on me. Just like Oakwood, everything had been seemingly designed for the single purpose of intimidation, the faceless architects responsible having no ethical dilemma over form versus function. Likewise the inhabitants themselves, uniformed, regulated, cracked, all empathy syphoned off by the real brains of the machine – ancient laws and flawed systems laid down by our long-dead forefathers. Difficult to believe these men were all cooing babies once.

Fancy spoke as we neared the entrance. 'DI Russell's your man. He knows you're coming.' He stopped. 'I'll maybe catch you for a drink later in the week, eh?'

'You're not coming in?'

'I'm not invited, dear chap.'

'You're going to wait out here, then?'

'Heavens, no. I'll ring a cab, pop back to the uni. Thanks for the ride. That Aretha's a gem, isn't she?'

'Steve, what's going on?'

'You're here to learn a little more about Rattigan. Allen's been in touch with the Met; they've rushed the stuff up here for your delectation.'

'What stuff?'

'The original file you were given was just a taster. Now Allen feels the time's right for you to know a little more about the kind of man you're dealing with. A sort of unexpurgated version.' He looked me straight in the eye. 'You're going to find out what he did to that girl. Word for word.'

'This DI Russell's going to tell me, is he?'

'No,' Fancy replied. 'Rattigan is.'

I waited ten minutes in reception before I met with DI Russell. Six-two, wiry, regulation haircut, black shoes, grey trousers, white shirt, brown tie, no jacket – introduced himself as Dave, before taking me up to the second floor into a small side office.

Next he brought in a tape recorder and a box of cassettes. 'Had this sent up from the Met. All the tackle they have on your man Rattigan. Gave it a listen myself last night. Quite a headcase.'

'He has his moments.'

'I'm sure he does, sir.'

'Excuse me,' I asked a little nervously. 'Don't get me wrong but is this normal?'

'Normal, sir?' He had a practised way of saying 'sir' which ironed all the respect out of the word. I imagined he perfected the technique interviewing suspects. His cold professionalism chilled me.

'I feel like I've been thrown in at the deep-end, rather,' I said, miserably failing to befriend him with a smile. 'These tapes, who asked you to get them for me?'

'Shrink up at Oakwood,' he confirmed.

'Dr Allen?'

'That's the one. He rang my guv'nors, who put a call through to the boys at the Met. They fished it out and sent it over. Saves you a trip to Scotland Yard, doesn't it?'

'Yeah. Thanks.'

'Pleasure, sir. That answer your question?'

I nodded. 'Here I was thinking I was a special case.'

''Fraid not. Done this sort of thing before for you' – he savoured the word – 'students. Part of the data-gathering programme we're all involved with, constabularies, prisons, judiciary. Lets us have a little peek into these people's brains, or what's left of them. Supposed to save us a lot of time when we're messing around with offender profiling.' Then he smiled. 'I think it's a load of old cobblers myself, but if it keeps the guv'nors happy, then I'm a happy bunny too. I'll leave you with it. I'm in room nine if you need me.'

He left, barking orders at some poor recruit loitering in the corridor outside. I stared at the small black machine on the desk in front of me, and the box of cassettes, each carefully labelled and dated. Here they were, then, the initial interview tapes taken during Rattigan's detention immediately after his arrest for the murder of Helen Lewis.

I cleared my throat, before rubbing both sweating palms along the seams of my trousers. Did I really want to hear it, any of it? After all, I'd studied the file, night after night, read the grim criminal history of the man, from petty offender to institutionalized tramp. Knew as much as I needed to know, surely, about that final explosion of unrestrained violence on an innocent young woman. However . . .

Taking a notepad and pen from my briefcase, I slotted in the first tape and pressed the button marked 'play'.

A man's voice, procedural, contained. Introduced himself as DI Shot from Bethnal Green nick, then announced – for the benefit of the tape – that he's there with his colleague, DS Williams, to interview Frank Rattigan in connection with the murder of Helen Lewis, on the 14th September, 1988.

Enough. I turned the machine off. It was all too real. I suddenly couldn't bear to hear his voice, his whines, his sickness.

I sat breathless in the tiny room, staring at the tape recorder, wishing I could run, but knowing I had to stay, had to endure it . . .

Play . . .

SHOT: Care to tell us, then, Frank? Care to tell us what the bloody hell happened in there?

RATTIGAN: You don't know?

WILLIAMS: We want to hear it from you.

RATTIGAN: Hear what?

WILLIAMS: For God's sake! We pick you up in Helen Lewis's house, and there's bits of her all over the shop! You topped the poor cow, didn't you?

RATTIGAN: Why have you got your cock out, Sergeant? I'm not going to suck it, and I know that's what you want me to –

SHOT: Shut it, Frank! You're doing yourself no favours. Don't play games with us, pal.

RATTIGAN (calmly): All I'm asking is that Sergeant Williams puts his penis away.

SHOT (irritated): For the benefit of the tape, Sergeant Williams is fully dressed.

RATTIGAN: He's playing with it!

WILLIAMS: I'll start playing with you in a minute, you murdering bast –!

SHOT: OK, Sergeant, that's enough! (Pause, during which Rattigan is clearly heard sniggering in the background.) Let's recap a little, shall we? Eleven-twenty this morning, we get call from a Mrs Anne Lewis concerning her daughter. She's worried, hasn't been able to contact her all weekend. Apparently the phone's not working. We decide to investigate.

Upon arrival at her address, a uniformed officer gets no response from the front door, so checks round the back. He peers through a set of French windows and sees what he initially suspects is a bloodstained corpse lying on the sofa. It's you. He calls for backup, which arrives, breaks into the premises, and discovers that you are very much alive. The same, however, could hardly be said of Miss Lewis. With me so far?

RATTIGAN: What more do you need to know? I mean, how fucking dense are you?

SHOT: You're saying you killed her, are you?

RATTIGAN: You've got to be as thick as pigshit to think anything else, right?

SHOT: Just you? On your own, killed Helen Lewis?

RATTIGAN: And the team.

SHOT: Team?

RATTIGAN: Arsenal. Very good, those lads. Very professional. Lot of kicking went on, you see. Took nearly four hours just to get one leg off . . .

SHOT (sighs): OK. This interview suspended at . . . two-twelve, p.m. pending psychiatric investigation of the suspect.

There was a twelve-second pause on the tape, before the interview restarted with the same formal introductions. Four hours had elapsed. This time, Rattigan appeared more subdued, and another officer, DCI Moira, had joined the team.

MOIRA: Recognize this, Frank?

RATTIGAN: Envelope.

MOIRA: Want to know what's in it?

RATTIGAN: Money.

MOIRA: Two out of two, clever boy. Now, before we go any further, would you tell me if you see any one of the officers present with his penis out?

RATTIGAN: You're starving me!

SHOT: The money. Yours, is it?

RATTIGAN: Friend's.

SHOT: Looking after it for someone, were you? Lot of loot, Frank. Nearly a grand in there.

WILLIAMS: What friend? Another one of your 'mates' from the Arsenal?

RATTIGAN: What's he talking about? Dickhead!

MOIRA: He wants to know . . . we all want to know, how a shabby dosser like you ended up with all that cash in your coat pocket.

RATTIGAN: Seems fair.

SHOT: Well?

RATTIGAN: Someone gave it me.

SHOT: Helen Lewis? That what you're saying, is it, Frank? She give it you, did she? Eventually?

RATTIGAN (laughing): She gave me nothing. But I really gave it to that bitch, didn't I? Didn't I, eh? Really gave it to her.

MOIRA: What do you know about her, Frank?

RATTIGAN: I know how her insides work. How they used to.

MOIRA: Why her?

RATTIGAN: Feed me.

MOIRA: Why her!

RATTIGAN (suddenly animated): She was there, right. I'd had a look at her gaff, thought I might pile in there and squat it out for a week or so. Looked like the place was unoccupied. Next I know, the fuckin' front door's opening, and the bitch just calmly walks in. No alternative, really. Just went to work on her.

MOIRA: She was an air hostess. Did you know that?

RATTIGAN (angrily): You think I fucking care! You think I give a shit about the stupid tart?

SHOT: What we're saying, Frank, is that Helen Lewis had a good job. Few bob in the bank. Nice house. You break in, and next we know she's dead, and you're found with nearly a grand in cash.

WILLIAMS: You tortured her, didn't you? Tortured the poor girl so's she'd tell you where her money was, right? What happened first, Frank? Good-looking girl, she was. Fucked her, did you? Fancied a quickie before you started hunting for the cash?

MOIRA: How long were you in the house?

RATTIGAN: Three days.

MOIRA: During which time you killed her, right?

RATTIGAN: She killed me years ago.

MOIRA: You knew her, then, did you, from years ago? You sought her out?

RATTIGAN: Christ's sake! You arseholes are so stupid. You don't get it, do you? I didn't have to find the bitch. She's always been around. Smiling at me. Know what I'm saying? (Pause) I mean, it's no good, is it, eh? To smile like that, and then . . . do nothing.

SHOT: I don't know, Frank. Maybe you can tell us what you mean. I'm confused. What makes a smile useless? I don't have a problem with a pretty woman smiling.

RATTIGAN: It was the first thing that went, you know, her fucking smile. (Laughs) They say, don't they, 'Just wipe that smile off your face'? I did the next best thing, didn't I? Couldn't be doing with all those screams. Found them, have you, the lips?

SHOT: Not really our job, Frank. We're looking for something else. The reason. Your motive. You going to tell us?

RATTIGAN (laughs again): What, and end all the fun? Just when we're all getting on so fucking famously? But from where I am, you clever boys seem to have it all worked out, don't you? The money, isn't it? Bit of rape, then I kill her for the cash. Sounds very plausible to me. Highly likely. Hurrah for the police! Trebles all round!

Moira suspends interview.

8

The tape rolled on, turning slowly in the black machine on the cigarette-burnt table. Outside, suburban birds tried their best to divorce me from the tinny voices, a natural melody of harmless song inadequately competing with Rattigan's sickening confession. But there was no comfort to be had from their happy twittering. Birds go on, regardless. Birds sing before every execution.

I began to see Allen's purpose in sending me there a little more clearly. I had the benefit of a better insight, now. Rattigan had told me everything, and it chilled me to the bone. A significant part of me wanted nothing more to do with the Beast of East 16, leave him and his mind and motives be – as if I'd opened an abandoned manhole cover and found it clogged with all the shit from humanity.

However, another equally significant part urged me on, directed me down into the stinking mess of the man with dark, whispered promises of what lay waiting there. Truth was, the more I knew about the man the less it all made sense; the more I felt there was to discover. About him. And perhaps myself into the bargain.

I hated myself, but was honest enough to admit I was hooked. Addicted – as surely as I'd been to the booze.

Here's a condensed version of what I heard that morning, taken from my own notes written at the time.

There are seven interviews in all, taken over a period of three days after Rattigan's arrest. As each is terminated and another begins, new pieces fall into the puzzle as the investigation gathers momentum. A total of six officers and three psychiatrists take part at various times, each determined to make some sense of Helen Lewis's apparently needless death.

And always the repeated question: 'Why?'

And Rattigan's 'answer': ''Cause she was there. Pretty as a picture.'

. . . Police at Bethnal Green (headed by DCI Moira) quickly establish the previous movements of Frank Rattigan prior to the attack. An address found on the suspect's clothes links him to Welland Farm, Suffolk, where further enquiries reveal he was working (cash in hand) as a fruit-picker during the week before the murder.

Two other pickers are tracked down and interviewed, when, in exchange for anonymity from the DHSS, they not only confirm Rattigan's whereabouts, but go on to add that whilst picking plums, a green Jaguar XJS drew into the farmyard. The driver seemed anxious to speak to Rattigan in particular. The farmer, a Mr Bob Jenkins, verifies the incident, but cannot say whether the Jaguar's driver sought out Rattigan specifically. It was Friday the 9th September, 1988.

In response to this, Rattigan would only say that the driver was lost and needed directions. He had no idea who the man was, and only sought to offer what help he could in the circumstances. However, both pickers were under the impression that the driver knew Rattigan personally. The suspect and the driver spent several minutes in conversation among the farm's outbuildings, before the driver left the scene.

The next day, Saturday the 10th September, both pickers confirm that Rattigan had simply disappeared. They were glad – he had struck them as a 'weirdo'.

Rattigan's next sighting is at a café less than three hundred yards from Helen Lewis's terraced house in Stratford, East London, on Sunday the 11th of September. Somehow, Rattigan has travelled the best part of one hundred and thirty miles to sit in a grubby café drinking tea. When questioned about this, he merely offers that he was 'bored shitless picking fucking fruit', insisting there was no connection between his sudden departure from the farm and the conversation with the driver of the green XJS.

Investigating officers interview the café owner, who confirms Rattigan spent three hours in the café. He surmises the dirty man was 'just another dosser' . . .

. . . Seven o'clock on Sunday evening and, according to Rattigan (who is by now talking quite freely to investigating officers), he sets off down Stratford High Road, turning left into Manor Gardens, a row of elegant terraced homes, set relatively quietly in the East London suburb . . .

. . . By eight, he's scouted the street for the most suitable property to break into and squat. Records found by investigating officers confirm that Rattigan had a long and varied criminal history, including several prison sentences for breaking and entering. Within minutes he has gained entry to number thirty-seven, saying the lack of lights, intruder alarms and visible neighbours made the home of Helen Lewis an ideal choice. Once inside, he draws the curtains, disconnects phone lines, then cooks himself a pizza and chips from the freezer . . .

. . . Ten o'clock that night, and Rattigan is woken from sleeping on the sofa by the sound of the key turning in the front door. Helen Lewis, a twenty-two-year-old BA air hostess walks unsuspectingly into her hallway after working a seventy-two-hour transatlantic haul to LA via Copenhagen . . .

. . . Panicked, bleary with sleep, Rattigan quickly rushes the terrified woman, pulling her into the darkened lounge, where her screams force him to knock her unconscious using a cricket-ball-sized onyx paperweight . . .

. . . She's out for maybe fifteen minutes at the most, during which time Rattigan manages to find a roll of three-inch insulating tape in one of the kitchen drawers, which he then wraps around her entire face, before using a biro to roughly puncture the tape at the juncture he suspects is closest to her nostrils. Rolling her over, he binds both wrists behind her back, before returning to the kitchen to find the chicken-scissors he will use to cut off her clothes . . .

. . . At no stage during any interview on the tape does Rattigan answer questions as to his state of mind during those first few minutes, save for the one admission that he felt he had to 'do her'. Detectives repeatedly ask him to explain further. Rattigan refuses . . .

. . . Helen Lewis is now naked, save for the grey insulating tape mummifying her head, wrists and legs, from the ankles to the knees. She can't move, despite her struggles, and a slight trickle of blood begins to run through her shoulder-length, thick, black hair on to the beige carpet.

Rattigan spends several minutes watching her struggle, then his attention is drawn to an oval photograph set on the mantelpiece above the gas-effect fireplace – Helen Lewis, ravishingly youthful and professional in her BA uniform. She is smiling . . .

. . . It takes him longer than he thinks to cut the lips from her face. The 'operation' is risky, as it involves removing the plastic gag, and stuffing the protesting mouth with the victim's discarded underwear before he can proceed in relative silence. During the action, Rattigan sustains a deep cut in his left hand. A police forensic officer will later confirm the wound correlates closely to bite marks consistent with Helen Lewis's dental records . . .

. . . Rattigan has to use much more tape to keep the bloodied mouth closed, the adhesive slipping under the gushing gore. Fortunately for the victim, she has again passed out. Rattigan lifts the unconscious body into a sitting position, propped up next to a cream sofa, in order to ensure 'the bitch didn't choke on her own fucking knickers' . . .

. . . Rattigan goes back into the kitchen and has a cold bottle of Becks from the fridge. He spends several minutes arranging a variety of implements with the precision of a consultant surgeon on the expensive working surface. In a cupboard under the stairs, he finds a vacuum cleaner, tears the electric lead from the junction where it meets the innocent machine, then pares away the black flex to reveal the red and blue wires within. In seconds he has exposed the glinting brass brushes of the conductor wires.

He returns to the lounge, and plugs his ten-metre flexible cattle-prod into a socket normally home to a Tiffany lamp bought from Camden Market. Blue sparks shoot angrily from the exposed copper wires. He is ready to play . . .

. . . Rattigan is again asked at this point as to his intentions. DCI Moira and DI Shot continue to imply that Rattigan's aims were torturous as well as murderous, and repeat their contention that Rattigan acted as he did in order that Lewis would reveal where money and valuables were hidden in the house. How else would he have gained access to the large amount of cash he had on his person when arrested? Rattigan scoffs at this suggestion, maintaining that if money was his aim, why would he have gagged his quarry, butchered then silenced the mouth which would have led him to it? . . .

. . . Back at thirty-seven, Manor Way, Rattigan reckons it's about eleven p.m. on the first night of the attack when he brushes the soles of Helen Lewis's feet with the electrical wires for the first time. He is amazed at the animating effects 240 volts have on an apparently lifeless body. But she is alive. Muffled screams and a pathetic attempt to struggle from the wires only serve to vary the electric assault. Rattigan is most pleased when he creates what he calls, 'my own human jumping-bean'. Switching off the power, he pushes and tapes first the blue, then the red wire up into the two holes underneath the victim's nostrils. Then, by simply retreating to the socket, he is free to switch the contraption on and off as his heart desires. On, off. On, off. A second or two at a time. Nothing too lengthy that it would 'take her out of it too sudden, like'.

Rattigan estimates he bores of this after ten minutes or so, returns to the kitchen for another Becks, then surveys the glinting knives, forks and can-openers laid so precisely on the marbled surface, racking his brains for more 'fun' as he does so . . .

. . . Consumed with new possibilities, Rattigan sets to work on an improvised set of leg chains, using lengths of grey insulating tape twisted into strong plastic ropes. Returning to the living room, he is delighted to see Helen Lewis has attempted to slide on her naked belly towards the door. He frees her legs from the original tape, then applies the leg 'irons' and forces her to stand, satisfied with his improvised design. She can move, shuffle, but can only take the tiniest of steps. She shakes uncontrollably and wets herself once more, as Rattigan explains they're going to play 'hide-and-seek'.

Even better, he spots a pair of state-of-the-art cordless headphones sitting on top of a polystyrene mannequin's head next to the television. Taking the bloodied chicken-scissors from the floor, he clumsily cuts two holes in the side of her tape-swathed head, revealing whitened ears. She sits for this, as her legs have given way.

Next, he tapes the headphones in place, taking several minutes to work out how to operate the expensive-looking hi-fi set in the corner of the room. Eventually, he manages to tune it to Radio 3, and there is the rewarding sound of muffled orchestral music powering into Helen Lewis's ears. A red light glows on the side of the headphones . . .

. . . By now, the sixth interview conducted at Bethnal Green Police Station, investigating officers seem to have lost the will to question the suspect further. The tape is ominously quiet, save for Rattigan's calm description of the remaining hours of Helen Lewis's life . . .

. . . Midnight, and 'hide-and-seek' begins in earnest. Rattigan arms himself with a knife and a battery-powered travel-iron, then proceeds to raise Helen on to her feet once more. Naked, taped, arms bound behind her back, assaulted by unstoppable sound, she is spun violently round and around, Rattigan struggling to complete the task and keep her on her feet. Job done, he stands back, watching her shuffle giddily on burnt feet. Inevitably, she crashes to the floor, and Rattigan is straight in with the iron . . .

. . . He 'plays' until one o' clock. The broken air hostess is now suffering from multiple burns, deep wounds, extensive bruising and scratches. During the last sixty minutes, she has twice tried to hurl herself through what she desperately hoped were the living room windows, but each time Rattigan has been there, waiting, knife in hand. Both nipples have been sliced off in 'penalties'.

He's amazed at how much he has enjoyed the game, sometimes standing just inches from her unknowing, taped face, knife and iron at the ready, sometimes watching from a distance, smothering his giggling delight as she painfully collapses over another item of furniture he has silently placed in her way.

Eventually, after another Becks, he feels his first yawn of the evening. He's tired. Reluctantly, he grabs the girl, who thrashes surprisingly strongly considering the evening's entertainment for which she's been such an amusing, if not reluctant, hostess.

He takes her upstairs into the bathroom, dumping her on the black and white lino-tiled floor, before filling the bath with three inches of cold water, then placing her, stomach down, buttocks up, into the freezing bath. Hands still taped behind her back, she has to strain considerably to lever her head out of the water, in order to breathe through the blackened nostril holes on the bloodstained tape which still covers her face.

Rattigan leaves her there, listening to something suitably appropriate by Vaughan Williams, as he pads contentedly into her bedroom, then slides himself under the lilac bedspread and crisp lemon-scented sheets . . .

. . . Nine the next morning. Rattigan's up and ready for more 'fun', having slept soundly. There's a spring in his step as he makes his way expectantly to the bathroom. However, all is not well, his hopes are soon dashed. Rattigan discovers to his dismay that his new toy has died during the night, and is now head-down in the pinking water. Her bowels have finally given way. A stinking yellow turd floats in the scummy water between her legs.

Depressed and angry at this unexpected forestalling of proceedings, Rattigan wanders downstairs and has a bowl of muesli with some live yoghurt.

He takes the premature termination of his fun and games very personally indeed, and spends the next two days reducing the stinking corpse to porridge . . .

On Wednesday, the fourteenth of September, 1988, just as Rattigan is snoozing on the bloodstained sofa downstairs, a lone PC, sent to check on Miss Lewis after relatives report her phone line dead, stumbles upon a scene of complete carnage. Stopping only to vomit in the rosebushes, he then calls for immediate backup. Minutes later an arrest team storms the malodorous premises, and takes Rattigan to Bethnal Green. He makes no effort to evade his capture.

Upon arriving at the police station, Rattigan informs the duty sergeant that he's glad he's 'out of that fucking gaff. The food was shit. All microwave stuff, and health rubbish'.

9

DI Russell joined me in the silent room.

'Will you be requiring lunch, sir?'

I shook my head. 'Lost my appetite a little bit.'

He sat, watching me in a manner which possibly betrayed a deeper interest. 'What do you reckon, then?'

'How do you mean?'

He lit up. 'You've met the bloke. Is he lying, or what?'

'I've no idea,' I answered honestly. 'From what I know, he left the body in bits. Broke two toes kicking one of the legs out of its socket. By the time the pathologist got what remained on the mortuary slab it was anyone's guess what had really happened. Rattigan gives us the only explanation. And with no other witnesses, we more or less have to take his word for it.'

Russell took a deep drag. I could sense he wasn't really listening, simply nodding, looking for a gap in the conversation, waiting to break in. 'How much do you know about the case, then, sir?'

'Only what's written in the Home Office file. Dr Allen forwarded me a copy. It contains a good deal about the murder, subsequent investigation, court case.'

'Really?' He scratched the side of his face. 'They find any other prints in the house?'

'Besides Rattigan's and the girl's?' I shook my head.

Russell exhaled, stared out of the window. I had the impression he was as intrigued about Rattigan and his motives as I was. 'Tell you one thing,' he said. 'Listening to those tapes, it just sounded too real for me. As if he was bored by it all, wanted to be charged and banged up there and then. Sick man.' He paused again, seemingly gathering his thoughts. 'Though it struck me as I listened, maybe he played them all for suckers. Not that it's my case, or anything.'

'Please,' I encouraged, sensing the beginnings of something. 'I'd really value a professional opinion.'

Russell turned to me. 'This goes no further than the two of us. It isn't my job to speculate.'

'Of course.'

'I wouldn't have been happy to have been on the investigating team.' He stood and walked to the window, stubbing out the cigarette in a pub ashtray lying on the sill. 'The moment your man comes out with the torture stuff it throws a massive spanner in the works.'

'Because he's potentially insane?' I offered, surprised Russell was willing to open up so candidly.

'The boys are more or less obliged to call the shrinks in. He admits he's guilty, says the whole thing's completely random – she comes home, he's squatting there, he kills her – leaving the investigating team to look to the psychiatrists for a motive. Whole thing disappears right out of CID's hands, suddenly property of the brain doctors, motive, the lot. Which they supply – Rattigan's a psycho, and she was just unlucky. He's charged on the confession, and the investigation stops in its tracks.'

'But you think there's more?'

'The money,' Russell replied cagily. 'Like I say, it's not my case, never likely to be, but I reckon the Met called the shrinks in a little too early. It just doesn't sit right. The green Jag, another pointer. You've read the file, right? Got more of a handle on this than I ever will.'

I nod, attempting to recall the relevant details. 'Police put out a nationwide alert to all forces to trace all movements by green Jaguar owners on the day Rattigan had the conversation at the Suffolk fruit farm.'

'Must have been thousands.'

'Hundreds. Anyway, before any progress is made, Rattigan is charged with murder.'

'Exactly what I'm saying. Any real truth is buried because Rattigan freely admits his guilt. In my mind, the car has to be the link. One minute he's screwing the benefit system picking plums, the next he's had a quick chat with someone in a green Jag, and disappears. Turns up in East London, doing the nasty on the stewardess with nearly a grand in cash.'

I said nothing, waiting for the punchline.

Russell leapt into the pregnant pause. 'Contract job,' he said authoritatively. 'Just a hunch, mind. And my opinion's worth stuff-all.'

'Even so,' I flattered. 'I could do with all the professional help I can get.'

Russell nodded, and I wondered briefly how much of a buzz he was getting out of enlightening me with his wisdom. 'Maybe the fella in the Jag gives Rattigan the cash to play games with the girl. Air stewardess, flies the world. Possibly had international connections. Or suppose your man gets the wrong address? Maybe the whole thing's just one big mistake. He tortures the girl for whatever information the Jag owner wants, but it's the wrong girl, but he's too intoxicated to care. Might explain why he went to such lengths with her.'

'Maybe,' I replied.

He sighed. 'God only knows what the deal was, but I bet you this . . .'

'He has the money before he even arrives?'

Russell nodded 'Nearly a thou, in an envelope? No one keeps that sort of money under the mattress, do they?'

'Someone pays him?' I asked. 'To torture Helen Lewis?'

'Listen,' Russell warned. 'This is strictly off-the-record. Just my speculation.'

'I'm grateful, really.'

He sat again. 'Maybe the Jag owner knows Rattigan's desperate for some readies. I mean, your man's spent enough time inside, perhaps even made some pretty heavy connections, offered himself out as a hitman. Who knows? Tell you this much, though, the Met were probably thinking the same. Then – bingo – Rattigan does his Hannibal Lecter impression and suddenly the investigation's pulled. I bet there weren't a lot of happy bunnies in CID when that happened. Too many unanswered questions, aren't there?'

'Such as?' I answered, resisting the urge to take notes, keenly trying to commit the conversation to memory. This was dynamite, the closest I'd come to finding a legitimate motive for the crime. At the time, I didn't really care if Russell's clandestine theorizing was totally off-beam. It was a start – a deviation from that dreaded word 'fun'.

'I'd have been interested in Rattigan's previous, for starters,' Russell replied. 'Any indications of past psychotic incidents on record. If this was a one-off, you'd have to ask yourself what had made him flip.'

'Or ask him.'

'Perhaps.'

'And it's really as simple as that? The investigation ceased once Rattigan was suspected of insanity?'

He coloured slightly, lit up again, taking time to formulate an answer. 'It's different these days. All I know is that for the investigation to be pulled proper at the time, it would have had to have been authorized from the top. Chief superintendent, CPS, whoever. Basically it would've come down to a "them" and "us" situation. CID on one side, shrinks on the other. Top brass and the CPS would've decided which way the balance went. Seems like the shrinks won the day. But I bet CID were a little confused. To my mind there was so much left to investigate, so many possibilities other than insanity.'

It was music to my ears.

'Look,' Russell said. 'You need to speak to the lads at the Met. Trace down the original investigating team. Maybe one of them could tell you what happened. I'm just guessing right now.'

'Right,' I replied. 'I appreciate your time. Really.'

'Just don't take any of it as gospel.'

'Sure. Listen, Dave, I've got to ask you . . .'

'Don't.' He held up a hand. 'Please. I know what you're going to say, and I can't help you. There could have been any number of reasons why. Personally, I think there was probably a bit of pressure applied. Nineteen eighty-eight, right? Care in the community's just taking off. General public whipped into a media frenzy claiming all the bins are turning hundreds of axe-wielding psychopaths loose on to the streets. Tough times.'

'Meaning there's a pretty big lever on the police to get a quick result with Rattigan?' I asked.

'Can't say,' Russell replied. 'I wasn't there. Now, if you'll excuse me.' He made to leave.

I reconsulted my mental notes. 'The case did make a lot of the dailies. They called him "The Beast of East 16". Headlines at the time were completely predictable. "Deranged lunatic slices innocent girl to bits" stuff.'

Russell paused by the door. 'We're talking about the bad old days,' he finally offered. 'Too much paperwork and external pressures for quick results. Mistakes were sometimes made . . . sometimes, mind . . . simply due to lack of resources.'

I struggled with the thread. 'Checking every Jag owner's movements would have been too expensive?'

He turned to me and began counting the following points on his fingers. 'One – Rattigan chops up the girl. Two – the papers put the pressure on. Three – your man freely confesses. Four – the Met charge Rattigan. Five – everyone's happy, general public feel a little more confidence in the boys in blue, top brass is ecstatic, even Rattigan's probably happy with the result, glad he's not facing life in the Scrubs. It's quick, cheap, and over very quickly.' He opened the door. 'Not that I ever said a word of that.'

I left a few minutes after.

I was back home by two.

Our neighbours were statistics of nineties Britain. Both properties were of equal size and design to ours, but one was home to a private day-nursery, the other a firm of solicitors on the ground floor, an architect on the first floor, and someone offering shiatsu massage in the basement.

Yet here we had lived for eight years, and there was something comfortingly familiar about the place as I crunched up the gravel and opened the large, pale-green front door, to stand silently in the darkened hallway.

For in those few seconds I was literally away from everything and everyone. Just me – and the faint cries of excited children playing next door, the occasional shudder as a heavy lorry thundered by. Quiet contentment smothered me, the smell of polish competing with breakfast's bacon.

I thanked God for a moment's respite from the madness.

Then made my way to the WP and began transcribing notes from the unscheduled morning at Police HQ. Two hours later, I was done. Guy and Juliet were back from school, absorbed in Playstation and phoning friends respectively. Neither bothered to come and see their toiling dad for reasons I fully understood. Theirs was a life full of possibilities and fun. I was just a father who spent his time absorbed in crime, would one day be called Dr Dad, and couldn't handle the complexities of computer games no matter how many times the aliens zapped me.

I yawned, switched off the machine, realized I needed to wake myself up. I had a choice – go down to the gym for an hour before Jemimah came home; or start cooking pasta with James Brown going full tilt. No contest – moments later I was down in the kitchen loading the best of the great man into the CD player.

I love preparing food. And it's not simply because I'm a little on the rotund side of lean. For me, it's a private ritual. I've always indulged in what Jemimah calls 'full-body cookery' – lots of flashing blades, crashing pans, dancing, singing. I'll be the first to admit that the results aren't always as palatable as the preparation, but then the eating is merely icing on the cake. The creation is key.

But that afternoon, James Brown was failing in his culinary obligation, couldn't shake or stir me as I stirred and shaked. Rattigan was always there, teasing, cajoling, making obscene suggestions. His face reflected in the heavy steel knives. His whispered insanity spat at me from stinging, frying onions. There were too many implements around, too many reminders of Rattigan's own brand of sick kitchen creativity. I doubted I'd be able to use a tenderizing mallet for some time.

And the Bolognese I cooked. So much pulpy, red, meaty sludge. Even bolstered by mushrooms, peppers, onions and herbs – it was her, Helen Lewis as last seen by the pathologist.

I began to feel quite ill, mind refusing to budge from the meal Rattigan had made of her.

I turned off the CD. Then hated the quickly descending silence. Checked my watch. Still another hour before Jemimah came home. For some reason I suddenly needed her badly. Her voice. Her wisdom.

The radio went on, and I silently prayed it wouldn't be playing classical. Just couldn't bear to hear that as well, seeing the naked, bleeding girl, wandering in my mind's eye – stalked, serenaded by classical. Classically killed.

But it was a discussion about football. I sat back down, relieved, glad of another's voice in the room. Invisible company. Poured myself a coffee, really wishing I could swap it for a glass of red. Just the one . . . to dull the day . . .

No way – not ever.

The subject had moved on to the fans. In particular the bad boys, the nutters. Incredibly, they'd managed to persuade a couple of them to turn up at the Beeb and be grilled by the show's resident, and audibly bored, psychotherapist.

It was all fairly standard stuff – predictable questions – neolithic responses. I was feeling a little improved, hungry even, and was just beginning to pen the first few mental lines of a letter to the show's producer offering my services as a highly paid, yet vastly more entertaining advisor, when . . .

. . . *Bang* . . .

It happened.

Almost a physical blow, a punch from nowhere, no one. And loud, so very loud, a cry, a scream, all too familiar, yet horribly unknown.

It lasted a split second, then was gone, leaving me feeling as if something dark and forbidden had passed right through me at sickening speed.

And then, as the nausea returned, I began to hear voices, a hideous collage of past and present. The young thugs on the radio proudly retold their favourite Saturday-afternoon street battles over the top of a sound-effects track denoting a similar scene. Which got louder, and louder, and . . .

Until I couldn't hear the voices any more, just this cacophony of drunken fear. I wondered if the show's producer had fallen asleep at the mixing desk, turned the track up too high. It had to be a mistake – all that violence, swearing now, bottles being thrown, and quite obviously . . .

It was in my head. Not the radio. The track was mine.

I began to slap my forehead, then pound it. Anything to rid myself of the noise. And it wasn't simply the disorientation, there was a real fear there, too. Growing, reaching out to strangle me.

What the hell was happening? An auditory hallucination? Was there such a thing? I was too spaced out to focus my mind. I just wanted the noise, the voices, to go. Wanted to run – but couldn't. Yet onwards they came, an army, wanting to hurt me, really enjoy hurting me.

I screamed but heard no sound, nothing above their terrifying din.

I was terrified. Absolutely scared witless.

Yet part of me knew this was coming. Here was where the answers lay, where I had to go to move on. Somewhere in the ruins of this half-remembered bottle-fight was an incident I had crushed, but now had to recall. An event which demanded to be heard, making its way stealthily from the past to shape my future.

When Jemimah returned, she found me in the kitchen, curled up, sobbing.

We had a takeaway that night.

10

After, when the kids had gone to bed, we talked.

I was exhausted. We'd eaten in a nervous family silence, and I watched the furtive glances which shot from one to the other. God knows how much Guy and Juliet had witnessed, or how long I'd been lying on the kitchen floor – but it was obvious they were just as disturbed as I was by their father's sudden unpredictability.

There was nothing I felt I could say which would make light of the situation. I was still so bloody confused, frightened. This is how it must have been for them when I drank, only now I was sober, had no excuse for what had happened, couldn't offer a slurred apology or explanation. Which made it all so much worse.

Unsurprisingly, Jemimah's first reaction upon seeing me was that I'd fallen off the wagon in a big way. I couldn't blame her, I obviously looked totally wrecked. It was only after she'd got close enough to cautiously sniff for whisky fumes that she held me, realizing something else was very wrong.

In bed, she did the same, comforting me, gently probing for some kind of explanation I was helpless to give.

'It's that bloody man,' she said. 'It's not good for you. For any of us.'

'This isn't about Rattigan,' I insisted. 'It's me.'

'What the hell happened, Adrian?'

I described what I'd heard as best I could, hoping that by airing the nightmare, I might in some senses be exorcizing it.

'Football thugs? Coming to get you?'

'And I couldn't move. Didn't know where I was. It was

all too loud. I wanted to run, but couldn't. Something held me there.'

'And you think that . . . ?'

'I don't know what to think. All I know is that one minute I was right as bloody rain, the next all hell let loose.'

'Perhaps you should see someone.'

'No,' I replied, missing the point. 'It was a sound thing. Just noise.'

'I meant,' she diplomatically replied. 'See someone who's maybe a little bit more of an expert on this.'

The penny dropped. 'A therapist?'

'Couldn't harm, could it?'

'Jesus, I don't know.'

'Think about it, yeah?'

'OK.' There was a long silence as I debated how much to tell her. 'I heard what he did to her today. Rattigan. Allen arranged for me to hear the tapes of his confession.'

She sighed. 'Well, is it any wonder you're cracking up? Was that really necessary?'

'It was a good thing, J,' I tried to assure her. 'I spoke to a CID bloke. He agreed with me. There's more to the case than first appears.'

'Adrian,' she calmly replied. 'Don't you think you're becoming rather obsessed with all this?'

'Obsessed?'

'I don't think it's doing you any good. Comparing yourself with the man, constantly struggling to rationalize him.'

'It's what I want to do, J. What I've grafted so hard for.'

'But maybe,' she said. 'Sometimes it's best letting some things go.'

'I just feel I have to.'

'Why?' Her eyes pleaded with mine.

'Because . . .' But I had no real answer to give, just a pitch-black feeling which couldn't be put into words.

'Please,' she said. 'Talk it over with someone. I'm really worried. We all are.'

'I'll try. Really.'

We cuddled some more, before turning out the light. She was asleep quickly whilst I struggled to do the same. Even exhausted as I was, I somehow couldn't shake off the fear that whatever had found me in the kitchen was gathering itself, waiting to return.

Over the next few days, I threw myself back into my work, hoping Rattigan would keep my own ghosts at bay. There were people to contact, appointments to arrange, research to be carried out.

I started with Russell's tip. Tracing Moira, Williams and Shot from the original Met police enquiry was fast becoming a priority, but there were no takers. OK, so in retrospect I can admit that I was being somewhat naive, but at the time I seriously believed that if you called up to speak to a police officer, you'd at least have a slim chance of talking to him.

I had no chance, stalling at the very first, 'And what might this enquiry be in connection with, sir?' hurdle. I mentioned Rattigan, the year of the arrest, and was told the officer I wanted to speak to in each case wasn't available. I accepted the excuses, thought nothing more of it. Made a note to try again, soon.

I reread the transcription from my morning's session at Essex Police HQ, and was once again plunged into the sick darkness of Rattigan's world. The 'Whys?' and 'What ifs?' returned with a vengeance.

And the deeper I immersed myself, the more I found I was almost mentally defending the man. That he wasn't a 'Beast'. That even as he inserted the bare flex into Helen Lewis's nostrils there had to be some insanely logical motive for doing so. Twisted, psychotic, indefensible – but a reason, nonetheless. But the harder I tried to make sense of the horror, the more I began to doubt my abilities to ever rationalize its causes and beginnings. And all the time one solution refused to go away.

Perhaps Rattigan really *was* evil, overpowered by dark forces, slave to their obscene commands and desires – a robot killer, obeying orders from hidden voices deep within his mind. Maybe all was exactly as he boasted.

He enjoyed his 'games'. Had no conscience regarding his immoral behaviour. Maybe the tabloids had got it right.

Dismayed, I tried a new tack. A very risky procedure. Stupidly, I thought myself into the part. Like perhaps an actor might have done, desperately searching for some motivation, a handle drawn from my own experience in a lame attempt to understand why he inflicted such pain.

I waited until the house was empty, then simply went with what I imagined to be his feelings. It became a power trip. A ghastly fantasy – the domination of one human being over another. The inadequate rapist's psyche. Rattigan always claimed he never had sex with her, that the act was never on the agenda. And the longer I 'became' him, to my shame, the more I began to understand the vehemence of the denial. Sex was way down on the list. Domination took the honours. Rattigan's pleasure came from being able to do whatever he wanted to another human being. Having the time, the space, the comfort to take it further, prolong the moment . . .

. . . But I was going too deep. In absolutely the wrong direction, against all I had been told, learnt and warned against. There is never any place for personal comparison in the science of the mind. But I couldn't stop it . . .

I saw Rattigan with a hard-on, one hand lazily pumping his dripping cock, the other raising a heavily bloodied claw-hammer in a gradual arc above Helen Lewis's taped head. Because I assumed it must have turned him on, led him tripping along an orgasmic high-wire, the power, naked flesh, time, imagination and equipment.

Then, one day, Amy arrived, like the bad memory she was. I was confused, incredulous. I hadn't thought about Amy Jordan in years, yet there she was, perfectly preserved.

And worse, it was no longer Helen Lewis that 'Rattigan' played with, but Amy.

I tried to erase the scene, but she wouldn't go, wouldn't return to whatever forgotten locker of my memory she had appeared from. My mind spun back the years to enlighten me. I saw her sweet-sixteen, standing in the flashing glow of the evening ferris wheel – Amy, my girl, out for a night at the fair, and her, giggling nervously, chewing on her bottom lip, telling me she didn't want to kiss that night. Or any other night. But one of her friends fancied me, she'd introduce me, I'd like her . . .

. . . And how I hated Amy so completely in one blithe instant, choked on the juvenile anger of teenage rejection, watching her walk arm in arm with her new, tall, slim, older beau, away from me . . .

. . . We were back in an instant. Stratford, East London, a front room I'd mentally furnished myself. It was Amy I saw as Rattigan placed the hot iron between plump thighs. Then he turned to me, questioning, waiting for approval. I controlled him, and he controlled her. He simply waited. And waited . . .

I hurried to the bathroom to be sick. I felt faint, giddy, dead. For I knew that at that moment I had crossed. Stepped over the line from academic voyeur to mental participant. Lent my own appalled imaginings to a scene ten years past.

Yet there was a strange excitement there, too, born out of the belief that I was finally privy to some inkling of understanding, a gleaming nugget of violent insight which had evaded me thus far.

The answer came with a sea of faces from my own past – bank managers, schoolteachers, bosses, the ex-girlfriends who had chucked me . . . and Rattigan, most especially Rattigan – all of whom I felt had interfered with my life, drove their own knife in. All of whom, I now realized, I could easily replace Helen Lewis with in my own mental retelling of Rattigan's crimes.

It wasn't enough just to hate these people – you had to *love* hating them to pull off the kind of damage Frank Rattigan freely confessed to. You needed to immerse yourself in their suffering, revel in their distress. Just as he'd done.

In some senses I felt re-energized, vital, alive. I reread the file, bathed in the new light of this revelation, digesting every line, every report, every photograph.

It took a further two hours, during which time my eyes ached from ingesting the small black type. But it was there, time and time again – Rattigan's trigger – 'pretty as a picture' – an innocent-looking photograph standing on a mantelpiece in Stratford, ten years previously.

Helen Lewis, head and shoulders, smiling.

And the first thing he did was cut the lips from her face.

Above all other things, Rattigan loved to hate her smile.

11

Edited transcript of third interview with Rattigan at Oakwood, RECREATION SIX. Rattigan, 'Warder-Orderly Denton' and myself in attendance.

(Nine minutes.)

RAWLINGS: Tell me about your father, Frank.

RATTIGAN: You see, the question you have to ask yourself is this, fat-boy. What the fuck are you doing here? Eh? I mean, really doing here?

RAWLINGS: Asking questions, Frank.

RATTIGAN: Being a good little student, is it? That how you justify it, is it?

RAWLINGS: Like I said before we started, I ask a set series of questions which form the basis of a data-gathering exercise. In turn, I'm sponsored by the Home Office for the completion of my thesis.

RATTIGAN: Pay's good, is it?

RAWLINGS: I don't think that's . . .

RATTIGAN: Only, this is what I can't suss. Call me stupid, but you ain't like the others they've had in here. Ain't no fresh young pup eager for a few quid. You're older. Expensive shirt's covering that gut, ain't it, fat-boy? Not the money you're here for, is it? You've got a few bob sorted away. Must have.

RAWLINGS: I need the experience, Frank.

RATTIGAN: Oh, pardon me. Experience. And how are you enjoying your 'experience'? Our little chats? Get a buzz out of it, do you? Bet you do. Bet you can't wait to tell all your pals about your new mate Frankie, eh? Wets your wife, does it, knowing her old man's gone face-to-face with the Beast of East 16? It's all a laugh for you, ain't it? Come to the human zoo and play the hard man taming the animals. Doesn't wash with me. You're soft as shit.

RAWLINGS: Like I say, I have a thesis to write.

RATTIGAN: Yeah, I caught all that bullshit last time. Some crap about evil not really existing – the papers make it all up. Yeah?

RAWLINGS: I feel that as a notion it gets in the way.

RATTIGAN: Listen to Dr Freud, here.

RAWLINGS: And that most . . . acts like yours are explainable. Traceable, if you will. Be it brain damage sustained before or after birth, or an accumulation of traumatic experience during childhood. Maybe both. But what I'm saying is . . .

RATTIGAN: Do tell . . .

RAWLINGS: No one is necessarily 'evil'. Even you, what you did to that girl . . . has physiological and emotional roots.

RATTIGAN: You don't know sweet FA, do you?

(Seventeen minutes.)

RAWLINGS: So, are you going to tell me about your father?

RATTIGAN: He was an auctioneer at Christie's. Went to work in a lemon-yellow catsuit, and was fired for crapping on an antique table.

RAWLINGS: He was hung as a murderer, wasn't he?

RATTIGAN: You know so much, what the bloody hell you asking me for?

RAWLINGS: I want to know what you thought of him.

RATTIGAN: He was a stupid drunk who got what he deserved. They topped him, good and proper. Enough for you?

RAWLINGS: What's your best memory of him?

RATTIGAN: (long silence) The fear. On his face. The night before they strung the bastard up. Sweating, he was, screw on either side. And there was Mum, doing the tearful bit, trying to control us kids. But I just looked at him, playing the hero . . . I reckon he shat himself when he went through the drop.

RAWLINGS: That night, did you know what was going to happen to him the next day?

RATTIGAN: Don't take me for a dickhead. It was all over the bleedin' papers, talk of the street for months. Turned me into a right royal celebrity. Got my first proper feel off a girl because my old man had killed a copper, and I wasn't even ten years old. Susan Cooper, 'bout fifteen, right fucking bike. (Laughs) And there's me, grubby hands down her knickers, knuckle deep in wet cunt, and me old man to thank for it.

Yeah, now you mention it. Susan Cooper.

RAWLINGS: Sorry?

RATTIGAN: Best thing the useless bastard ever did for me.

RAWLINGS: Any other memories? Any . . . happier ones?

RATTIGAN: Oh, here we go. The same old fucking merry-go-round. Let me save you the time. I've had that many wankers asking me about my mum and dad, and I'll tell you what I told them. They were both cunts. But then every fucker was in them days. First it was the war, and every man in the street was after proving he was unfit to die for his bleedin' country, then dipping all he could into the black market. My old man was no different. Pulled the dodgy-back number on the draft doctors, saw out the rest of the war in Mile End, pissed out of his head.

RAWLINGS: And your mother?

RATTIGAN: Ditto. Same as a thousand other East End mums. Scrimping, struggling to get by, doing whatever to make the coupons stretch to feed us three kids. No two, there was only the two of us, then. Me an' me older sister.

RAWLINGS: Maybe you felt overlooked, unloved in some way?

RATTIGAN: Jesus Christ, do give the deprived-childhood number a rest. You weren't even born then. Us kids had the time of our bloody lives. Great gangs of us hunting for bits of Jerry bombers, crawling into gutted warehouses. There were times when it weren't always a holiday. Some kids would be sent letters telling them that their old man had copped it somewhere, or they were to be evacuated down west. But mostly it was an adventure.

RAWLINGS: Did you see much death?

RATTIGAN: Few bombs landed in our road, but it was mostly old folks who seemed to buy the farm. Anyone with half an ounce of common sense would be down the shelters. Us kids, we felt . . . immortal, I suppose. Death didn't happen to us.

RAWLINGS: But your father . . . ?

RATTIGAN: That was after the war. Four years or so. Like I say, I couldn't really give a toss. They were going to top him, that was that. Fuck-all I could do about it. Was worse on me mum. She was eight months gone with Jimmy, then. Pressure of the trial an' all that – bloody wonder she didn't loose the little sod. But he clung on in there, born five weeks after Pierrepoint did the job on my old man.

RAWLINGS: So Jimmy never met his father?

RATTIGAN: No fucking loss there. No loss.

(Twenty-six minutes.)

RAWLINGS: How did you feel when your mother died?

RATTIGAN: Ain't I heard this a million times?

RAWLINGS: Sorry. I'm simply here to ask these questions.

RATTIGAN: And when are we going to get to your own questions? The ones I know you really want to ask.

RAWLINGS: In time. So, your mother?

RATTIGAN: How did I feel when the useless old bird croaked? Nothing, really. Must have been in 'seventy-eight. I was doing a stretch in Durham nick for ABH. I done someone, can't remember who, got six months for it. Anyway, they took me to the guv'nor, who tells me Mum's just dropped off her perch. That's it, really – screws escort me back to the wing.

RAWLINGS: Did you cry?

RATTIGAN: She was brown bread, you useless twat! Nothing I could do about it. We all die, friend. It was her turn at the gates, that's all.

I mean, it weren't as if we were close. I'd upped and on me toes by the time I was sixteen, summer 'fifty-six. Hadn't seen her for the best part of twenty years.

RAWLINGS: You never even dropped by? Cup of tea, Christmas?

RATTIGAN: Me older sister, Ellie, played nursemaid, popping in regular to check she was coping with Jimmy an' that. Not that she needed to, me Uncle Johnny was seeing to me mum, if you know what I mean. She was sorted.

RAWLINGS: Tell me about 'Uncle Johnny'.

RATTIGAN: Just a geezer. Took a fancy to me mum. Was always round at ours, ever since I was a nipper. Then after they'd done for me dad . . . well, I guess he saw his chance to get in there on a more permanent basis.

RAWLINGS: They married?

RATTIGAN: Fuck knows. I never took that much interest. I'd sometimes drop by Ellie's, and she'd fill me in on all the latest, but it was like, so bloody boring.

RAWLINGS: And your brother? Jimmy? You never saw him again?

RATTIGAN: Listen, I was all over the place, dealing, getting by. That's how it was. The war unloaded half a million dead-eyed pricks in a 'land fit for heroes', and all they had was demob suits and a ration book. Everyone was out looting, nicking whatever. And the coppers were as bent as the rest. Used to organize the betting on the street fights. I got noticed as being tasty with my fists, got myself into some shitty outfits as hired muscle. Went all over the country. Did time in most of the jails.

But Jimmy, yeah. I used to meet him sometimes after school, maybe. Once every six months or so. Just checking on him. It was the sixties, and the big firms began carving London up on both sides of the river. The fucking Maltese arrived, then all the wogs and Pakis. Fuck 'em. I was doing three years in the Scrubs for an altercation with a Western Oriental Gentleman, and thought, 'That's it. No more running with scallies and wankers.' I went solo. Misjudged it. Times were harder than I thought. Ended up a bleedin' tramp, didn't I? Never took the booze, though. Gentleman of the road's one thing, useless fucking wino's another.

RAWLINGS: Tell me about your relationships with women at this point. Your younger days?

RATTIGAN: Oh, I know where we're walking with this one. Just because I had a bit of fun with the hostess – I'm down on all cunt, right? Or maybe you reckon I had the voice of the Almighty in my ear, telling me to have a go at 'em all with my toolkit?

Weren't like that, pal. Just cunt, wasn't it? Skirt after a young lad with a bit of a local reputation. I had a few, then got bored by it all. Couldn't understand the other mugs' obsession with it. It was just so simple. I had a few dodgy connections, they wanted a new blouse or something, I fucked 'em for it.

RAWLINGS: But there was no one . . . special? A first love, maybe?

RATTIGAN: Look, you stick it in, shoot your load, then give 'em something. Just a fucking trade. 'S no love there. No boy-kisses-girl-next-door stuff. I had it whenever I wanted it, on tap. After a while I thought, what the hell's so brilliant about this? Just a wet wank, innit? Had a few pro's since. I mean, I'm human, you know? Still get randy on occasion. But love? Never entered the equation.

Ask yourself this, the next time you're on the job with your old lady. Do you love her, really fucking love her – or is it all just physical sensation?

RAWLINGS: I think the two things are interdependent. The better the love, the higher the sensations.

RATTIGAN: Bullshit. You're afraid. Your bollocks are telling you to fuck every woman on the street, but you won't do it because you're too comfortable with the wife and kids. It's not love, it's routine. Safe. Boredom disguised as something fantastic.

Listen. Shared a cell with a fella in Norwich. Young kid, he was, just married. Doing nine months' bird for handling. And, fuck me, every night he'd prattle on about his missus, how he was going to reform for her, how he loved her, she loved him, their love would see them through. (Laughs) Four months into his stretch, he gets the old 'Dear John'. Turns out an HGV driver's moved into the marital home and is offering her nightly comfort. Nearly pissed myself.

'Course, this kid then spends the next few weeks telling me how he's gonna have the driver put away. Then he goes very quiet, like. Mute for the last month or so. I see the anger rising, and know what's on the way.

Sure enough, he's only out for six weeks before they haul him back inside, only this time it's five years. Turns out he tracked 'em both down to a boozer, laid the trucker out, then performed a little facial surgery on his loved one with a broken glass. Over a hundred and fifty stitches. But when he walked back inside – you could tell he was happy. All the tension had flowed from him.

True love runs deep? With her nose hanging off her face, I bet it ran deep. I fucking bet it did.

(Forty-two minutes.)

RAWLINGS: I'd like to ask some questions of my own.

RATTIGAN: This is what we've been waiting for.

RAWLINGS: I've recently listened to tapes of your 'confession' made at Bethnal Green Police Station – the murder of Helen Lewis. What I can't understand is this – nowhere on your records is there a history of this level of sustained violence. Yet with her, you . . .

RATTIGAN: They had to take her away in eight bags. They tell you that? Took 'em most of the day to find all the bits. And do you know what they kept asking me? Had I fucked her? Like they didn't understand nothing. I even heard some poor bastard had to comb her pubes to see if any of mine were on there. What a shit job, eh? Looked like a tiny bit of hairy steak, and this fella's poring over it looking for my pubes. Jesus.

RAWLINGS: Were you disappointed, when you discovered she'd died during the night?

RATTIGAN: S'pose. I had lots planned. Shouldn't have drunk all that pissy bottled lager. Sent me to sleep too early.

RAWLINGS: Frank . . . I keep going over and over this in my mind, maybe you can help . . .

RATTIGAN: Be a pleasure, old chap.

RAWLINGS: You break into a house, the owner comes back, and, instead of simply leaving, or tying her up – you spend hours and hours torturing her, a complete stranger, a defenceless young girl . . .

RATTIGAN: Behave! Don't make my heart bleed with all this pious crap! I was having fun, for Christ's sake! She died, so what? You never even knew the bitch. Why pretend you care? You give a kid a toy, it breaks, you bin the bastard. Same story.

RAWLINGS: And that's how you saw her – a toy?

RATTIGAN (sighing): Why doesn't anyone believe me?

RAWLINGS: Because I'll tell you what I think, Frank. I think you had so much hate in you that night, and something in Helen Lewis set it off. I think that like the young man who attacked his wife in the pub, you have to love something completely before you can hate it as utterly as you did. You enjoyed your 'games' because you loved hating her. Revenge.

RATTIGAN (laughs): Now you come to mention it, she did once spill a cup of coffee on my lap on a short-haul flight to Crete! Fucking hell, I thought – I'll have that clumsy cow one day, just you wait and see.

RAWLINGS: Tell me about the money, Frank.

RATTIGAN: It's all in the file. The law's got it all worked out, didn't you know? I tortured her until she told me where it was. Nothing to add.

RAWLINGS: And the green Jaguar, the man who visited you at the fruit farm the previous week?

RATTIGAN: Geezer stopped for directions. I obliged, considerate as always.

RAWLINGS: You knew them, didn't you? Knew them both – the driver and the girl. And however much you try to convince me the whole damn thing was random and fun, and what a hard man you are – it's all a front. You went to that house deliberately. God knows why. But I'll find out. I really will.

(Rattigan dissolves into giggles.)

12

'An evil little bastard.'

The old schoolteacher looked at me with damp grey eyes. 'Yes, I well remember Rattigan. And I'm sorry, Mr Rawlings, believe me, I'm not a God-fearing man – but Rattigan, he was evil.'

It had taken me eleven days to track down the retired headmaster of St Cedric's School for Boys, Mile End Road. Eleven days since my last meeting with Rattigan.

Driven by an increasing hunger to uncover the metamorphosis of boy to Beast, I'd contacted the Inner London Education Authority as a PhD student asking for a list of schools operating post 1945 in the area closest to Rattigan's home.

During this time, I was becoming increasingly unnerved. Try as I might to quash the base feelings inside, I was beginning to see it now, with ever more terrifying clarity. I *had* to make some sense of Rattigan's madness, had to frame his awful act in some cloak of reason, no matter how flimsy. Because otherwise the world, *my* world became senseless. If I could calmly sit in my own house and think myself into all that horror so comfortably – what kind of beast was I?

It seemed my only hope lay in 'normalizing' Rattigan's attack on the girl, digging out that which the police investigation had been so speedily and confusingly denied. I had to find a motive for the murder of Helen Lewis beyond one man's desire for 'fun' and 'games'. If I could put the Beast of East 16 to sleep, perhaps my own ghosts would lie down and die alongside.

So research began in earnest. First to the ILEA. Fortunately for me, my call was answered by a Mrs Bhaku, who, once

95

I'd explained a little more, seemed to throw herself whole-heartedly into the role of archive detective. In just three days, she sent me a list of six possible schools (four mixed, one state secondary, one grammar) all attended by 'Rattigan, F's' during the period, according to the microfilmed, handwritten attendance ledgers.

Indeed, further to this, Mrs Bhaku had correctly assumed that a pupil of Rattigan's notoriety would possibly be remembered by any living ex-members of staff, and if 'we' struck lucky . . .

I phoned Mrs Bhaku immediately, thanking her profusely for her help. She seemed offish, until it clicked that she thought I was ending our research tryst. Wonderful woman – she had nine addresses of retired staff living in East London, each of whom had taught at one of the six schools during 1945–55.

I hung up, punched the air, raced round to Interflora and sent a large bouquet to the Archives Dept, ILEA.

. . . Strange, now I reflect on this brief brush with euphoria. The sudden wave of victory, as I felt the thrill of tracking him down. The *real* world, *real* history. Technology, telephones, microfilms, people, communication – how wonderful it felt to have my head out of textbooks and self-analysis. No theory here, just action. No illustrations of brain abnormalities, no case histories arduously linking trauma with trauma – just action, doing it. In total safety, too – Rattigan rotting behind Oakwood's huge walls; me, on the outside, foraging, beyond his reach, fighting to free myself from his foul influence . . .

The same day I sent eleven copies of a covering letter to Mrs Bhaku's addresses, setting out the intentions of my thesis, and politely requesting more help.

Three days later, a Mr Eric Saunders rang me at home to confirm he was headmaster at Rattigan's 'school', but doubted whether he could be of much help, since the 'offensive youngster in question' was mostly truant during the time of his supposed education.

Saunders invited me over to his basement flat in Upton Park, should I wish to pursue the matter further. I had struck gold.

The flat was neat, small and bright. Old items of furniture keenly maintained with polish and thread. A gas fire hissed comfortingly in the yellow-tiled fireplace. A square, wired cage was home to a pair of singing canaries, serenading their eighty-two-year-old owner, while the traffic rumbled indifferently outside.

He made me tea, cup shaking in the bone-china saucer as he set it before me. I sat in a stout dining chair, notebook out, pen poised above the blank page, watching as Eric Saunders settled in his favourite armchair.

'In 'forty-five,' he said without prompting. 'I was discharged from the RAF with an officer's teaching qualification. I had the option to stay on, I was only thirty, but instead took a "civvy" post as deputy head at Mile End. No glamour in the rank, Mr Rawlings – simply no other bugger'd take the damned job.' He laughed gently to himself. 'Head too stuffed with postwar ideals, I'm afraid.'

'Sorry?'

'Usual idealistic nonsense. Thought I could make a difference to the city's poor. Little sods ran bloody great rings round me. Nothing, Mr Rawlings, nothing I had learnt teaching conscripted pilots and ground crews prepared me for the ghastly privilege of trying to educate poverty-stricken children.'

I felt I ought to contribute. 'Guess some things never change, eh? Kids are still running round like wild animals in a couple of schools up north.'

Saunders studied me carefully. 'The system was inadequate, Mr Rawlings, not the children. These days, I'm not so sure. I think it's still primarily a discipline problem. Teachers simply aren't allowed to . . .'

Here it comes, I thought, retired headmaster's standard wish to bring back the birch. So I was surprised when he said . . .

'. . . love them enough.'

'Love them?'

'It's a fact, Mr Rawlings, an inescapable human truth. Without love, the infant dies. Give it warmth, food, shelter as much as you wish – but without love . . .'

'You . . . tried to love these kids? Rattigan?'

97

He sipped from his tea cup. 'Heavens, no. I was too damned young to appreciate anything but my own self-importance. We had twelve hundred kids, orphans, returning evacuees, and locals, all crammed into one of the only remaining schools in the district. It was an absolute bloody mess – Army arriving to build more temporary classrooms, Labour government doing the usual trick of throwing someone else's money at the problem – and most importantly, a tide of kids completely uninterested in any form of education.

'You could see it writ large in their snotty faces. What was the point? Why bother to learn, trust these adults who'd just spent the last seven years in a cataclysmic conflict whose only gain was to destroy their homes, families, communities?

'It was hopeless. Still, we pressed on, banging Latin verbs into their bemused little skulls, times-tables by rote. Utterly ridiculous. But they had the last laugh, thank God.'

'They did?'

'The sixties, Mr Rawlings,' he answered brightly. 'My young, disillusioned charges discovered sex, drugs and rock and roll. At last they had their own culture. A miracle – from the glowing embers of the bomb sites came the phoenix of teenage rebellion – and in its wake, liberation. You have a lot to thank them for, Mr Rawlings.'

'Right,' I hesitantly replied, wishing I'd had Mr Saunders as my headmaster, wondering if he'd taught the basics of joint-rolling in his study after school. The views of the man were so at odds with his appearance. Yet, ironically, the retired teacher was still teaching. Only this time, I was the pupil. I'd learned once again, never to judge a book by its cover.

As he went on to confide in me, though, these views were tempered by time and experience, the lonesome thoughts of a fragile eighty-two-year-old. Wisdom accumulated via a lifetime of mistakes and misunderstanding.

I finished my tea. 'And Francis Rattigan,' I pressed. 'Twelve hundred pupils, and you still remember him?'

The wrinkled eyelids closed in pain at the memory. 'He is, Mr Rawlings, what I would call "my exception". I firmly believe that every other disruptive child it has been my unpleasant duty to teach, would have responded to a simple cocktail of love and encouragement. But Rattigan was way beyond anyone's help.'

Silence fell heavily over the spartan lounge. Even the canaries appeared to respectfully hush their melodic chirrups and whistling.

I shifted in my seat. Saunders peered right back, waiting. 'You know what he went on to do?' I said eventually. 'What happened?'

'I follow the papers. Tabloids occasionally.'

'I need to know more about him. As he was then. If he had any . . . ?'

'Traits?'

I nodded.

He bit delicately on a sweet digestive. 'Those,' he said, after meticulously chewing and swallowing, 'are something I'm afraid you'll have to educate me on, Mr Rawlings. I well remember the phrase "sick psychopath" being bandied about in even the more trustworthy broadsheets. It is a sad omission of my vocational lifetime, Mr Rawlings, that Mr Hitchcock's near-immortal shower scene has left me with the most rudimentary understanding of the term "psycho".'

I swallowed hard, rubbing both palms together under the table, feeling for all the world like a sweaty fourth-year giving a science report to the head.

Saunders, empathetic as ever, offered a kindly smile. 'A layman's explanation would suffice.'

Right. 'I suppose if I was to reduce it to its simplest terms, then the psychopath represents one branch of recently identified sociopathic behavioural disorders . . .'

'In recognizable English, perhaps?'

I flushed slightly, wishing I had a ready definition. 'An individual such as Rattigan would mostly act without the conventions of our learned morality. He does what he does simply to please himself. He has no "inner voice", to challenge his actions. He becomes bored very easily, and while most likely exhibits above-average intelligence patterns, will never use these to the benefit of any other individual but himself.'

'What lesser people such as myself might well call an evil man, perhaps?'

I smiled back. 'Most studies agree that the brain separates its functions at the temporal lobes. There's a doing side, and a being side. The common psychopath will most likely have an enlarged "doing" side, and faulty connections to the "being" or "I am" side.'

'He operates with no social conscience?'

'Just doesn't occur to him. He sees something he wants, he takes it. It's very . . .'

'Animalistic?'

'Exactly. He knows he's causing pain, but only registers the pleasure it gives him. There's no empathy for the victim.'

'It all sounds hideously mercenary.' The elderly gentleman pronounced each word crisply. 'And Rattigan, he conforms to all this . . . ?'

'He's had the standard battery of psychiatric tests and brain-scans. Although, temporally, his brain seems pretty much the same as yours or mine. In its physical make-up, anyway. The point being, he should function, should have a conscience.'

'So he has no excuses for the way he is?'

'Research is in its infancy.'

'And now you come to me, to look to the past for possible answers?'

'Sociological and environmental factors have enormous influence over various mental functions during childhood years.'

Saunders rose from his chair, and walked slowly to the birdcage, adjusting the height of a hard white cuttlefish as he spoke. 'Enterprising little shit, I'll give him that.'

I found myself flinching at the swear word. 'Rattigan?'

One of the yellow birds had decided on a bath, settling in a bowl of water in the bottom of the cage, fanning its wings in the cool liquid. The old man's eyes never left it. 'They executed his father. Nineteen forty-nine, 'fifty, sometime around then. Drunk, by all accounts, pushed a young police constable through a shop window. Made quite a stir locally. Anyway, a couple of weeks after the sentence, one of my staff caught Rattigan selling a blow-by-blow account of the hanging to a group of his eager peers. The whole thing, as if he'd been stood on the side of the scaffold, watching his father plunge through. Some of the younger children were quite traumatized, parents complained. Rattigan had, of course, embellished his gory pantomime to include some truly sensational details, all of which must have found form in the vilest recesses of his devilish imagination. He charged tuppence each for his fictional account of the execution. Had a pocket full of coins when he was brought to my study.

'Now, I dare say, in these enlightened, liberal times, a well-meaning social worker or suchlike would say the child had the beginnings of a fine entrepreneurial career, that he ought to have been encouraged, not punished. But to me, what he did was simply evil. No excuses, Mr Rawlings.'

'He was disciplined?'

'I thrashed him myself. It lives with me still. Oh, I've had the grave misfortune to flog many a bare backside, Mr Rawlings, but . . . this was different. There was no gain from it. No lesson sinking in. It was just a meeting. One power over another. A battle, if you like. He stood bent over my study table, drawers down, grinning. Then straining. I managed two strokes before he defecated on the floor.'

I had little trouble imagining the scene. Rattigan's fearful smile had haunted many of my nightmares, too.

Saunders turned slowly from the cage. 'He killed a woman, didn't he?'

'An air hostess.'

He sat back in the creaking armchair. 'He had a sister, you know. Lovely girl. Some years older than him. Bright, alert. And a younger brother. Hard-working mother, despite the terrible loss she suffered. But I seem to remember she married again. Happiness came to her eventually. Some years after the execution. Wonderful man, too. Policeman.'

My hand ached from taking shorthand. ''Uncle' John? 'Policeman?'

Saunders nodded. 'Local man. Sergeant. Old school. Give the kids a clip round the earhole for any lip. What was his name now?'

I waited in silence as he trailed the memory. 'No. It's gone. Wonderful chap, though. Something of a local celebrity. Awarded an OBE, eventually.' He thought again for a moment or two. 'Yes. I seem to remember something about a gas explosion. Terrible shock to us all. He risked his own life pulling a family from the rubble. Real hero stuff, whole damn house could've come down on him any moment.' His eyes caught mine. 'All in the local archives, I expect.'

I made a note to track the story down. 'And Rattigan had already left school at this time?'

'Probably. My memory's not up to much, these days. Besides, the hateful child was hardly ever there anyway. Only seemed to interest him when he could make trouble.'

'What sort of trouble?'

'Whatever he could think of. Assaulting other pupils, staff, anything. He had no respect for the cane. No respect for any of us. The one bad egg in a lot of three children. Even after he'd left, he'd periodically return – local gangster by then, schoolboy's hero – waiting for his younger brother by the school gates, smoking Woodbines, charming the young mothers with various items which had no doubt fallen off the back of any number of lorries. And nothing we could do. We were all terrified of him.'

Forty minutes later, I was stood on the Eastbound platform of Upton Park tube station, my mind a mass of swirling images.

Once on the rumbling train, I sat quite still, the tiniest beginnings of a smile creeping slowly over my face.

The research was paying off. I was getting somewhere. I believed I had a lever into the faded mechanism of Rattigan's insanity. A three-pronged attack – a stranger in a green Jaguar, a woman's smile and the little brother he kept coming back for.

The little brother he must have loved.

13

As I was already in London, I decided to meet Jemimah for lunch. We ate at an Italian place on Greek Street, me filling her in on the morning's meeting with Saunders.

At times I could sense I was losing her. The eyes started to cloud over, wandering from mine to listlessly scan the restaurant. I ploughed on, trimming the narrative, doing my best to edit and enliven what was obviously boring her rigid.

At length, she said, 'I want to go on holiday.'

'Sure. Me too. As soon as . . .'

'Now.'

'Now?'

'Skiing. Somewhere fresh and clean.'

'Christ, J. This is a bit . . .'

'Sudden?' Her eyes met mine.

'Yeah. Sudden.'

'Wouldn't you like to go? Just the two of us?'

'Eventually, yes, of course. It's just . . .'

She turned away. 'A fantasy,' she softly replied. 'Just a fantasy I wanted you to share for a moment or two.'

I reached for her hand, but she withdrew it. 'Sorry, J. I'm not with it, these days. When the thesis is done, then we'll get away. For real, like you said. Just the two of us. Hell, why not make it skiing? God, with my centre of gravity, I'm sure I'll end up in foreign traction, but why not? It'd be fun.'

'Stop it,' she replied. 'You're trying too hard.'

I signalled for the bill. She produced the agency plastic. 'I just wanted us to have a silly conversation,' she said. 'Away from your work, my work. Just us. Like we used to. It was an idle dream, Adrian, our starter for ten. I never wanted it punctured by reality.'

'Sorry,' I replied. 'Guess I've goofed, rather.'

She signed the credit slip, handed it to the waiter. 'I've got to get back.'

'Sorry I never took you on to the virgin-white snow, J.'

'So am I,' she said, before air-kissing my cheek and making for the door.

In previous times, I'd have headed for the nearest pub for the grand liquid tour of the pumps and optics. I hated unresolved situations, especially between Jemimah and myself, detested living with the silently building feelings before we spoke again.

And as was often the case, I knew that when the time arose for the emotional postmortem, neither of us would begin the process with any real honesty. Inevitably, we would silently agree to skim round the edges, move on, resolving nothing. Over the years we had become expert cosmetic surgeons of our own relationship, gathering around us the appropriate trappings in order that others might be convinced of our material success. But the real issues, our fundamental differences lay quietly simmering between us.

I'm sure we both felt this – though naturally, neither would have the courage to admit it to the other. We just simply went on, both realizing it was too late to pick over the bones of past hurts, arguments and injustices.

Many's the time when I wondered why Jemimah stayed so loyal to me. What kept her bound into a relationship with so little depth, so shallow an intimacy? Then, one day, I understood. I watched as she left for the job she loved, kissed the children she adored goodbye, stepped out of the house she'd laboured so hard to turn into her dream home, then drove away to the station in the company Merc. Together they formed the cornerstone of her life. She was blissfully happy with it all. And if our relationship wasn't ever set to be fantastically invigorating or intolerably exciting – then that was a small price to pay. Her marriage was merely a part of her life – not its centre. She carried on as Mrs

Rawlings because it would be too much bother to change anything.

And with this revelation came my own role within it. How much was I to blame? How easy had it been for me to carry on in a marriage which required so little effort on my part? Why had I stopped romancing the woman who had so completely, breathtakingly stolen my heart? When had complacency crept in? I had answers, a theory for Jemimah's situation, but very little save for laziness to account for mine.

Truth was, I would never have thought of having a conversation about an imaginary holiday. She did. It vividly illustrated the gulf between us.

Minutes later, I found an Interflora on Wardour Street, then had a bunch of flowers sent over to the ad agency, hoping they'd beat her back to the office. Six red roses – hell, I was trying.

It had started to drizzle. A faintly nauseous smell began to rise from the pavements, something which I immediately recognized from long ago. And Jesus, it did seem so long since I'd worked in London. Two lifetimes at least – the drunk's and the aspiring doctor's.

I began to wander, unwilling to go home. What waited there for me, but yet another afternoon writing up notes, transcribing conversations, phone calls to police officers who never returned mine? In short – Rattigan. The man was strangling the life out of me.

The food at the Italian had been on the bland side of seeringly dull, but I could still taste our closing conversation. Jemimah had simply wanted to escape – just for a few precious minutes. Wanted me with her, instead of with him.

Sod Rattigan – he could wait. I needed an afternoon off.

I decided to make my way through the throng of tourists, damp shoppers and grim, suited professionals to Tower Records at Piccadilly. Check out the new arrivals at the soul section, maybe get some Wilson Picket in my ears at one of the listening posts.

I cut down Brewer Street, alive with the bustling market, peepshows, sex shops and clip joints. The place has always fascinated me, with its bizarre mix of sleaze and pseudo-sophistication. Many years earlier, I'd worked in a big ad agency close by, and would often wander out of the office to enjoy the gaudy carnival of London's Soho in sad swing.

It was barely past two, but already the girls who worked the strip clubs sat in tattered doorways festooned with exotic untrustworthy promises of what awaited in darkened basements below.

'Four pounds, darling,' one of them said, all peroxide blonde, heavy stockinged thighs and eye make-up. 'Chance to get out of the rain, ain't it?'

I smiled, then felt suddenly forced to ask, 'How long have you been doing this?'

''Bout half an hour, love,' she replied, chewing gum, eyes constantly flicking behind me, looking for more punters. 'Plenty of girls downstairs.'

'No,' I said. 'How old were you when you first started?'

She stared blankly back.

I repeated the question, making the connection in my head as to what had compelled me to ask in the first place. Something Rattigan had said about sex – 'Just a trade, innit?'

'Too bloody long, darling,' she replied. 'You coming in, then?'

'No,' I said. 'But thanks, anyway.'

'Suit yourself.'

At which point I should have left, had the previous courage of my convictions to leave Rattigan alone for the afternoon. But I couldn't. Something about him turning up at the house with all that money, waiting, perhaps, for a girl to come walking through – to trade?

'Listen,' I said. 'Don't take this the wrong way, but . . .'

She cottoned on quick. Shook her head. 'Sorry, love. I ain't for sale.' Then brightened. 'Come inside, though, and I'll see what I can do. That good enough for you? You're getting very wet out there.'

'No, no.' I was flustered. What the hell was I doing? Research, I tried to persuade myself. 'I'm just interested in prices.'

'Come downstairs, we'll talk money.'

'What would I get for a thousand?'

The tired eyes dilated. 'A bleedin' grand?' she gasped. 'Just about anything you like, darling.'

I never made it to Tower Records. Got the tube out to Liverpool Street, then train back to Chelmsford, fired up. Maybe I'd seen something Russell and the others hadn't. OK, I was prepared to accept Rattigan might have arrived at Helen Lewis's house with the cash, but perhaps it wasn't anything to do with any 'contract job'. Maybe he borrowed it for his own pleasure.

I'd often read tales and seen so-called documentaries about the secret lives of air stewardesses. Was there a remote possibility Helen Lewis was a high-class hooker? That the man in the green Jag gave Frank the address, told him the whereabouts of a good-time girl who specialized in something a little more unusual than straightforward sex. S and M, maybe? Rape fantasies fulfilled for a thousand?

Perhaps it was nothing, a wild stab in the darkness of his insanity. But I had to consider the possibility, like all the others. And better still, this one actually felt plausible. He'd paid for his 'fun'. Then got too carried away, started hurting for real.

I was home by four, working by four-fifteen, consulting textbooks on sexual deviance, dominance and related behaviours.

I hardly noticed the kids coming home, or Jemimah arriving back with six crushed red roses.

She stood at the office door for a while as my fingers flew over the keyboard. But when I looked round to talk to her, she'd already gone back downstairs.

14

'This is OK. But you look appalling, friend.'

'Just tired, that's all,' I said.

Four days after my meeting with Eric Saunders, and Fancy handed me back the first draft of my thesis, stuffed with all its confusions. We sat in the dimly lit uni. video editing suite, as he compiled a tape for his next undergrad lecture entitled 'Man's inhumanity to man?' A bank of monitors hummed before us at eye-level, all sets frozen on the one image – the bleak grey face of a woman collaborator, paraded through the streets of Paris after the liberation. Head shaved, bare-shouldered, she looked zombied by the screaming, pointing crowd which surrounded her, almost resigned to the inevitable.

I retrieved the manuscript. 'It's just a first draft.'

He smiled. A technician silently coiled cables in the humid studio next door. I watched him through the dark glass, broad back, T-shirt, goatee beard.

'Be careful, Adrian. There's no doubt in my mind you've got what it takes to honour the proposition. We don't have to be Einstein to work out the media always conforms, sometimes even shapes the political agenda of our times.'

'But?'

'Your proof hinges on the one case. Rattigan's.'

'So?'

'You've got to come up with some hard facts. Hinting there might have been some tabloid pressure placed on the police to get an early result with the man hardly qualifies.'

'My source didn't want to be named.'

'DI Russell, right?'

'Maybe.'

He chewed at his bottom lip. Then said, 'There's no way you can ever disprove something as fundamentally culturally entrenched as "perceived evil" in just a few weeks. Chances are, you'll never do it. Ever. Jesus wept, if you did, you'd put the entire mechanism of behavioural science on the scrapheap. But you're having a stab. And it's OK. A little . . .'

'Confused in places?'

'Your words . . . but adequate.'

I fought against inhaling second-hand cigar smoke. 'I just feel that if I can prove the papers inhibited the investigation, then I can make the connection.'

'Being?'

'That newspaper editors get quick and profitable copy from sensationalizing events such as the murder of Helen Lewis. Which, in turn, inhibits proper investigation and rigorous understanding of what actually occurred.'

'You're talking like a cautious back-bencher on *Question Time*.'

I ignored the quip. 'And in order to do that, I need to know the truth, what the police were denied.'

'But that isn't the only problem, is it?'

He knew me too well, a disadvantage at times like these. 'Life isn't so smooth back at the ranch.'

Fancy's eyebrows twitched. 'Ah.' He paused for a moment. 'Finding an answer to what Rattigan did means a lot to you, doesn't it?'

I nodded, aware he was watching closely.

He cleared his throat. 'Listen, Adrian, I'm not sure what you're getting yourself into, but I want to warn you against getting too involved. Don't let it eat you up like this. Jemimah OK? The kids?'

'Fine,' I lied, then met his gaze and realized what a pathetic attempt I'd made at deception. It was pointless to hide anything from the man. He gave me the space to elucidate, and before I knew it, I was telling him of the auditory nightmare in the kitchen. My fingers idled on the mixing desk, sliding the faders up and down. 'Be great, wouldn't it?' I mused. 'If we could make human personalities like this. Fade in a bit of compassion here; drop a tad of cruelty there – just recompose ourselves according to the perfect mix.'

'You're waffling.'

I stopped playing with the technology. 'Know what I said to Jemimah, later that night?'

He waited.

'I told her I'd get help. Therapist or something.'

'But you haven't, have you?'

'Don't worry, I'm not about to throw myself under a number forty-two, or something. Oakwood and the uni.'s precious reputations are safe.'

'For now.' Fancy's demeanour changed, became suddenly more serious. 'I couldn't do what you want to do, Adrian. Realized that a long time ago. Face to face with the beasts, day after day. Striving to find some sort of mental connections between intent and action. Couldn't spend hours wondering about the mental make-up of a man who calmly wanders into a school armed to the teeth, then lets loose on innocent children. Because, to me, that implies forgiveness. Goes against all my animal instincts. There are very few people who have the drive to see through the "evil", dissect the being from the action.'

I stared back into the blazing blue eyes, uncomfortable in their righteous glare. 'We all have to find our own niche, I suppose.'

Fancy slapped a hand on the battered draft of the thesis. 'Rattigan fascinates you. Admit it. You rack your brains trying to understand what could bring a man to that. His past? His physiological functions? Evil? You have no idea. But still you persist. Despite the doubts. Contacting old schools, firing your own questions. It bugs you, worms its way in, the one question you refuse to face.'

I squinted uncomfortably, gut suddenly aching for a malt whisky, craving its comforting stickiness – distancing me in sips from the here and now. 'How did you know about my visit to the old teacher?'

'A woman called Mrs Bhaku contacted the university to verify your credentials before carrying out a search on your behalf. Perfectly normal procedure. Nothing sinister in that.'

The anger rose. 'You saying I'm paranoid, now?'

'Calm down. I'm saying you have a big question to ask. The same one I ran from many years ago.'

'Which was?'

'You're drawn to it, Adrian. Right the way down the line. Remember, I know you. Seven years I've watched you. Fired ad-man turns up as a mature student after a psychology degree. Don't you see? *You* took that decision, made that choice. MA which followed – more of the same. Now this, forensic psychiatry – the desire to unravel the darkest shit the mind has. All choices you took.'

'Just how it was, that's all. I was interested.'

He shook his head. 'Listen. Collective unconscious, you remember that much from the drivel I shovelled down your throat as an undergrad?'

'Voice of intuition,' I replied, parrot-fashion, still smarting from the urge to drink again. 'See a stranger walking down the street, get an odd feeling, cross the road. A contention that generations of genetic memory are maybe passed down in their own mental DNA cycle at conception. Fear of the dark – the caveman listening to the howling of distant wolves . . .'

'And you,' Fancy interrupted. 'Were drawn intuitively to the Rattigans of this world. Your choice. Your intuitive desire.'

'And yours?' Anything to deflect the intensity.

'Irrelevant.' He sat back down, lit another cigar, the voice calmer, levelled. 'Look, don't take this the wrong way, but the reason you have to know so much about people like Rattigan . . . is that you . . . fear you are just like him.'

'No way.'

'The question you have to ask is . . .'

'Rattigan's already come up with that one. What am I really doing with him?'

'And your answer?'

'Asking more bloody questions. Being paid for it. First time in years. Jesus, you're giving me all this stuff about me being like him, and . . .'

'Then why are you so angry about it?'

'Mother of God, Steve! You think I'm capable of doing what he did? Sod off!'

His voice remained calm. 'You know what the detective does, when he arrives at the scene of the crime? He looks for evidence, then a motive. The reason why . . .'

'Oh please!'

'He sees a dead body, then considers the possibilities. Hate is one. A thoroughly credible motive. He knows this because he has hated himself. Hated someone enough to want to kill them, sometime. He puts himself in the mind of the murderer, seeing where his own emotions might dovetail with the killer's.' He gripped my arm. 'I ran from the realization, Adrian. Bolted all the way to my hidey-hole here at the uni. Didn't want to delve too deeply into the world of the psychotic – because I didn't want to know where the urge was coming from, or how much of it belonged to me.'

A long silence. Fancy flicked a switch on the edit-panel at his fingertips. The face unfroze, and we watched in silence as the grey, baying crowd clumsily hung the topless woman from a nearby lamppost.

'You've got to remember, first and foremost, that I'm your friend. Shit, Adrian, I'm worried about you.'

'Don't be, I'm fine.'

Forty minutes later, Fancy and I had retired to one of our regular haunts, the Rat and Parrot, a large pub set on Duke Street, Chelmsford. A crowd jostled at the long L-shaped bar, office types after bottled lagers, alcopops for their giggling secretaries. Corporate brass and floorboards, a dumb-waiter bringing standard pub lunches up from the basement, barmaids taking plate after plate of lasagne and baked potatoes to laughing executives. Just as they'd always done. Strange how unsettling normality can seem when the mind chooses to wander in another direction. Fancy and I had drunk here many times, but that day the pub felt totally alien, as if I was visiting it for the first time.

I nursed an orange and lemonade while he enjoyed his second pint. I knew my fingers were wrapped too tightly around the warm glass, my eyes wandering to the alluring upturned shorts bottles I sometimes glimpsed behind the bar. It took all the willpower I had not to order a double malt.

Conversation thus far had been painfully stilted, as if the whole edit-suite chat never existed. Obliterated the moment we agreed to 'pop out for a swift one'. I felt under inspection, analysed.

'Look,' he said. 'It's really none of my business, but when you were telling me about the voices you heard . . .'

'It just happened. God knows why,' I snapped, searching the crowd of faces, wondering if any one of them had ever thought a fraction of the things I had when 'in character'. I doubted it – for their sakes. 'I'm not a schizo, for God's sake.'

'I never said you were.'

'So can we drop it?'

'Were you ever involved in any football violence?'

'Of course not. Haven't been to a game in donkey's years. Bores me bloody rigid.'

'But you used to go?'

'Way back. With my dad.'

'And you were how old?'

'Eight, nine.'

'And you never saw any trouble?'

'Nothing. Now, please, drop it.'

He held up his hands. 'Easy, Adrian.'

'Wish to God I'd never told you.'

'But you did,' he said. 'Didn't have to – but you did.'

'Please,' I begged. 'Forget it.'

He nodded slowly. 'Everyone's looking out for you, Adrian, that's all. Remember what I was saying? The need to understand being driven from within? You can pay a high price for the answers.'

'Thanks for your concern. But you don't have to worry any more.'

Fancy made a show of eyeing up a young girl, turning to me with raised eyebrows and false male bonhomie. Then afterwards, 'All I'm saying is, you've got a whole career in front of you. Twenty years to solve the Rattigans of this sick world. Qualify first. Allen's impressed with you. Admires your tenacity. But it's misplaced. Even you admit it's starting to eat into your personal life. Just ask the questions, finish the thesis, get the PhD, then sit back and wait for the job offer.'

'And leave Rattigan till later, right?'

'Now's not the time.'

I thought about this for a while. 'I get the impression,' I said slowly. 'That friend or no friend, all you're really concerned about is whether I make an arse of myself and cause the uni. and Oakwood some embarrassment.'

'You're being unfair.'

'I'm being honest.'

'I'm concerned about you as a friend.'

'Fine. Let's leave it at that.'

He finished his pint, declined the offer of another. 'How's it going with him, anyway?'

'Rattigan?'

Fancy nodded.

'I'm sure it's a sexual motive.'

'"Sure"?'

'Convinced it might be.'

'You got this from him?'

'Partly.'

He stood, placed a hand on my shoulder. 'Just be careful, Adrian,' he said. 'Understand where it's all coming from. Even the lamest idea has its beginnings in the originator.'

'Sure.' I finished my own drink, then left with him, fighting the almost overpowering urge to stay and drink for real.

15

Edited transcript of fourth interview with Rattigan at Oakwood, RECREATION SIX. Rattigan, 'Denton' and myself in attendance.

(Twenty-seven minutes.)

RAWLINGS: (After finishing preselected questions) And now I'd like to ask you some things of my own, if I may?

(Rawlings takes out a series of women's faces cut from magazines. All the models are smiling. He places them in front of Rattigan.)

RAWLINGS: The name Eric Saunders ring any bells?

RATTIGAN: Why, is he Quasimodo's brother?

RAWLINGS: Your old headmaster, from Mile End. I went to see him the other day.

RATTIGAN: Fucking bully for you.

RAWLINGS: Says you were an evil little bastard, Frank.

RATTIGAN: Me an' a thousand other kids.

RAWLINGS: No. You stand out quite clearly in his memory.

RATTIGAN: I don't remember him.

RAWLINGS: He says you sold stories of your father's execution to other pupils.

RATTIGAN (sniggering): Yeah, that's right. Now you mention it, I do remember that. Fucking hell! Why I never made it to a millionaire is beyond me.

RAWLINGS: He also says you used to terrorize both pupils and staff, and even once shat on his office floor.

RATTIGAN: It's all coming back to me. The cunt was trying to stick me. The look on his mug was priceless. Anything else, fat-boy? You've no idea how this little trip down memory lane is cheering me up.

RAWLINGS: Hardly a 'normal' education, wouldn't you say?

RATTIGAN: Hardly normal times.

RAWLINGS: What I'm saying is . . . that sort of behaviour – disruptive, aggressive – tends to be treated a little more seriously today. Social Services are alerted, investigators sent in, the pupil interviewed, home life studied. What would they have found, Frank, if they'd gone to the Rattigans' home?

RATTIGAN: Well, not me, for starters. I was out with the boys most of the time. The old man was always falling over pissed on someone else's doorstep, and me older sister was . . . around, I suppose.

RAWLINGS: What about 'Uncle' John?

RATTIGAN: What about him?

RAWLINGS: He was a policeman, wasn't he? Something of a local hero. Apparently he saved a mother and two children from the aftermath of a gas explosion. Dug them out with his bare hands before the fire brigade arrived.

RATTIGAN: Who told you that? Ellie, I suppose?

RAWLINGS: No, Mr Saunders. (Pause) Ellie's your older sister, isn't she? You thought I'd spoken to her?

RATTIGAN: She ain't got fuck-all to tell you. She hates my guts, and don't know fuck-all.

RAWLINGS: What is there to 'know', Frank?

RATTIGAN: Nothing. (Pause) John Templar was just another shithouse copper who quickly sussed my old man was a pissed-up nobody. They did the Air Raid Patrol together in the war. Spent most of it pissed on black-market beer round the allotments. Then Uncle John, he'd occasionally be at the house, wolfing down a bloody great plateful of grub, or something. That's all.

RAWLINGS: And when your father killed PC Scrimshaw . . . ?

RATTIGAN: He stuck by me mum while Dad was inside. Guess she'd taken a shine to him by then. Never really knew him as a person. Sure, I've heard all about the fucking heroics in the rubble, but that was long after I'd scarpered. But I guess the old girl made the right choice in taking him in. Wouldn't blame her, anyhow. Just a mum, you know? Knackered with life, too fucked to be bothered looking too deeply into it.

RAWLINGS: Scrimshaw and Templar? Did they work at the same police station?

RATTIGAN: Ain't this interview supposed to be about me?

RAWLINGS: Fair point.

RATTIGAN: Worse than the Old Bill, you are, fat-boy.

RAWLINGS: Did you ever wonder why your father did it, Frank? Why he attacked the policeman? Surely you must have asked yourself what was so bad about it that he couldn't even testify in court to maybe save his own neck?

RATTIGAN: I'm wondering why you're so keen on it.

RAWLINGS: Let's try something else.

RATTIGAN: Good-oh.

RAWLINGS: I'd like you to look at the pictures, study them carefully. What do you think they're saying, Frank? Anything to you?

RATTIGAN: Fuck knows. Bunch of tarts smiling, ain't they?

RAWLINGS: Rather like Helen Lewis, Frank. She had a smiling face, didn't she? In the picture? What was it you said – 'pretty as a picture'? But you hated her for that, didn't you? Hated that smile. Because however much she shook with fear in the house – the picture always smiled, didn't it?

RATTIGAN: Midnight maybe, many months from now. After all this. After you've finished fucking with my mind. The phone will ring . . .

RAWLINGS: What do the faces say to you, Frank?

RATTIGAN: Perhaps you'll answer it. Maybe the wife, yawning . . .

RAWLINGS: The faces.

RATTIGAN: They say nothing! Nothing at all! None of them, ever, ever does. Just faces. Just smiles. No words. Liars, all of them. Like her fucking lies. All bullshit!

RAWLINGS: How does it feel, Frank, to be locked up inside here with all the other crazies? To be classed as 'criminally insane'?

RATTIGAN: Meals are shit, music's piss and the company's crap. Then there's the endless stupid questions from arseholes like you.

RAWLINGS: They say you're a psychopath. You happy with that?

RATTIGAN: It's all bullshit to me.

RAWLINGS: What would have happened? The next day, if Helen Lewis hadn't died in the night? You had more 'games' planned?

RATTIGAN: Plenty.

RAWLINGS: So why didn't you run? Why stay there, doing what you did to the body, knowing you could have been caught at any moment? Didn't it bother you that a boyfriend might walk through the door at any moment? A lodger?

RATTIGAN: Why should I worry? They don't hang bad boys these days.

RAWLINGS: You already knew, didn't you? Knew she lived alone, would be coming home that night, alone. Knew you had a few days to have your 'fun' with her.

RATTIGAN: Prison-face.

RAWLINGS: Sorry?

RATTIGAN: You asked about faces, I'm telling you. Prison-face.

RAWLINGS: I asked you why you didn't . . .

RATTIGAN: It's an attitude. What was it that poncy writer said? Eyes are the window to the soul? More crap. Every fucker on the planet wears a mask. You learn that shit the moment they bang you up for the first time. You wear a prison-face, full stop.

RAWLINGS: OK. What does it look like?

RATTIGAN: Jesus! It doesn't 'look' like anything. It just is. Has to be. You, you just ain't got it. Know the first thing that happens the moment you step inside? They're all watching, screws, other cons, the whole bleeding lot. Watching the new arrivals, sussing them for weaknesses. And as you make your way to the cell in some other fucker's dirty underpants, two shitty blankets and a wanked-over sheet in your arms, a quiet goes down the wing. New man on the landing, let's have a pop. Might not happen for a couple of days, then suddenly, some scout'll bump into you – give you a string of verbals. And the others are all watching.

RAWLINGS: So you put the expression on, right? The prison-face?

RATTIGAN (laughs softly): Fuck, you wouldn't last two minutes inside. The moment the geezer gets fresh, you lash out with everything. Really tear the bastard up. And don't stop until the screws are holding you back.

You get a few weeks' solitary, then you're back out on the wings, and no idiot'll have the bottle to have a go after that. A few screws'll try, maybe mob-handed, late at night, bunch of 'em. But you just have to keep fucking 'em over until they drop you. They soon work out to leave you be. Word gets round – Rattigan's a headcase. See it in his eyes. Prison-face.

See – I couldn't give a shit what they call me, or where I am. They leave me alone. I get by.

The bloke who has no fear, always wins. He never feels the pain of the punch, 'cause he's too busy punching back.

RAWLINGS: That how it is, Frank? You against the world?

RATTIGAN: They leave me alone, I gives 'em no trouble. You ask any of the screws here. Good as gold, I am.

RAWLINGS: Helen Lewis . . .

RATTIGAN: What is it with you and her? Fucking obsessed with the bitch!

RAWLINGS: She didn't represent a threat, did she?

RATTIGAN: That was different. She was fun.

RAWLINGS: Because she smiled? Was 'pretty as a picture'?

RATTIGAN: Because of what she didn't do.

RAWLINGS: Tell me what she didn't do.

RATTIGAN (stands): That's it. Playtime over. See you next week, folks.

RAWLINGS: Wait! Just wait a minute!

RATTIGAN: No. It's over for today. It's boring.

RAWLINGS: Then give me a minute to bore you some more. Let me see if I've got this right, Frank. You tell me.

RATTIGAN: Still bored.

RAWLINGS: The man you met in the green Jaguar on the fruit farm was a connection. You knew him, had put out some feelers among your criminal network. You wanted something . . . a little unusual. Dangerously unusual. He arrives, whispers an address and a price. You go to Stratford – and the break-in, the attack – it's all part of a scenario, a plan.

RATTIGAN: You've been overdoing it, sunshine. Brain's broken.

RAWLINGS: My hunch is that Helen Lewis was complicit in some kind of rape fantasy of yours. A 'game' she charged big money for. A thousand pounds. But something went wrong. Seriously amiss. It all got out of hand. Maybe you went too far, killed her, then spent the next two days in a rage, completely destroying the body you had payed so handsomely to hate. Only now you really *did* hate her, because she'd ended your game by dying so inconsiderately.

Getting closer now, are we, Frank? A little too near the mark? Like you said – you know about whores. All a trade, isn't it?

RATTIGAN (grinning): All right, Sherlock, where does a mug like me get a grand from, eh? And if she's a high-class whore, then she's going to have a pretty big nigger pimp watching very carefully what she's doing with all that cash. I would've been turned over and mugged the minute I set foot through the door, prick! Fucking rape fantasy, Jesus! (Laughs) Is that the best you could do? Amateur!

RAWLINGS: Then, when you realized the girl had died, you panicked, knew what the punishment was for sex-offenders, the beatings they get from other prisoners. So you don't run, but pulp the body, get yourself arrested, then concoct all this torture crap in order to sound as psychotic as possible – knowing a spell at Oakwood is far preferable to prison. Right? You're a smart man, Frank, a loner, habitual offender, you know the system backwards. It's not going to take too much effort on your part to play the role.

RATTIGAN: If I'm as smart as you say, surely I'm gone the moment the bitch is away with the angels?

RAWLINGS: The man in the Jag. You can't trust him not to run to the police. Plus you were spotted loitering in the area. Your fingerprints are all over the house. It's only a matter of time before you're picked up. Better to stay there, play the madman – God! I bet you loved all that Beast of East 16 stuff, didn't you, eh?

RATTIGAN (slowly): Know what you should do, fat-boy?

RAWLINGS: What?

RATTIGAN: Try it. Just do it. Doesn't have to be a woman, either. Easier to handle, but I suppose a kid'd be the same. Dwarf, even. The point is they have to be . . . less than you. Smaller, weaker. Find one, disable 'em, then . . . have some fun.

RAWLINGS: I don't think I need to, Frank.

RATTIGAN: And do you know what the best part'll be? About an hour into it, when you realize you're so far along the line, there's no other way it can end. But here's the kick, fat-boy. Only you decide when. And how. They're yours, to do what you fucking well like to them.

It's the thrill of the universe. Playing God for real. Sex is bollocks by comparison. I mean, fuck 'em if you want, really want to, but my bet is you'll discover lots of other tricks better than sex.

Try it. Do it. You want to 'know' me? You have to 'be' me.

What's the worse that can happen, eh? Chances are the filth'll tumble you and you'll end up in some shithole like this, surrounded by cunts like me – but it won't matter, son – 'cause all you'll be thinking about is the next time. Better games to play.

It's a mind-fuck. The best kind. And when you come – believe me, it lasts a lifetime.

(Long silence.)

RAWLINGS: Tell me about your brother, little Jimmy. Why did you keep going back for him?

RATTIGAN: Forget my family. They're nothing, history. Do something for yourself, something you've always promised you'd do. 'Cause you're a man, right, or supposed to be? So forget all the polite fucking chatter and student bullshit – be one! Start punching and kicking, feel the buzz of it. Just like all the geezers who go and give the Frogs a good seeing-to at the World Cup. Should be given fucking knighthoods. Warriors, they are. Hard bastards you don't fuck with.

Try it, then come and talk to me about being a psycho. Ain't nothing to do with dicky brains. Simply about honouring what you are, what nature gave us. Best killers in the fucking world, men.

Go on. Make the leap, fat-boy. It's a wonderful fucking landing!

(He sits in total silence until the end of the session.)

16

Judas threw the coins down in the Temple and left; then went off and hanged himself.

The chief priests picked up the coins and said, 'This is blood money, and it is against our Law to put it in the Temple treasury.' After reaching an agreement about it, they used the money to buy Potter's Field, as a cemetery for foreigners. That is why that field is called 'Field of Blood' to this very day.

Matthew 27, verses 5–6

There was a six-foot bearded surprise waiting for me in Dr Allen's gloomy office after the session. Warder-Orderly Denton – or Dr Millar, as I now knew him.

He sat to Allen's left, grim-faced.

I sat too, deflated, embarrassed Rattigan had so easily bettered me in RECREATION SIX. I'd had time to reflect on the prostitute theory I'd put to him, realized its many flaws and implausibilities. He'd been right, of course. If bizarre sex for cash had been on the agenda, chances are someone else would have been around to look after the girl's safety, count the money, police the whole sordid enterprise.

Indeed, in the aftermath of the session, I'd been more or less forced to admit to myself that the very idea was little short of ludicrous. But the money still bothered me. Russell's clandestine theorizing as to its origins still made some sort of sense. I felt convinced Rattigan had it on him when he arrived. That the green Jag owner was a vital link. That Helen Lewis was a deliberate target. But if not for sex – then what? I was back to square one – a student on a tightrope of conjecture, with little in the way of hard facts for a safety-net.

Allen's labouring tones punctuated the heavy silence. He was less than pleased, telling me I had no 'right' to bring visual aids along to interview sessions without prior approval from Dr Millar and himself.

I apologized, half-heartedly, promised to adhere to the rules in future.

Next he offered me a drink. Not coffee, but alcohol. Specifically malt. I declined. But the choice unnerved me. 'You seem to know a great deal about my past preferences, Dr Allen.'

'Past, Adrian?' he answered softly, then added, 'I've been talking to Dr Clancy.' No surprise there. 'He's worried about you. Specifically, your approach to your work here with us.'

All the time Millar merely observed.

'It would be a shame, Adrian,' Allen mused. 'To earn yourself an unprofessional reputation at the beginning of what promises to be a distinguished career.'

The set-up was starting to rile me, reminding me of the day I was fired – the same benign expressions, careful choice of appropriate language. 'Please don't worry on my account.'

Allen opted for his best professional patronizing smile. 'Perhaps you misunderstand your role here.'

'Perhaps I do.'

'Then allow me to explain. You represent little more than a decoy.'

He watched for my reaction. I struggled to keep a neutral expression.

He went on. 'Dr Millar performs the lion's share of the work during the interviews. He's vastly experienced and gauges Rattigan's responses in order that we may compile the next set of questions. Your own questions are of little significance. Except,' he added deliberately, 'when they become dangerously unprofessional personal opinions.'

'What can I say?' I meekly offered. 'I'm learning.'

Allen nodded. 'I've been told of your "theory" regarding Rattigan and his expensive sexual preferences. Quite bizarre, Mr Rawlings.'

I swallowed hard on a dry throat. Maybe a shot of malt

would've been a good idea. No – they were testing me. Fancy had obviously noticed my wandering gaze at the pub and duly reported it back. I just hoped to God he hadn't shot his mouth off over the voices I'd heard in the kitchen. 'I just wanted to ask him. I read an article focusing on the secret lives of air hostesses. Of the six interviewed, four were prostitutes specializing in unusual sexual –'

'I'm afraid,' Allen replied tersely. 'The world of forensic psychiatry relies on proven techniques a little more rigorous than magazine articles.'

Millar nodded in agreement.

'I'm sorry,' I apologized. 'It won't happen again.'

'I do hope not,' Allen said. 'It might pay to remember you're here as a student merely gaining insight into the running of this institution. The amateur sleuthing has got to stop. Rattigan's a killer. Convicted. Most probably psychotic. His only interest to us is his medical maintenance.'

I shifted uneasily on the institutional chair. It was time to make some sort of defence. 'But don't you ever wonder why he did what he did? What drove him to put a stranger into eight body-bags?'

'You honestly think he'd tell you?' Millar asked.

'I don't know. Maybe, yes.'

'By going to see his old schoolteachers?' Allen scoffed.

'That was background,' I insisted. 'Research for the thesis.'

'Which proposes what?'

'That people like Rattigan are too easily dismissed as evil. Especially by the popular press. Which in turn inhibits thorough investigation into the root causes of their crimes.'

'Very noble, I'm sure.'

'I just have this feeling,' I continued, hoping they wouldn't see the sweat breaking on my upper lip. 'That if I can discover what really drove Rattigan to kill the girl, then it would prove invaluable to the argument.'

Allen toyed with a pen between his lips. 'And what did you learn from your visit with the headmaster? What fresh insight did it bring?'

'That Rattigan's capable of love.'

'Big conjecture, Adrian. Huge.'

I hung my head slightly. 'I'm sure he has feelings. Deeply buried, maybe. But there, nonetheless. And if there's even the vaguest chance he's capable of love, then –'

'What?' Millar interjected.

'It makes a mockery of the "fun" motive.'

The bearded man shook his head. 'Love? Rattigan?' he said. 'Once, maybe. But not now. He has no need of it. You know as well as I do that hate is all that sustains him, Mr Rawlings. He hates me, you, this institution, everything. And before you rebuke me for being uncaring, please remember Dr Allen and I have a hundred and seventy-six other inmates to worry about, plus seventy staff working in a potentially dangerous environment.'

'I never intended to rock the boat,' I said quietly.

'And discovering whatever reason why one of them may have gone berserk ten years ago is of little significance to us. His demeanour whilst under our care, however, is.'

I said nothing.

Allen seemed to almost be timing his next point. 'Dr Clancy also tells us of a strange episode in your kitchen.'

Shit! 'I think I was tired. Overworked, that's all.'

'We have to be very careful, Adrian,' he warned. 'If you're finding this process at all . . .'

'No,' I said quickly. 'I understand your concerns, but there's really nothing to worry about.'

'I can be sure of that, can I?'

'Absolutely.'

'Fine,' he replied, smiling. 'Then I think we all understand one another.'

I nodded, eager to be out of there.

Allen rose. 'You'll receive a transcript of today's session in due course. Sorry to have kept you, Adrian. From what I've gathered, you're most probably keen to return to the thesis.' He almost savoured the moment. 'I'm sure there's a lot of work to be done, yet.'

I left Oakwood wondering who I loathed more – myself for uninformed speculation, Allen and Millar for their patronizing attitudes, or Rattigan – for winding his way so completely into my failure.

But it was none of the above – someone else entirely, an individual I'd once considered a personal friend, shared many a laugh, problem and emotional dilemma with over the years. Fancy – I despised him the most for trading an intimate secret.

They'd known about 'the voices' I'd heard. No matter how hard I'd tried to dismiss the episode as a stress-related one-off, he'd gone right ahead and told them. Most probably within minutes of returning to the uni.

I turned on to the Mll, heading south for the domestic comforts of home. And the longer I thought about it, the less I felt Fancy was to blame. It had scared me rigid at the time, and he was most probably right to report it back to Allen. Perhaps I *was* slightly unstable, unsuitable for Oakwood's graduate training programme. After all, what answers did I have? The 'crowd' had simply arrived, done their stuff, left me a gibbering wreck in my own home. And since? I'd buried my head in another man's insanity, refusing to confront their fearful origins, petrified the screaming mob would return when I least expected them.

I drove home with the car stereo at full blast. Simon and Garfunkel live in Central Park did their musical best to divert my mind. Even succeeded for a while.

But when I heard the words, 'Hello, darkness, my old friend,' I silenced them.

Intuition told me I had enough darkness in my life already.

17

There seemed little else to do but return to the research, complete the thesis.

Of all the things that bothered me with the Rattigan business, two remained uppermost. Firstly, his own admission that he had suddenly decided to 'go solo' while serving three years for a racially motivated assault in Wormwood Scrubs. His 'argument', that life in the big firms had become too hectic when foreign villains arrived seemed flimsy, to say the least. Here was Rattigan, hired muscle, a nut-job, born to the task, wallowing in the criminal respect of his rank, suddenly slipping away from the fast money, to end up a tramp? If my suspicions were right, Rattigan still had plenty of connections, certainly at the time of the Helen Lewis murder. The owner of the green Jaguar being just one of them.

But Rattigan, a tramp? The records proved it, the file bore it out. Numerous arrests for vagrancy, fights in hostels, threatening behaviour, countless probationary violations. In later years, as his behaviour gave more evidence for concern, there were several abortive attempts to enrol him on fruitless anger-management courses. Social workers passed the buck back to the probation authorities, who, in turn, batted his case back to the social workers.

The records showed that for most of the three years preceding Helen Lewis's death, Rattigan spent much of his time living rough, ekeing out a meagre existence when he could, begging, working on the fruit farms, petty thieving – standard stuff in the life of what Rattigan referred to as 'the gentleman of the road'.

So I remained unconvinced, felt sure something else must

have motivated the decision. Maybe Rattigan had crossed his own mob, been expelled from whatever firm was paying for his services. Perhaps he'd been found out for a grass, then forced to survive on his own. Maybe the green Jag owner was a copper, seeking Rattigan out in the calm of the fruit farm to pay the ex-hard man a few bob for some inside information?

But I had no answers for any of it.

Which brought me to the second ill-fitting puzzle piece. Rattigan's anger at the mention of his sister, Ellie.

She ain't got fuck-all to tell you. She hates my guts and don't know fuck-all.

Leaving aside the possibly intentional double-negative (Rattigan was an intelligent Beast – choosing most of his words with deliberate care), I was left with only one course of action.

To find her, and talk to her.

Back to the detective work.

It took eleven days before I had an address. The first step was to contact Rattigan's solicitor for the murder trial, an exhaustive trek around the overstretched Legal Aid system. I had a name from the file, Martin Bellamy, and, God bless the man, he still worked for the beleaguered, subsidized justice organization, albeit in a rather more superior position than in 1989.

Two days later I sat in his dilapidated London office and took up twenty minutes of his valuable time stimulating his memory. He glanced through my copy of Rattigan's file, shook his head sadly several times, then had Rattigan's Old Bailey case notes whisked up to him from some unseen repository in the creaking building.

As we compared notes, memories began to resurface. Martin Bellamy had loathed the man he was legally required to act for, remembering him to be surly, uncooperative, gloating, at times seemingly unbalanced, unkempt – and above all else (at least to his way of thinking at the time) little short of evil.

'There was something in him,' Bellamy recalled, frowning as remembered intuition fought with professional conduct.

'No. Forget that. The problem was . . . there was nothing in him. No remorse. I remember he had a perfect understanding of his legal position, details of his arrest, the crime itself . . . and I suppose that was the worst for me. I was used to muggers, squatters, drunks as clients – suddenly I had this grinning murderer on my hands.' A long pause. 'He told me he did it for fun. I'll never forget that.'

'You ordered the psychological tests while he was on remand?'

'Had to. The Crown had already run a series of its own using police shrinks. They found him to be a dangerous sociopath who was most probably unaware of the moral ramifications of his actions. All we had to do in defending him was convince the jury that he needed treatment in a secure unit, as opposed to serving life in a prison. It was a difficult time – the public still remembered Sutcliffe and the voices from God, but Rattigan didn't have any of those schizophrenic illusions. No fantastically insane motive for his actions. Like he said, he just did it for fun. We had to prove that that was enough to make him insane in the eyes of the law. Because you'd have to be, wouldn't you? Three days he spent –'

'His sister,' I interrupted politely. 'Ellie? She never testified at the trial, never came forward as a character witness. Why?'

Bellamy gave a short, wry laugh. 'She would have buried him. Hated him. Elaine Horton. Lived up north somewhere. We contacted her, went to see her. I remember her saying it's a pity Rattigan wouldn't go the same way as her father.'

'Why the venom?'

'She never told. Said the whole thing was a no-no from the off. We gave her up as a dead loss. His mother was dead, stepfather too . . . and I think there was a younger brother,' he consulted the ageing file, flicking through the brittle typed pages. 'James Rattigan. Another drifter. Registered as a drug addict by the Manchester police authorities. Useless as a character witness. Prosecution would have picked more holes in him than a string vest.'

'You met him, Jimmy Rattigan?'

Bellamy shook his head. 'No point. He was a dud. All we had was a severely dysfunctional family. Father hung for the murder of a policeman, mother dead and buried, two sons known as villains and vagrants, and a sister who wasn't prepared to testify.'

'Plus the silence from Rattigan himself, right?'

Bellamy nodded.

'When he was arrested, he had nearly a thousand pounds in cash. Now, the police –'

It was Bellamy's turn to interrupt, time at a premium. 'Alleged he tortured the girl for the money.'

'Did you believe that?'

'The problem was we didn't know enough about the girl's lifestyle. We didn't know if she would have kept that amount of cash in the house in the first place. We talked to a couple of her old boyfriends, and none could remember her keeping that sort of money. She had an exemplary work record.' He flicked through the file again. 'British Airways. Three years as a cabin stewardess. Wages always paid straight into a numbered bank account in her name. Even her relatives in Wales thought it unlikely she'd have much spare money lying around. Out of character.'

'So . . . ?'

Bellamy nodded, catching the drift. 'The money could well have been his, or possibly as he said at the time, a friend's. However, fingerprinting showed it to be covered in his prints. And hers.'

This was new. 'Hers?'

He shrugged. 'Who knows? Maybe he got her to count it before snapping her fingers off.' He sighed heavily. 'But that's the point about all this, isn't it? No one's ever going to know what happened. The body was so unrecognizable that forensic testing was virtually useless. DNA testing wasn't as sophisticated then. All we had to go on was his word, his version.'

'You tested him for signs of psychological sexual deviancy?'

'Of course. The confession he detailed upon arrest contained many deviant overtones, sexual torture among them. However, no semen that could be forensically matched to

Rattigan's was found on the body, the clothes he was wearing, or in the house itself. In the end we were forced to go along with his own admission that he'd done the whole thing "for fun". In court, the torture theory gradually fell apart, and of course Rattigan used the occasion to act the total moron with Oscar-winning aplomb. The jury saw a foaming madman, evidence of what he'd done for pleasure; and when our independent psychologists came in with their evidence, were more or less directed by the judge to return a Guilty Via Diminished Responsibility verdict.'

'You think he was faking it?'

'Probably not. The man's most likely a psycho. He's where he belongs. Mad, bad, both, who knows? His crime was unimaginably terrible. One of the worst I've dealt with.'

'One of?'

The phone rang. Our meeting was in danger of overrunning. He muttered one or two impressive-sounding legal phrases into the plastic mouthpiece, then replaced the receiver. 'You chaps. You don't see it like we do.'

'I'm sorry?'

'Human beings malfunction. Probably a hundred billion reasons why. You can't pigeonhole insanity, because that would be truly insane.'

I made a half-hearted gesture of acknowledgement, a shrug, followed by a forced smile. 'Elaine Horton,' I asked innocently. 'Don't suppose you still have her address, do you?'

He gave me Elaine Horton's address. She'd moved five years previously. I rang the new owner, asked for her address and phone number. He seemed hesitant, suspicious of my motives. But I was fortified by the buzz of amateur detection and the waffle flowed easily. Long-lost cousin on a surprise visit from America, whatever. He left me hanging on for four minutes, before returning with the information I wanted. I thanked him, thinking how easy it all was. Too easy, so far.

I considered calling the new number straightaway, wondering if I'd have to repeat the deceptively easy process of deception. Maybe she'd have moved on again, emigrated, died. God only knew. The only way to find out was to try.

I rang the number, watching through the office window as the soundless shapes of toddlers played in the garden of the day-nursery next door. I sat quite still, receiver to my ear, double-glazed from their suburban micro-cosmos, seeing a bigger boy push a smaller one to the ground. The mouth opened, but I heard no screams. Next, a woman dashed to his aid, righted him, distracted him with a brightly coloured ball. The older boy watched from a few feet away, waiting for the next time.

Three rings and she answered. The merest trace of a buried Cockney accent lay smothered by a phoney middle-English accent.

'Mrs Horton?'

'Speaking.'

'I'm sorry to bother you. My name's Adrian Rawlings and –'

'I don't want anything, thank you. Not today.'

'This isn't a sales call, Mrs Horton. It's about your brother.'

'Jimmy? What's he . . . ?

'Frank.'

'Frank?'

'I wondered if I could –'

'Police?'

'Sorry?'

'Are you from the police?'

I laughed, trying my best to thaw her out. 'No, Mrs Horton. I'm a postgraduate student currently researching a doctorate thesis . . .'

No dice. 'I'm afraid I've nothing to say to you.'

A gamble. 'And if I was the police?'

The lock out. 'Good day. Please don't bother me again.' She replaced her phone.

The thesis began to resemble a freaks' gallery. My study had its own incarnate air of fools, ghouls and sickos. Ed Gein, Dahmer, the Wests, Brady, Hindley, Nilsen and a dozen other assorted monsters lay around in condensed, sensationalized paperbacks, fighting for desk space with research reports on temporal brain dysfunction and screaming tabloid headlines.

I remember a conversation I had with a stranger in my local pub one lunchtime. I needed to get out of the house for a breather. Just an orange juice and a change of scenery. He was simply another punter in the bar, mid-fifties, drinking brandy. We got chatting about all sorts. He wanted to know what I 'did'. I didn't see the harm and told him. He was hooked. We chatted for over an hour. At some point I suggested to him that mental illnesses should really be considered in the same light as physical ones. That the paranoid-schizophrenic muttering gibberish by any bus station in the land deserved the same sympathy and understanding as the bloke with the broken leg down the road.

At which point he looked at me with near-total derision. 'Point is, mate,' he explained. 'Geezer with his leg in plaster ain't likely to kick you to death with it, is he?'

The work – the research – continued.

I remember having tea with a Church of England bishop, earnestly prepared to donate an afternoon of his time championing the Christian side of the debate.

As I could have predicted, he gave me the expected theological line – good and evil, light and dark, day and night, universal balance, spiritual harmony.

'I accept all that,' I said, eventually. 'But if God's such a wonderful being, the Father who loves all His children, why bring Lucifer into the scheme of things in the first place? Why not waive a bit of his omnipresent power and do away with the evil once and for all?'

He regarded me in the same patronizing manner as the man in my local pub had done. Then added, slowly, deliberately, 'The way of life is a journey of temptation, Mr Rawlings. Christ Jesus showed us that. God gave us His only son so that he might die for all our sins, and show us the true way to the Resurrection and the Life.'

'Forgive me,' I diplomatically replied. 'But I still feel you haven't answered the question.'

'Life will answer your questions, if you are open to the answers.'

'And how do I do that?'

'Open yourself to Christ.'

'OK. But can I ask you this? Do you believe in evil as a force?'

'A way of temptation.'

'Psychopaths – those born with malfunctioning brains? Are they evil, or God's children?'

He nibbled on a digestive, smiling, enjoying the debate, donation of his indoctrinated wisdom. 'There is always redemption through God's love.'

I left soon after, all previously held views confirmed. The man appeared to drift around in a quasi-bubble of his own goodness, a security afforded by professional comforts. I cynically wondered how quickly it would burst if a Rattigan tracked down his wife and set about her as he'd done with Helen Lewis. At what point would the smiling bishop finally snap, tear off the dog collar and cassock, eyes ablaze with real living fury, wrench the whirling drill from the Rattigan's grasp and set about taking an eye for an eye . . . ?

A tabloid newspaper editor refused to see me. But I'd expected that. You don't make appointments to see them. You do something, they come to you. One by one. Until someone else does something a little more sordid, more spectacular, more 'evil'.

More profitworthy.

Elaine Horton, on the other hand, proved too much of an allure. Too complicated, too bound in with it all. Three minutes after our inital call, the phone had rung again. A man's voice this time, northern accent, brutally challenging.

'Whoever the fuck you are, get your stinking nose out of other people's business. OK, pal? Want your fucking back broke?'

He hung up. I immediately dialled 1471 to trace the less than friendly caller. Surprise, surprise, the call came from Elaine Horton's number. She'd done exactly the same as I had – traced the call to pin me down. Then got someone else to threaten me. Which he'd done very successfully. I was terrified. She knew at least one very heavy-sounding heavy. A doubt flashed across my mind for a split second, an urge to leave everything where it was, hide from her as I'd chosen to hide from the baying crowd.

But then I realized that she had to be just as scared to set the man on to me in the first place. I must have been some kind of threat – me, a stranger, a student, a thirty-nine-year-old, soul-loving nobody. Just the one enquiry about big brother Frank and, as James Brown would've said, she'd 'let loose with the abuse'.

Which made me even more determined to find out why.

18

It was about this time that I first saw him. Some isolated moment during those eleven frantic days. A glimpse of someone standing near my car, parked in the loose-chipped uni. car park. Perhaps ten metres away, waiting.

Just a corner-of-the-eye thing, a shock of short sandy hair. Scruffy – an older man, mid-fifties, Rattigan's age, standing with the air of one who doesn't drive, loitering for some indefinable purpose.

Two days later, the same scenario. Only more disquieting somehow. I'd just wandered out from seeing Fancy once more, and there he was again. A quick peek at his face this time as he scanned mine. Hair wet from a recent downpour, shabby charity-shop overcoat, black shoes, one sole coming loose at the toe. Our eyes met for an instant, locked across a steel sea of curving car roofs. His face appeared to be almost criminally urgent, deep-set eyes darting, and for a moment I wondered if he was a lookout, casing the car park while a younger accomplice removed stereos unseen elsewhere.

I even nodded at him, the old coward's trick, turning the blind eye, distancing myself from his intentions. You just do your own thing, mate, don't mind me, I ain't seen a thing. He hesitated, seeming to consider returning the gesture, then turned and walked away.

It was only when I saw him for a third time that things took an unexpected turn. This was much closer to home, as I walked from Chelmsford Central Library late one afternoon and caught sight of him on Broomfield village green. Just standing. I saw him first and stopped, thirty yards away on the other side of the thundering road, only to discover he was directly opposite my house, simply watching. I felt a slight tingling of dread as I realized he knew my address. My throat had also dried.

What now? Walk inside and spend the next half-hour watching from an upstairs window? Or balls it out? I'm no hero, believe me, but something compelled me to take the latter option. Curiosity, perhaps, a rising anger, even. What if our last meetings were all coincidence? Was I being strangely egotistical in assuming the man's interest was in me? Only the one way to find out.

I crossed the road and walked nervously towards him. He turned when I was less than five steps away. Our eyes met again. It was my cue to start the dialogue, but here I ran into another problem. What was I going to say? Small talk? Or straight for the obvious?

Why beat about the bush? 'Excuse me . . . erm . . . Are you looking for something?'

'Adrian Rawlings?'

The last thing I wanted to hear. 'Yeah. What do you want?'

'That's my question.'

I stopped, anxious for distance. This close his eyes were bloodshot, face almost yellow-ochre in the early-evening twilight. Mad, I thought instinctively. Gentle mental. Pavement zombie. Dangerous.

'How do you know my name?'

He turned, walked away. Relief flooded over me. Then he stopped, turned back. 'They watch me,' he said quietly. 'Got to be so bloody careful. I had to check you weren't one of them.'

I went for the collusion line, hoping he didn't have a kitchen knife hidden under the torn overcoat. 'Big Brother, isn't it? George Orwell had the whole deal figured out in nineteen forty-eight.'

His face contorted into sudden misunderstanding. 'What you talking about?'

I backtracked fast, anxious not to upset him further, wishing I'd taken option two – watching from the bedroom, maybe calling the police. 'Nothing, really,' I quickly replied, offering my most unthreatening smile. 'Rubbish, I suppose.'

He frowned, studying me closely. 'We need to talk.'

'Sure.'

'You've been asking a lot of questions. Careless talk costs lives, Mr Rawlings. Especially careless talk about Frank Rattigan.'

The name struck deep. 'You know about Frank?'

'Too much,' he replied. 'But not enough.'

'Listen,' I croaked. 'I don't wish to appear rude, but who are you?'

He smiled, baring tobacco-stained teeth. 'A casualty of their corruption. Though the official line would be that I'm a routine paranoid-schizo who cracked up under the pressure. We'll talk, when the time's right. Now's not right. Later. I just needed to know you weren't one of them.'

'How do you know him?' I was suddenly desperate to make the connection.

'He ruined my fucking life.'

'How? Please, you must . . .'

'Just watch your back. You're getting into something very serious.'

A bus made its plodding way slowly behind him, and he began walking quickly towards the bus stop. I was completely frustrated by the double-talk, unanswered questions. Who was he? What did he know? How had he found me? I followed as the bus floated wearily into the stop. The doors hissed open and he took a step inside.

He turned back, beckoned me over. I'd already caught up, curiosity at bursting point. Did he want me to ride with him? Lend him his fare? What?

I stood by the folding doors, glimpsed the driver looking just as bewildered as I was.

The stranger passed me a piece of paper, then paid his own fare and walked quickly towards the back of the bus. In seconds the doors slid shut and I watched helpless as the green and yellow bus began the next stage of its staggered journey into town.

Then read the note: *I'll be in touch. Former DCI Nick Moira.*

19

Dazed, I recrossed the road and let myself into the house.

My first impulse was to ring the Met again, tell them I'd just been waylaid by a lunatic posing as one of their key CID men back in the late eighties. But previous calls had all been politely dismissed, what hope was there that this one would be taken seriously? I made myself a coffee, retired to the office, and pondered.

What if the dishevelled stranger really *was* Moira? Then how in God's name had he tracked me down? My memory struggled to reassemble the conversation. He was nervous, flitting between paranoia and veiled references to Rattigan and others. More worryingly, if he wasn't Moira, why claim that he was?

We'll talk, when the time's right.

When? What would he do? Bowl up and ring on the door? Signal me clandestinely from the uni. car park? What did he have to say? How had Rattigan ruined his life?

Why hadn't I simply followed him on to the bus, pressed him further? Though I was forced to admit that the feeling of relief as he left was greater than the urge to uncover what he may or may not have known. A part of me even hoped that that was the last I would see of him, in order that I might dismiss the episode as an innocent exchange with a mixed-up man. For to acknowledge that he was who he'd claimed to be would have surely meant accepting the rest of it. He'd talked of dark agencies, mysterious 'theys' and 'thems'. And scared me. I was just a student, for Christ's sake. I wanted no part of his madness. No part of any of it.

My thoughts were already preoccupied with Elaine Horton.

I had no space for 'Moira', his ramblings. Besides, what could I do? He was gone, I had to move on.

I just wished he hadn't mentioned Rattigan by name.

Next morning, I'd forced the incident to the back of my crowded mind. Simply didn't have the space for it, was already considering following another trail – to pay a visit on Elaine Horton, née Rattigan.

As older, hostile sister to the Beast of East 16, I was convinced she'd provide me with valuable insight as to his background. I deliberately hadn't told Jemimah about the threatening return phone call I'd received from Elaine's address, nor my meeting with 'Moira' either. She was smack bang in the middle of a new business pitch, and it seemed cruel to offload my worries on to her already overworked shoulders. I well remembered the stress of pitching from my own agency days – there simply wasn't the room for domestic distractions.

Instead, I asked her if it was OK if I disappeared for a couple of nights, pop up to Manchester on a fact-finding mission. She agreed, too wrapped up in her own worries to object. In retrospect, I wish she hadn't. But that's negating my own responsibilities and choices. Jemimah was never to blame for that trip. Ever.

On the morning I left, I made sure I drove both Juliet and Guy to school. I needed to hold them both, much to their embarrassment. It's a curiously flat feeling, when you wish to embrace a child, and they just want to break away, join their friends. Though who could blame them? Here was the man they called 'Dad' – who they most likely still mistrusted from numerous whisky binges – now asking for paternal affection. A sad fool whose new party-piece was to crack up in the kitchen when the footy was on. Still, they tried their best to play doting offspring, didn't flinch too obviously as I kissed them, promised to help their mother until I returned, and never asked why or where I was going.

I went back home, phoned Jemimah at the office, keen to hear her voice once more. She was in a meeting, occupied.

So I packed and drove north. Stanstead, M11, Huntingdon,

switchback of the A14, M6, outskirts of Birmingham, on towards the forwarding address I had unearthed from Martin Bellamy a few days previously. I stopped for petrol and a Manchester *A-Z* at Cowley Services, flicking through the index to match a street name with my intended destination.

Ninety minutes later I arrived in Wilmslow, Greater Manchester, the Three Degrees serenading me into its moneyed luxury. Quiet avenues played secure hosts to large houses. The tentacles of inner-city deprivation seemed to have stopped well short, uncertain of their withering influence in this football players' homeland. I found one car in ten that wasn't a superior German make or Japanese four-by-four.

I parked some distance from the address I'd been given, wondering how it could have all gone so horribly wrong for Frank, so materially right for big sister Ellie.

Her home appeared to be almost nakedly detatched, unshielded by trees and fences. Just a low brick wall and a neatly trimmed front lawn separated the opulent property from its equally pricey neighbours. I had no idea of northern property prices, but in Essex it would have gone for close on a quarter of a million. The whole place appeared hushed in some sort of quiet reverence – no birds, children, cars, just silence.

I stopped, frozen, unable to confront what lay waiting just a short distance away. Just how stupid was I actually being? Elaine Horton obviously had a quick line to telephonic thuggery, what if she lived with some scarred neanderthal only too willing to disturb the suburban serenity with a thousand painful symphonies played out on my hopelessly unprepared body? I'd never been any good with my fists, somehow managing to talk, cajole and run my way out of trouble – now would be a lousy time to start learning how to fight.

But I was there, having driven the best part of two hundred miles to talk to Rattigan's older sister. Little for it but to leave the car and make my way towards the house.

And I really, really wanted a malt. A double.

The door opened at the third time of asking.

No words at first, not even an enquiry. Just a pleasant female face, squinting behind the tiny gap afforded by the security chain.

So I started. 'Mrs Horton?'

Still nothing. She waited.

I tried not to appear obvious in studying her face. On closer inspection, she looked worn and worried, struggling to maintain the polite facade. Pale-grey eyes twitched nervously. I wondered if the shock of blonde hair was dyed, or a wig. 'My name's Adrian Rawlings. We spoke on the phone the other day . . .'

'Oh.'

I tried the 'putting hesitant clients at their ease' smile. 'Look, I didn't really get the chance to explain . . .'

A glimmer of recognition crossed the anxious face. The penny began its journey . . . 'You're the man who rang here asking about' – and dropped – 'Frank?'

'That's right. I just wondered if I could . . .'

'No. I don't think so.'

Deep breath. 'I want to ask you some questions, Mrs Horton. I'm researching a thesis for my psychology doctorate, and your brother's case forms a –'

'He's no brother of mine. Good day.'

'Mrs Horton, I've come a long way. From Chelmsford. I'd really appreciate just a few minutes of your time.'

She forced a smile, keen to appear unflustered. 'I'm sorry. I have to go out in a minute.'

'I'll wait in my car, then. What time are you back?'

She looked beyond my shoulder, struggling to see the car I'd parked way beyond her eyeline. 'Can't say. I'm sorry. Goodbye.'

The door closed.

I waited five seconds.

Then took another deep breath, opened the letterbox with shaking fingers and crouched down on one knee.

'Mrs Horton. I'm not a security-conscious bloke. But I do tape all my calls. I really don't want to upset you. But you should have gone ex-directory, Mrs Horton. I've got the lot on tape – the abusive phone call the minute after we spoke, then confirmation from the BT computer that the call came from your number.'

Another silence. Then: 'Go away! This is harassment. I'll call the police!'

'Go ahead. I've got the tape in the car. Let's let them sort it out, shall we? You really want that, Mrs Horton? I don't.'

'Leave me alone.'

But I wasn't having any of it, hadn't driven all that way to be so easily rebuffed. 'I need to talk to you about Frank. Believe me, I don't want to cause any bother.'

'I'm warning you . . .'

'What? You going to get your charming friend to "get my fuckin' back broke"? Come on, Mrs Horton, I'm not a threat. Just a student. Ten minutes of your time, then I'm gone. Promise.'

There were muffled footsteps from the other side of the door. I quickly stood, realizing my hands shook uncontrollably. The door opened. I half expected to be staring up the nostrils of a twenty-stone son or minder, but it was Elaine Horton who fiddled with the chain, cursed in broad Cockney, then allowed me in.

The accent was slipping fast, lapsing back towards its vocal origins. 'Five minutes, max,' she announced. 'Any funny business and I call the police.'

I stepped gratefully into a hallway odorously rich in air-freshener and carpet deodorant. 'Thank you,' I replied, gratefully. 'Thank you very much.'

20

She reluctantly showed me into a spacious living room, indicating where I should sit on a beige leather sofa. The room was predominantly cream-coloured – carpet, curtains, walls. It all seemed considered, even Elaine Horton's outfit matching the interior – cream skirt, blouse, shoes.

She looked nothing like her brother. Tight lips replaced his fleshy grimace. Seven years older than Rattigan, at sixty-five, she was thinner, taller, tanned.

There was no offer of a drink. She waited and watched. My gaze was drawn to a great cluster of framed photographs crowding the large mantelpiece, strangers frozen by chemical emulsion smiled from behind thin-layered glass. In some, I recognized a younger Elaine Horton, still vibrant, laughing.

I placed my briefcase on a low coffee table, opened it, and began to arrange one or two items alongside. A pen, notebook, photocopy of Rattigan's report . . .

Twenty seconds passed in the uncomfortable silence. I cleared my throat, checked my watch. It was nearly three, and outside the fading light had already begun to give way to the beginnings of another winter night. 'Like I say, I won't take much of your time.'

'Indeed you won't.' She sat across from me, lit up from the heavy round onyx lighter. Rothmans – just like her brother. 'But if it's about Frank, there isn't much I can say. You're wasting your time.'

But I didn't think so. The body language was too tense, too guarded. 'Why did you have me threatened over the phone?'

She never even flinched. 'That was my husband. He gets

a little anxious at times. Overprotective.' She sucked on the cigarette, tip glowing fiercely. 'I told him it was a stupid thing to do. But he wouldn't listen. I'm sorry if he caused you any distress. He's not a bad man. Not like Frank. Frank's a cancer on this family, Mr . . . ?

'Rawlings. Listen, Mrs Horton, do you mind if I record this conversation, only I have a micro-cassette, and it would save me . . .'

'I don't think my husband would appreciate your being here, Mr Rawlings. He doesn't work far away. One call and he'll be back in minutes. Don't push your luck.'

So I began a clumsy shorthand, trying to maintain an eyeline and scribble at the same time. 'It's a thesis, Mrs Horton. I'm using Frank's case as a study aid towards under-standing the relationship between . . . well, let's just say, cause and effect.'

'Can't say I'm really that interested, Mr Rawlings.'

'It wasn't my choice. I kind of ended up with him. Numer-ous studies are undertaken using incarcerated offenders. You end up using who's available, who the hospital thinks are suitable.'

'And what do you think, Mr Rawlings? About Frank?'

'I don't know enough about him.'

'You've spoken to him?'

'Several times.'

'Well, you must know he's a psychopath, then.'

'Conventional testing indicates he might well be.'

She narrowed her eyes. 'But you're not so sure?'

'He told me not to see you. Told me you didn't know anything.'

'First time he's told the truth in fifty goddamned years. All those drugs must be doing him some good. He's an habitual liar. Takes people in. Always has.'

'Like at school? Selling stories of your father's death?'

'A leopard doesn't change its spots, does it?'

'Maybe he has. You just said he's finally told the truth for once.'

She had two more quick drags, speaking as she exhaled. 'I can't help you. Whatever it is, I can't. He's sick. Best left where he is. He was always heading where he ended up. Bad by birth. People needed only to say something to Frank and he'd do it. I suppose he thought it'd get him respect. They'd say, "Listen, Frank, so-and-so needs sorting out", he'd go and work them over. Dreadful. He had no conscience about it. He was proud of his job, proud of his reputation.'

'But that was later,' I pressed. 'He can't always have been like that. Not as a young boy.'

She pointedly stubbed out the cigarette, seemed to hesitate for a moment, then sat in the armchair opposite. 'He was in trouble the moment he could walk. The war was on. Children ran wild, looking for shrapnel, souvenirs, running in gangs.'

I went with a hunch. 'But not you?'

'Couldn't, could I? I was seven when it started, thirteen by the time the Yanks finished it. Mum needed me around the house. Jobs to be done. Washing, cleaning, cooking. Dad was out hustling, trying to beat the rations. All the local men that were smart enough avoided being drafted. So he was down the pub most times, cutting deals.' She looked at me with near contempt. 'You . . . people these days, you've no idea what it was like. No concept. It's all microwaves this and computers that . . .'

'But Frank was out, getting into trouble?'

'Causing it, mostly, by the end of the war. Truanting, breaking in, chucking bricks, fights. Most weeks we'd get a knock on the door. Dad'd be out, and John, a family friend, would be holding him by the scruff.'

'John Templar? The man your mother married after . . .'

'Dad died.' A long pause. 'Yes. A good man. Policeman – hero. There was a gas explosion. He dug survivors out with his bare hands.' Her eyes drifted to the window. 'Made all the papers. "Hands of a Hero" – and they printed this life-size shot of his blistered hands, and underneath the story of how he'd saved those lives before the roof caved in. 'Course, I'd left home then, married. But he was a good sort. Took us all on, including Jimmy. Three East End kids. Not many'd do that for the love of a woman. Not in those times.'

'And your father? He was a friend of Uncle John's, right?'

She nodded. 'More than that, I'm afraid.'

'It goes no further. This is just for me.'

'He was his nark. Local grass. Templar had caught Dad up to no good a dozen times. Finally persuaded him to start trading a few names in return for turning a blind eye. Dad had no choice. I didn't realize any of this at the time. It only began to make sense a long time after. My first husband was a local rogue, Mr Rawlings. It was common knowledge that John Templar had Dad in his pocket. Mum didn't say a thing. Guess she was just pleased at the extras Dad would sometimes bring home.'

My wrist began to ache from the shorthand. 'And Frank just continued to run riot?'

She nodded again. 'A wildcat. Sometimes Templar would take him into our front room, take his belt to him. I'd be somewhere in the house, cleaning or something. Mum'd come and tell me Uncle John was teaching him a lesson.'

It seemed incredible, despite the agonies of the wartime past she was describing. 'She approved? Another man beating her son?'

'They were hard times. Templar gave it out because Dad wasn't there. Besides, Dad didn't believe in that stuff. Thought kids ought to be understood. Got beaten black and blue as a kid himself. Swore he'd be different with his own kids. Too soft by half.'

'Did he know what Templar was doing?'

She paused to light up another Rothmans. 'No idea. Can't ask him, can we? I was only a child myself. Frank was a little sod who got what he deserved. It was all for his own good. You can't let children run rings round you. Kids were always given a belting in those days.'

'But Frank continued to get into trouble?'

'No matter how hard he was beaten, next week he was back for more.' She looked away, the glimmer of a smile crossing her taut face. 'Oh, I know what you're thinking, Mr Rawlings – that old sentimental stuff about the aggrieved child who just needed to be shown a little love. But not Frank. Plenty had tried to "understand" him. Then given him up as a bad lot, like all the rest. Don't forget he was a big child. Stocky, strong. Prided himself on being able to take a beating, then dish it back, ten times as bad. Eventually, he became unmanageable. Too big for any of us in that house. Got into stupid bits of business with the other local crooks. The fast road to easy money, I'm afraid – flash suits, women and cars.'

'Your mother? Couldn't she control him?'

She laughed sadly. 'It wasn't like the Krays. Frank couldn't give a fig about anyone except himself.'

'He spent a good deal of time in various institutions?'

'And he deserved every day of every sentence. But the whole thing was a holiday to him. Just another chance to prove himself.'

'Did you visit him often?'

'Once or twice.'

'How was he?'

'Disturbed. Mad, I suppose. This was the early seventies. I went to see him a couple of times when he was doing a stretch in Norwich, I think. Could have been Doncaster. Anyway, the governor calls me in after the visit, and asks me the sort of stuff you're asking me now. There's some sort of psychiatrist there as well. They told me they thought Frank was a psychopath. Well, I didn't know what the hell the word meant. Looked it up when I got home though. Made a lot of sense, really.'

'How so?'

'Maybe it was in his genes. From birth. I mean, Dad went barmy in the end. Belted that poor policeman through a window.'

'You don't feel that PC Scrimshaw's death could be put down to a fatal accident?'

'My father was drunk. The records bear it out. He went for him. Totally out of character. Just snapped. Refused to tell the court why. I don't think he knew himself. Except maybe he'd always had that rage in him and spent his life sitting on it, damping it with the drink.'

'You feel your father let you down? Not taking the stand?'

'This isn't about me, Mr Rawlings.'

I blushed slightly. 'Right. You're right. I'm simply trying to gauge . . . how perhaps Frank was feeling. Losing his father like that?'

'Like I said. Frank never gave a monkey's about anyone except himself.'

'And your mother, pregnant as she was? What did she make of your father's silence?'

She inhaled slowly, paused, held the smoke deep down inside for a moment as if drawing on a joint. 'I suppose she accepted it. What could she do? Apart from going through all the appeal channels, letter to the Home Secretary, all that sort of stuff. But, you know, it was like he was already dead. We saw him once or twice before they . . . carried out the sentence. But I don't think he ever gave her any answers. Or if he did, she never told us kids. It was her business in the end.'

I paused for a second, gathering my thoughts, realizing we were fast running towards the end of her five-minute deadline. 'When the news broke about Frank's murder of the air hostess . . .'

'No. I wasn't surprised. History repeating itself, perhaps. Same as his dad. The big court case, him saying nothing.'

'You went to the Old Bailey?'

'No point. One of his defence team had come to see me, ask if I'd be a character witness. I told him what I told you. They didn't think I'd be much use.'

'But you could have told them you suspected Frank was insane. Your testimony would have propped up their Diminished Responsibility defence.'

She almost laughed this time. 'They didn't need me. Frank could manage to convince the entire Vatican he was the Pope if he wanted to.'

'He was faking?'

She looked me straight in the eye. 'He's mad, Mr Rawlings. No question. But bad mad. He knew what he was doing. Said he enjoyed doing what he did to that poor girl. My brother is a devil incarnate. No mercy, no remorse. He's just bad, through and through. That's the end of it.'

'But do you think . . . ?'

Her eyes blazed. 'When in God's name are people like you

going to realize what ordinary folk already know? How long's it going to take? How many more kids have got to be taken, raped and murdered before someone finally catches on? The world is full of bad people. My brother is one of them. Lock them up, throw away the bloody key. Make it safe for the rest of us.'

I tried a last-ditch defence of my intended profession. 'Mrs Horton, there are millions of neurological connections made in the brain of which we have no understanding. Likewise, there are numerable instances of sociopathic disorders stemming from a combination of traumatic childhood experiences and debilitating cerebral functions . . .'

No dice. 'And what about the victims, Mr Rawlings? How many people spend their time investigating what we feel, eh?'

It was time to go. Besides, I was convinced I'd made sufficient progress. The revelation that Frank was beaten by a family friend had already afforded me a tiny glimpse into the confusing origins of his madness.

I started to pack up. 'Many studies are already done on victim reactions. Post-Traumatic Stress Disorder is now a recognized psychosis simply because . . .'

The ferocity of the response caught me by total surprise. 'Always got a smartarsed answer, haven't you? Like bloody politicians. Get real, Mr do-goody Rawlings. Open your eyes. Best thing you could do, you and your kind, is to invent a machine which scans these monsters' brains at birth, then does away with them if they fail the test. That's all we want. A safe place to live. It's nearly the next millennium, and we've still got people like you harping on about "understanding". Why bother? When bastards like my brother wouldn't know the meaning of the word? Shoot them. Shoot every one of them at birth.'

I finished packing away in silence, then stood, feeling her anger subside, the storm over. I rose from the sofa, intending to walk away, out through the front door towards the sanctuary of my car. But my eyes were elsewhere, drawn to one particular photograph on the crowded mantelpiece.

Oh, my God.

Then another look, just to be sure.

Heart rate suddenly increasing.

Shit. No mistake.

I looked away, anxious that she hadn't seen me glimpse what should have been hidden, well hidden from my prying eyes. But Elaine Horton was already standing in the hall, making small talk now, apologizing for the outburst, asking to be excused, saying she was tired, the whole business made her confused . . .

I stepped out into the quiet avenue. The front door closed behind me. I began the short walk from the house back to my car, holding the image in my head, trying to appear calm, just in case she was still watching . . .

There were many photographs on the mantelpiece that day, an instamatic tableau of the Hortons' past. Most featured Elaine with a younger man, arm in arm, kissing, standing on the steps of the registery office, confetti swirling around. No kids, just him and her.

The shot which had made the hairs on the back of my neck almost stand on end was ostensibly as innocent and charming as its companions. A summertime memory. A decade ago, judging by the fashions. Husband and wife, champagne glasses raised, by the beach.

A car park by the beach.

Sitting on the bonnet of a gleaming new car.

Maybe toasting their good fortune, their latest purchase.

A green Jaguar.

21

Two hours passed . . .

Mostly, I sat stock-still, brain on 'pause' after glimpsing the photo. Just a split-second glance had separated me from turning back for Chelmsford and staying where I was, an inanimate man in an inanimate car.

The more I brooded, the more I began to wish I hadn't seen the damn thing, for that one photo demanded too many answers, raised numerous fresh possibilities and conumdrums.

But I *had* to push on. For me.

OK, I thought, if it really was the same green Jag at the fruit farm just days before the murder, then I had to accept that Elaine Horton was probably keeping some serious secrets from me. Which would also explain why her husband was keen to warn me off. Maybe he was the driver, the man who had supposedly 'asked for directions' all those years ago.

And if he was, and he used the occasion to give Rattigan the money, then chances are he could be a nasty piece of work, too. But how in God's name was I ever going to find out?

I contented myself with sitting and waiting for Mr Horton. At least get one look at the man who had so effortlessly scared the life out of me with his phone call. Then try and figure something out. What else could I do?

I began rereading Rattigan's file, reviewing the facts, piecing together what I knew to be true, then filling the gaps with what others had told me.

Born in March, 1940, the second child of Joseph and Mary Rattigan, Francis James Rattigan is quickly identified by the local Mile End community as a young troublemaker.

Neither parent seems able to control the child, whose

behaviour becomes more and more antisocial with each passing year.

Joseph Rattigan manages to avoid being drafted, and spends the majority of the war as a volunteer Air Raid Patrol warden, indulging in whatever black-market activities are presented to him. Somewhere about this time, he meets up with John Templar, a sergeant with the local police. Joseph agrees to do the officer a few favours, naming local villains, grassing on various plots and scams. In return, Templar turns a blind eye to Joseph's own illegal endeavours.

Over the years, Templar becomes a frequent visitor to the Rattigan household, often returning with young Frank, even being allowed to discipline the unruly child in his father's absence. The rest of the family, it seems, saw nothing wrong in this, and over time, Templar strikes up a relationship with Mary Rattigan, marrying her after the execution of Joseph in 1949.

At his trial for the wilful murder of PC Scrimshaw, Joseph Rattigan refuses to testify.

The death of his father appears to have little outward emotional effect on Frank. There is no remorse, no tangible regrets, all grieving as swiftly executed as his father. Between the ages of ten to twenty, Frank continues to exhibit behaviour patterns associated with the developing sociopath, seeking out, impressing and eventually being 'employed' by local villains as hired muscle.

At fourteen, he spends nine months in borstal for aggravated assault. During his time there, he attacks three members of staff, and spends up to seven months of his sentence locked in his cell, denied free association with other offenders.

At seventeen, he is back inside. Eight months, this time, with a stern warning from the court that any further offences committed during his detention will result in his first full prison term. That night, he headbutts a visiting female probation officer so hard that he breaks her nose and both cheekbones. As promised, the court orders Rattigan to serve eighteen months in Wandsworth Prison immediately upon his release from borstal.

When interviewed by the prison psychiatrist, Rattigan can provide no real motive for his attack on the woman. When told she lost the three-month-old baby she was carrying at the time, Rattigan is documented as saying, 'I did the fucking thing a favour. Imagine having a screw for your mum.'

Prison staff suspect Rattigan is behind several assaults on fellow prisoners, but are unable to prove anything. Victims appear too scared to openly name their aggressor, and Rattigan's stature begins to escalate. During this time, he receives no visitors, the reason being, his mother will explain later, that John Templar was reluctant to be identified as a police officer visiting a 'relative' inside.

During his brief periods 'outside', Rattigan goes back to the East End, staying and working with many of the criminal gangs whose incarcerated members he has so impressed with his capacity for seemingly unlimited violence.

It is now the early sixties, and apart from occasional visits to his old school in order that he may walk his younger brother, Jimmy Rattigan home, Frank enjoys a few brief years living off the fruits of his terrifying reputation, culminating in a three-year prison sentence for grievous bodily harm sustained by a Jamaican in Notting Hill, thought by Rattigan's firm to be trying to cut in on one of their protection rackets. The victim himself was no stranger to the workings of the judicial system, but was somewhat unfortunate to find himself serving a nine-month sentence for possession in the same prison as Rattigan the following year. Although wardens were fairly sure the negro's death was most probably unsuspicious, one or two did go on record during the subsequent enquiry voicing concerns that Rattigan's cell door appeared to be open shortly before the fatal fall.

Verdict – suicide.

Rattigan does twenty-two months of his sentence, before, astonishingly, being let out on 'good behaviour', stunning one or two of the more experienced prison staff. At the gates, he is met by a large black car driven by a former 'guest' of the prison. There are three grinning girls in the back. One of them tosses a champagne glass at gaping wardens as the car speeds off.

However, in eight months Rattigan is back inside on remand, no amount of underground connections able to convince the authorities to grant bail. But, seven weeks into his stay, charges are dropped, and under normal circumstances, Rattigan would have walked straight back to the waiting car. Unfortunately, in the intervening seven weeks, Rattigan has chalked up five fresh assaults, three of them on prison officers who aren't afraid to testify. Rattigan will later claim that this was unfair, as it had been proven that he was on remand for a made-up charge – that prison life had stressed him considerably and all crimes committed by an innocent man waiting on remand should be waived by judge and jury as 'misdemeanours incurred while intolerably persecuted'.

He got six years for the attack on the three officers, one of whom will see out the rest of his life in a wheelchair.

Rattigan did all six. No parole – no good behaviour. Twelve further assaults are pegged to his record. Rattigan is moved from prison to prison, and has now been classed as Category A – violent with dangerous sociopathic tendencies. He undergoes many hours of psychiatric counselling, treating each of his academic inquisitors with derisive contempt. Efforts by a succession of parole boards and prison governors to have Rattigan moved to a secure psychiatric unit are repeatedly blocked by the Home Office, whose own team of experts constantly conclude Rattigan is simply 'bad', not 'mad'. A battery of tests and interviews has shown his reading age to be that of an eleven-year-old with an estimable IQ of seventy-five. Whatever measures of insanity Rattigan needed to qualify for an indeterminate stay in a different kind of institution are never revealed.

Over the six years, Rattigan shows no signs of any desire to 'improve himself' at any level, refusing books from various prison libraries, and unwilling to accept any chores which might have led to increased privileges within the system. In his own words, he decides to 'go solo', withdrawing, refusing friendships, doing his time. Quite possibly, this decision was enforced by Rattigan's own violent unpredictability. Even the prison's hard men seemed unwilling to associate with the former villain.

October, 1972, he walks from HMP Norwich to start life over. This time, there is no car, no girls, no champagne.

The probationary authorities fix him up with an address and a job in a meat-processing plant. He puts frozen chickens into cardboard boxes for just three days, before walking out mid-afternoon. The works foreman, who was unfortunately vigilant enough to try to persuade Rattigan back to his post, receives a black eye and two broken ribs for his trouble. However, no charges are brought, the foreman stressing to police, 'The guy's a nutter. No way do I ever want to see that bastard again. He'd kill me.'

Rattigan spends the next three years on the streets, barely recognizable, dishevelled, moving from hospice to hostel, taking what work payed cash in hand, no questions asked – fruit farms, hotel kitchens, labouring, night watchman . . . During this time, he neither applies for nor receives any benefits of any kind.

Francis James Rattigan next comes to the attention of the authorities in March, 1978, when, after a brief court appearance for ABH (a young drug addict had his head repeatedly smashed against a steel sink late one night in the kitchen of a large Liverpudlian hotel), he is sentenced to six months at Her Majesty's pleasure inside HMP Durham. During his stay there, Mary Rattigan dies. As with his father, Rattigan appears totally unmoved, and even has to be persuaded by prison staff to send a note to the crematorium. It reads: *Mum. That's that, then.*

Over the next ten years, Rattigan spends four back inside for various offences. With overcrowding an ever-increasing problem, prison authorities become anxious at the thought of long-term offenders like Rattigan sharing a cell with two other inmates. A summer of prison riots, including the Strangeways rooftop protest, prove their concerns about the tinderbox waiting to explode. Rattigan himself was on C Wing during the riot, and whilst it is difficult to imagine he took no part, police surveillance of video footage taken by news crews reveal he never appeared on the roof – and, if he is to be believed, spent his time, 'Walking about a bit. Not bothering no fucker.' When riot police were eventually ordered in to restore order to the beleaguered prison, Rattigan was found alone in his smashed-up cell, sitting quietly. Allegations made by fellow prisoners in the aftermath of the abortive riot (that Rattigan had set about them with a metal bedpost) were difficult to prove in the light of so many serious injuries sustained by prisoners from the authorities' final, bloody storming of the prison.

Next stretch? Chelmsford Prison, 1982. More interviews, more evaluations.

TRANSCRIBED SECTION OF INTERVIEW CONDUCTED BY DR RICHARD IVANS, HMP CHELMSFORD, 1983. (Rattigan is serving two years for yet another assault.)

IVANS: Can you see a pattern emerging here, Frank? All this violence, prison sentences?

RATTIGAN: S'how it is, ain't it? Not my fucking choice.

IVANS: Perhaps . . . perhaps if you turned the other cheek, so to speak . . . acted, shall we say, less impulsively . . . considered your actions, their consequences . . . ?

RATTIGAN: I don't do nobody what don't deserve it. No fucker.

IVANS: I guess that would depend on your definition of 'deserve it', wouldn't it?

RATTIGAN: Give the man a gold star.

IVANS: So what would it take, in your opinion? A look? Is a look enough to . . . set you off?

RATTIGAN: Depends.

IVANS: The circumstances?

RATTIGAN: Look, what you got to understand is this. You know nothing about me. My life. You ain't lived it. It's fucking pointless trying to tell you my shit, because you ain't got nothing to compare it to.

IVANS: All I'm trying to ascertain . . .

RATTIGAN: People piss me off, I do 'em. Do 'em fucking proper. Then they leaves me alone. You fuck me, I'll fuck you. Yeah, sure, a look can set me off. And if it does, I belt the geezer one. He'll never look at me again. One less to worry about, ain't it? Out of my life, history.

IVANS: The . . . woman? The . . . erm, parole officer you . . . had an altercation with as a youngster?

RATTIGAN: Same story. Look, the whole world's full of hypocrites like you. There's always some cunt who'll stand up and say you shouldn't batter a bird. But it's bollocks, ain't it? Look around you. Women's getting the shit kicked out of them every day. It's just in us.

IVANS: In us?

RATTIGAN: Survival. Get your punch in first. Man or woman, don't make no difference. Woman can stab you just as easily as a bloke can. Don't matter who you belt, just make sure the bastard ain't getting up again. Then you're OK, see? Don't have to worry about it no more.

IVANS: Frank . . . I want to ask you . . . Hitting the woman, any woman . . . is it somehow a more . . . pleasurable experience?

RATTIGAN: Put it this way, chances are a bitch'll go down a good deal easier than a bloke. It's like anything. You beat someone, you feel good, don't ya? Do it with one smack in the mouth, and it's less effort for the same result. (Long pause.) But I know what you're really asking.

IVANS: Oh?

RATTIGAN: I don't get no extra special pleasure out of spanking a bird. Not 'cause she's a woman, like. I'm a survivor, for fuck's sake. I ain't no pervert. There's plenty of blokes in here who'd smack a tart then give her one. Ain't me. I'll clip her if she's in me face, then that's it. End of story.

Five years later, Francis James Rattigan will spend three days systematically torturing, murdering and dismembering Helen Lewis.
  For 'fun'.

22

And with 'the facts', came an endless list of 'supposes'.

Suppose the man at the fruit farm had been Elaine Horton's younger husband – Richard Horton? Suppose he'd given Rattigan the cash – had he also given him Helen Lewis's London address? Suppose the whole ghastly business was exactly as the Beast had described it? He'd simply killed the girl for kicks – and there *was* no other motive. Suppose I hadn't the insight, the academic prowess to reach inside and empathize with killing 'for fun'?

Or just suppose, Rattigan had a very different motive entirely . . . ?

I realized when the Japanese four-by-four passed me and pulled into Elaine Horton's drive further up the road what a fool I had been.

It was now early evening, five thirty. Richard Horton had come home. I'd been expecting him in the green Jaguar. But that was ten years ago. Come on, Adrian, get your crap together! The Jag was long gone. This was Wilmslow – suburban affluence. No one would be seen dead driving a ten-year-old car.

So what now? Leave the safety of the car and take my chances knocking on the Hortons' door a second time? I hadn't glimpsed enough of the bloke to see if he was as physically threatening as he was verbally, and I really didn't fancy my chances in a fist-fight. But I had to do something, felt convinced the answers lay within those four respectable walls.

I started to twitch – nerves. I was definitely bloody edgy.

I needed a drink too, very badly, and was finding resistance more and more difficult. Not that I wasn't aware that this day would eventually arrive. I knew full well I was always going to be tested by an addiction I felt sure I'd beaten. But then again, surely one little malt wouldn't hurt, would it? Just to prove I was over the goddamned stuff. That I controlled it, not vice versa. Just the one, just to prove I had it licked . . .

The four-by-four drove past again.

Richard Horton at the wheel? I had no idea, dusk's fading light and the car's speed denying driver identification.

So decided to follow the four-by-four.

I started up the Cavalier, giving the Landcruiser seventy yards before pulling out. Seconds later I was away down the street, chasing the taillights, not getting too close, trying to discern the sex of the driver as oncoming traffic fleetingly illuminated the body-shape.

A man, definitely. Richard Horton? Could be. Maybe the same man who met Rattigan two days before Helen Lewis's murder. But where in God's name was he off to? He couldn't have been home for more than fifteen minutes.

We turned on to a main road. Two cars slipped between us, and I was grateful for their unknowing intervention. Not for the first time that day, I found myself asking what the bloody hell did I think I was doing, chasing a strange car, for God's sake? And it wasn't as if I had an armoury of proven driving techniques learnt on a oil-drenched skid-pan, either. The sensible option would've been to have returned to speak to Elaine Horton alone. But something – instinct, perhaps – wouldn't let me.

Signs – green and yellow, spelt out unfamiliar places – Handforth, Cheadle Hume, Gatley. Then a battery of blue ones. Imminent motorways – M63, M56, M52.

Traffic lights. I watched him attempt to rush them. I thought I was going to lose him. But at the last, he braked, hard. Maybe he'd spotted the speed camera on the dark shell of the red light. I sighed out loud. Thank you, God. But how much longer could I keep it up, a virgin private eye, playing at pursuit.

Lights to green – he turned right, and I followed down twisting built-up streets, choked with Victorian terraced houses, overgrown privet hedges, wheelie bins . . .

We journeyed on towards Manchester proper, just two cars between us. And the longer the journey lasted, the more I began to enjoy it, almost revel in the absurdity of the chase, past caring if he suddenly stopped, leapt from the Landcruiser, raced up and demanded an explanation.

The signs said 'City Centre'. It was just me and him now, my two safety cars having dropped out a couple of junctions back. He drove on, I still followed. I raced two amber lights to be with him, whooping like a cowboy as we beat the red.

A flyover loomed up ahead, crossing our path, shielding big illuminated office buildings behind. He took a left, then a right, and we were definitely in the heart of Manchester now, driving past illuminated squares, the ornate town hall, and numerous floodlit buildings on both sides.

He turned off. Left down a small one-way street.

Next came the decision – turn left myself, and if he suspected I was following, he'd know for certain. Or drive on past, never knowing what I might have missed.

There wasn't the time to think it over – I simply did what felt right, trusting intuition again. I turned left, a black taxi hooting behind at my sudden, unsignalled manoeuvre.

It was a darker, narrower street, tall warehouses on either side. A nightclub on the left, doors closed, too early for business . . . and up ahead . . . no sign of the four-by-four.

I drove another fifty yards, then pulled over. Two hundred yards ahead I could see bright lights where the end of the street met a lighter, brighter, shop-clustered road.

I switched off the engine.

Where had he got to? Must've turned off. Side alleyway, anything. He surely couldn't have got to the end of the street before I turned in. Impossible, not without doing at least a ton . . .

I took two deep breaths, then stepped from the warm car, into sights, sounds and smells. It all felt sickeningly real, cold. The game was over. Whoever he was, he'd won, lost me.

I began walking back to where we both came in, looking

for a place he could have turned off. Nothing. I slipped on the pavement, aware my jaw shook from the icy cold – and maybe the fear, the lunacy of what I was playing at . . .

Next, I saw it, thirty yards further up to the right. A small turning, cobbled, just large enough to take a . . . Landcruiser.

There it was, twenty feet away, parked up on the tiny pavement, silent, waiting.

I waited a second, then moved on.

A group of youths approached my abandoned Cavalier. I watched in horror as they laughingly tried the doors. Please don't brick the windows!, I wanted to shout, but found myself struck dumb, unwilling to be discovered by them, or anyone else.

More laughter from the lads. Another ten seconds passed. I struggled to control my breathing, make it deeper, more regular. I felt the panic begin to rise. Something in the way their jovial obscenities echoed off the walls had terrified me.

It was the mob again, violent, unpredictable, the same gang who'd come so close as I hid in my kitchen. But this wasn't an auditory hallucination. These youths were real, threatening, dangerous if provoked. I felt useless, already beaten, paralysed until they'd finally left the scene. And then, so bloody relieved they hadn't seen me.

I glanced quickly at the darkened four-by-four. It was still parked up, maybe twenty-five yards from me. Chancing that Horton was long gone, I pressed myself against a recess in the wall to wait for his return. A wet wooden padlocked door supported my shaking back.

I waited five minutes before something happened.

Someone emerged from the far end of the darkened alley-way and made their way slowly to the Landcruiser. I couldn't be certain, but it didn't look like Horton. Even though I'd only had a few photos to go by, this figure seemed too stooped, cautious. I put him late forties, but it was difficult to be certain. I wondered if he was going to try and rip the car off, he looked furtive enough.

I checked my watch – six forty-five. My feet were beginning to freeze with the inactivity.

The inside light was suddenly flicked on. Horton had been

inside all the time! There followed an exchange, by the driver's window. Heated. Obscene gestures came from the visitor. A dosser, I assumed, begging for scraps from the rich Toyota owner. The situation seemed to calm. A handshake. Then suddenly he turned and began walking straight towards me.

I stepped quickly from my shelter, head down towards my car, praying he wasn't about to accost me for charity, either. An engine fired up behind me. Steeling myself, I risked a glance. The shuffling figure now headed away from me, back towards the beckoning bright lights. Then the Landcruiser passed me by, turned right at the top of the street, and disappeared before I could get back to my car.

I'd lost him – for good this time. He had too much of a lead.

So, I reflected wearily, that's it – game over. Again . . .

Unless the beggar knew any different . . .

23

I raced back to the car, keeping one eye on the figure further up the street, cursing the responsibility of the great metal box. I couldn't leave the damn thing where it was, and had little choice but to park it somewhere safe before I lost sight of Horton's visitor.

He'd already reached the top of the street, ten yards in front on the left. Inevitably, the one-way system forced me to turn right. I waited as long as I dared at the intersection, before slowly turning out.

A quick glance in the rear-view mirror. He was still there, further up, now sitting on a bench in what looked like a pedestrianized section of the high street. I was getting desperate to park before I found myself taken too far away from him.

And all the while thoughts of Rattigan's meeting with another stranger in the green Jag some ten years previously swirled around my head. Had I just witnessed something similar? What was Horton's 'in' on all this? Why the obsession with clandestine meetings in strange places?

Another two hundred yards and I spied it. The big P of a car-park sign. Maybe, I hoped, if I was quick enough, he'd still be there on the bench.

Two minutes later I walked out of the piss-stained concrete multistorey, struggled for my bearings, then headed back towards the brighter lights. Please, please be there.

It was all happening too fast. After weeks of inactivity, idle speculation and endless hours waiting for phone calls which would never be returned – here I was suddenly propelled into deeper waters, in just the one day. The speed of it all set me on edge. Maybe the encounter with the youths in the street, too.

But I was glad I hadn't crumbled like I did in the kitchen. I'd simply frozen, prayed and hid.

There he was. Sitting, alone on the green metal bench, stock-still, as others passed by, huddling under umbrellas, avoiding him. I walked up, sat down. Began.

'Excuse me. I was wondering if you could help me?'

'Fuck off.' It was a slurred nonthreatening northern lilt, undercut by a croaking giggle.

'Can I ask you something?'

He stared ahead, oblivious to the rain, the town, the wet life teeming all around.

'That man you spoke to just now, in the alleyway, round the corner . . .'

More giggles. 'What you talkin' about?'

'You met a man, just now?'

He turned to me for the first time, and I looked into his wet shambolic face. Stubble, creases, bloodshot eyes. 'Got any smokes?' He made a half-hearted attempt to mime smoking a cigarette.

'Sure,' I quickly replied, hoping he wasn't too out of it. 'You want fags, a drink?' I opened my wallet. 'Look. I'll get you a whole pack of fags. You want a beer? Something stronger? Let's get out of this bloody rain and go somewhere. Warm up. Yeah? Are you hearing any of this?'

He stood, thrust both nicotine-stained hands into his soaking greatcoat. 'Fucking police! Fuck off! Tossers! Go on, fuck off!', aiming his abuse at two sheltering uniformed officers who watched us, bored, from a shop doorway.

Then to my surprise he walked back to me, put an arm over my shoulder and croaked, 'You're on, pal. How about a bevvy or two, eh? You want answers, tell me the questions. Like how many people does it take to . . . fuck it, I don't know. Let's get some ale down us necks.'

He took me to a pub called the Shakespeare. It was half full. Two heavy-looking bouncers on the door agreed to our entry when I reluctantly persuaded them with five pounds each.

'Half an hour, pal,' the smaller one said. 'Any trouble and you're both out.'

'First question,' I said to my guest, removing his arm from

166

my shoulder as we made our way to a corner table. 'What do they call you?'

'J.S.,' he replied, grinning. 'Everyone knows J.S. Famous, is J.S.'

'The man in the car back in the alley. Did you . . . ?'

'Large vodka,' he ordered. 'And Bensons.'

I went to the bar, ordered the vodka and a large tomato juice for myself, got change for the cigarette machine, bought the fags, then brought both bribes back to the table. He looked half-asleep.

I sat down, watching as he slowly acknowledged the offerings. The soft interior lighting did nothing to disguise the blasted face. I could only guess what he looked like under a striplight. Shoulder-length wet grey hair tied into a soaking ponytail streaked the back of his damp overcoat.

I unwrapped the cigarettes, lighting one up before passing it on. A group of lads occupied a table nearby, sniggering over their pints of lager. My companion paid them no heed, but sank the vodka with one swift, well-practised action.

''Nother,' he belched, giving me a face full of halitosis.

'In a moment, J.S. I promise. I just want to know . . .'

The juke box exploded from unseen speakers placed all around. A strangled voice sang, 'Today is going to be the day when they give it right back to you . . .' The lads cheered as a group of rain-sodden, giggling girls made for the bar.

'Listen,' he said quietly. 'I know what you're after. But s'not a raw deal, pal. He don't do owt for any fucker. I gets . . .' He paused, eyes twinkling. 'Special considerations. But just me. Only me. Get it?'

'Not really, J.S. I want to know about the man in the car . . .'

'Fucking telling you, aren't I? It's not a raw deal. He just does for me. 'Cause I need quality. See what I'm saying? You wanna try one of the clubs down by the docks. Get you a half of skag for a twenty, most probably.'

I nodded, but wondered what use any of it was. It was like talking to an alien. 'But do you know who he is? The man in the car? Did you know he was going to be there? Just now?'

The grimy bloodshot eyes closed fractionally. He sniffed twice. 'I smell pig, pal.'

'Look, please, J.S. Please try and think . . .'

'Fucking law, ain't ya?'

'No. No. Please, listen . . .'

'I got to strain me spuds.' He stood, swayed slightly, looked back at the doormen. ''Nother voddy. Large one.'

He wandered towards the beige door to the side of the bar before I could stop him. I bought another round, returned to the table and waited . . .

Twenty minutes later, the pub was beginning to heave, but no sign of J.S. returning from the Gents. Twice I'd fought the urge to follow him into the toilets, both times persuading myself to wait another five minutes. After all, he'd seemed pretty certain he'd return for his drink.

His drink . . . there in front of me. My fingers drummed the table, legs shook beneath it as I tried my damnedest to ignore its lure.

One of the lads from the nearby table tried to attract my attention, the last thing I needed. They'd all had at least three pints of strong lagers with chasers to follow. Now's the time, I fearfully supposed, that they start picking on outsiders. I blended into the pub's young clientele as gracefully as Stevie Wonder at a Combat 18 rally.

He sat next to me. I glanced round, trying to appear as unthreatening as possible. Young thug, short-cropped hair, grey eyes, hard face. His mates bob heads behind, watching the action.

'This seat taken, mister?' Thick, Mancunian delivery. 'Only there's some blart at the bar wants to rest their brains, you with me?'

'I'm waiting for someone.'

'Jimmy Smack?'

'I'm sorry, I . . .'

'J.S.? The smackhead you come in with a while back?'

'Yeah. That's right. He's just . . .'

'Fucked off, pal. Ages ago. Shot up in the bogs and hoofed it out the back. He's taken you, pal. Police, are you?'

'No, I'm . . . he's gone, you say?'

The shaved head nodded, then twitched back towards the watching table. 'Our Darren went for a dump ten minutes back. Heard Jimmy doin' the business. Like I said – smackhead. Everybody knows him. Always on the fucking blag.'

One mystery solved. For J.S., now read Jimmy Smack – local heroin addict. And for Adrian Rawlings – read Naive Twat.

'So I was wonderin' like,' the young lad continued. 'Any chance of you buggerin' off so the girls can park their bums. Don't mean to be rude like, but he ain't comin' back. No fuckin' chance.'

I smiled, relieved I wasn't about to be bottled, but annoyed I'd been so easily duped. 'Yeah, sure,' I said. 'But do us a favour, will you?'

'Sound.'

'Where's my best chance of catching up with him?'

'Jimmy?' He whistled, contemplating the dilemma. 'Could be anyplace. He just sort of gets about. Probably trippin' out of his friggin' head somewhere. Won't have gone far, though. When that gear kicks in, you just got to get your head down, go with it. Not that I ever . . . you know. Bit of fucking whizz, maybe. That's me lot.'

'Yeah, sure,' I replied resignedly, finishing the tomato juice but somehow managing to leave the vodka. 'Thanks.'

He leant forward, lowered his voice. I struggled to hear over the cacophony of noise. 'Listen, if you're looking to score, Jimmy ain't the one. He's too messed up to deal. I know this bloke who –'

'No, you're all right. Honestly.' I stood, noticing the girl group already moving towards the table, feeling suddenly so terribly old.

The youth also stood, before making the all-too-obvious observation. 'Not from round here, are you? Like I say, Jimmy's part of the fuckin' furniture. All of us know the bastard. Plays a little violin thing in the Arndale sometimes. Fucking good, he is, too, when he's straight. No hard feelings, eh?'

'No.'

I'd taken two steps into the crowd, when his arm caught my shoulder. I turned, wincing, waiting for the blow . . . nothing.

'Easy, pal. They did an article on 'im, you know?'

'Jimmy?'

He nodded, winking at one of the girls as they moved past to the vacated table. '*Mancky News*. A while back. Did a series of 'em on all the local barm cakes. Looking into their past an' that. Thing about Jimmy's I remember was that they hung his fuckin' dad. Apparently it were before he was born. Poor sod. I mean, that'd do anyone's head in, wouldn't it?'

Jimmy. Jimmy Rattigan! Frank's younger brother. Jesus – how could I have been so . . . ?

The youth struggled to remember. 'Strung him up for beltin' a copper, or something. Day after the article comes out, he gets free drinks off all of us, poor bastard. Nice enough bloke – but hanging your old man – that's tragic, ain't it?'

'No,' I said, voice trembling, gripping his arm a little too tightly. 'That's amazing . . . incredible. Wonderful! Really, really wonderful! Thank you. Thank you so much!'

He stared in disbelief for a second, before flinching from my grasp. 'You what? Wonderful? Go on, fuck off!' he spat, nostrils flaring. 'You're another one, aren't you? Mad as he is!'

'Do you know?' I replied, feeling a bizarre rush of elation. 'You could be right about that.'

And I was out of there in seconds.

24

Stepping back on to the street, the surge of elation was quickly replaced by a teeming rush of disappointment. The rain fell heavily down from the dirty night sky. I had had them both – Horton and Jimmy Rattigan – then ineptly lost them.

It was time to think, consider, plan. First off, I hailed a black cab, and it took me to the offices of the *Manchester Evening News*. A uniformed night porter steadfastly refused my request to trace the article on Rattigan's brother. I was advised to come back in the morning, unless I had a story to give the night-shift editor now. I said I might well have, but needed to check something out first. I slipped him a tenner. He made two calls as I stood waiting in the large impersonal reception area.

He replaced the phone, said nothing. Went back to his own paper – the *Daily Sport*. So what was going on? My question was answered by the arrival of another man, name of Kevin something. He told me the paper did run a series of articles detailing the lives of some of the city's more 'colourful' characters earlier in the year. He asked me what bearing this had. I replied that I'd very much like to see the edition featuring Jimmy Smack. He shook his head – the archives were closed until morning.

'Fine,' I said. 'Could you tell me the name of the journalist who wrote it?'

He left again, returning some minutes later.

'Karen Allison.'

'Not working tonight, is she?'

'Nah. Sorry, pal. Freelance. Does the odd human-interest piece for us. Works all over the north west. Us, *Liverpool Echo* . . .'

'I need to speak to her. I might have something for her . . . related to the article.'

'Hang on.'

Another wait. Longer this time.

Three minutes and he returned, yellow Post-it note gummed to his thumb. 'Try her on this number. S'all I can do, Mr . . . ?'

'Rawlings. Adrian Rawlings.'

'Listen, Adrian, if there's anything you want to talk to me about . . . ?'

'No. Thank you. But thanks very much for your time.'

'No worries.'

Back outside, I turned right, remembering the cab took me this way, feeling I was somehow being drawn back to the city centre. I found a phone box, dialled the number, waited, then listened . . .

'Hello. You've reached Karen Allison's phone. I'm sorry I'm not available to take your call, but if you'd like to . . .'

I tried the pager, mobile – nothing. Then called the answerphone again, asked to meet her – mentioned Jimmy Smack, left my name – then realized I had no contact number – bollocks! I felt suddenly very stupid talking inadequately to a machine in a draughty phone box in a city which couldn't care. The rain began to subside. I needed to find somewhere to stay – a guesthouse, hotel, whatever, just so I could rering Karen Allison's number then leave mine.

I decided to definitely visit the *Evening News* archives in the morning – swot up on Ms Allison's impression of 'our Jimmy'. Then hopefully meet the woman herself.

Which brought me back to finding a bed for the night. Where to start? I couldn't believe how hopelessly ill-prepared I was. And cold, so very cold.

Money. I needed to find a cash machine and replenish reserves, access a couple of hundred of Jemimah's corporate wages. Jemimah! Of course. It was only right I let her know what I had planned. Sighing heavily, forehead on the wet, tobacco-stained Plexiglas, I punched out our number.

'J?'

'Hello, stranger. I wondered when you'd call. How's it going?'

'You wouldn't believe it if I told you.'

'Where are you?'

'Still here. Trying to find somewhere to stay the night.'

'How long is all this going to take, Adrian?'

'I don't know. I'm finding out stuff all the time, but as fast as I do, it all seems to be slipping through my fingers.'

'Just remember you aren't Columbo.'

'Wish I was, J. He always wrapped it up in ninety minutes.'

'So are you coming back tomorrow?'

'Jesus, I hope so. Kids all right?'

'Fine. Guy's been abducted by aliens and Juliet's joined the local Hell's Angels chapter.'

'Kiss them both good night for me.'

'Adrian?'

'J?'

'Not drinking, are you?'

'What makes you say that?'

'You sound funny.'

'Just bloody cold and tired.'

'Hey, it's grim up north.'

'Grimmer than grim. I can't wait to . . .' Which is when I began to hear it again. Softly at first, drifting, a distant chorus of disapproval voiced by a vast unseen army.

'Adrian? You still there?'

'Yeah, sure. It's just . . .'

'What?'

Silence again. Gingerly, I opened the creaking phone box door, letting in the rush of passing cars on the wet road. Nothing. Nothing outside. Which meant it had to be inside – in me, again. For God's sake, not now!

'Adrian, talk to me.'

And they came again. A faraway chant, full of menace, youth, danger. 'Can you hear that, J?' I shouted above the traffic. I held the receiver into the night sky for a few moments, panic in my voice. 'Did you hear it?'

'Hear what?'

I gripped the phone too hard, felt my legs begin to shake. 'The crowd. The football fans.'

'Look, Adrian, are you OK?'

'Did you hear them?' I shouted. I had to know that they were real.

'I don't know. I . . .'

My heart-rate soared. Despite the bitter cold, I felt the first traces of sweat run down my back. I was light-headed, giddy in my fear. 'I've got to go, J. Before they find me.'

'Adrian!'

But I was out of the phone booth, running, feet slapping the wet pavements, freezing air tearing at my throat. A hundred yards and I had to stop, sit, unable to take another step.

Again the crowd came taunting. A vast 'Aah' hit me with the force of a verbal tidal wave. And there was more, other sounds, closer voices, swearing, laughing. But these were from within. I was alone, sitting in a doorway, yet surrounded on all sides . . .

. . . Now it was light, warm, a summer's afternoon. Panic on all sides. Dad was with me, breaking into a run by my side. They were after us. God knows why, but there wasn't time to stop and consider anything, except saving ourselves. And so we ran, further into nowhere, pursued by the baying mob . . .

. . . I stood. Shook my head. Fought with reality. It was a Wednesday. Obviously City or United had a midweek game on. Twenty thousand fans were most likely packed into Maine Road or Old Trafford, roaring their boys on. Nothing more.

Yet still it terrified me so.

I wrung my hands, knowing I had to move on, find money and shelter, if only temporarily. Get my head together. Rid myself of whatever irrational fear had risen up to strike me down.

I found a cash machine. A pub. Went straight to the bar and ordered . . . a double malt.

Then drank it, before ordering another.

And another.

My thoughts refused to be ordered. Dad – I'd clearly seen him, felt his fear as he pushed me along the familiar street. We were hunted, he and I, for no reason other than simply being there – at the game all those years ago.

But the memory was too painful to confront in full. I felt spun around, suddenly victim to an event I'd crushed in order that I wouldn't have to face it in its full violent glory. But it was so close, so keen to reveal itself, my part in whatever had happened, that I knew resistance was useless. It was stronger than me, stronger than the boy who . . .

I tried switching thoughts, dragging my mind back to Rattigan, changing channels. All the time thinking, 'That's it, then. End of story. Rattigan business solved. Man's a junkie – just like his brother – seeking refuge in street-shit to obscure the scars of a dysfunctional family.' But nowhere on Rattigan's file did it mention heroin addiction. OK, so his forearms didn't look like a pin cushion, maybe the murdering creep smoked his shit over tinfoil – chasing the dragon, or whatever the street-hip junkies called it.

And Horton most likely supplied the gear. Drove round in a succession of top-of-the-range motors, dealing. Special rates for family. Perhaps that was the deal – the meeting at the fruit farm. Richard Horton drove the best part of one hundred and fifty miles so Frank could score before heading off for the bright lights looking for a squat, shooting up, and starting to lose it – big time. Then broke into Helen Lewis's house higher than he's ever been and began his games . . .

No reasons – no motives – just fun. As he'd always maintained. Heroin-related fun. No evil, no birth-defected brain, no hidden agenda – just the hallucinatory lunacy of heroin.

Drunk, I wondered if that was all psychopathy was, a medical conspiracy to prevent us from breaking out, giving into baser drives, wallowing in the emotional depths of simply being, eating, fucking, taking . . .

Rattigan was angry from the moment he was born. Dropped into a world at war, brought up by parents who simply couldn't care, he ran wild. In his own twisted way he 'lived'. I saw that now, clearer than anything. The world owed him damn-all, and he used the whole goddamned place as his playground.

Perhaps he had needed to whack himself full of junk that night ten years ago, giving himself a heroin parachute before he made his 'leap'. But maybe for him, the way to live – was simply to kill.

I bought crisps and nuts as I staggered back to the bar, realizing I was drinking on an empty stomach. I considered phoning my alcohol counsellor for advice, but I was past the moment, and past caring. The malt had settled me, allowed me to refocus, move away from my own demons and concentrate on Rattigan's.

I felt sick, ridiculous, ashamed. But at least I wasn't terrified. Not for the moment, anyway.

It was way past midnight when I stumbled on the club, somewhere on the city's east side. I was drunk, depressed, confused, alone.

But I can't use that as an excuse for what happened.

25

Sound, sweat and smoke assaulted me.

'Welcome to Babyluuuun . . .'

I stumbled down the damp peeling stairway, malt-shot eyes adapting to the waiting gloom, booming bass and drums punching my diaphragm, unable to turn back – feeling almost as if I'd been journeying to this place for some time. That this hell was somehow my destiny, the last refuge from the baying crowd in my mind.

I remember paying the reefer-smoking Jamaican far too much for entry, but I was past caring, lured to the basement underworld, the forbidden safety beyond. In the darkened room shapes shifted slowly to the pounding beat . . . fifteen, maybe twenty night people at most – dispirited souls catatonically choreographed in a haze of exhaled dope.

Again the slow drawling voice reverberated over what passed for music – 'Welcome to Babyluuuun . . .'

I could just about make out the bar, far right, lit by a single flickering bulb, manned by one of the fattest men I've ever seen. Sweating drips of his disgusting excess fell slowly from matted black hair on to the worn wooden surface. I waved a note in the air, and he poured me a double from a bottle somewhere under the counter. No half measures . . .

I leant against the counter, wallowing in the whisky's warmth, turning to the others, watching the iridescent glow of white eyes, teeth, trainers and T-shirts turning purple under the weak ultraviolet which pooled the minuscule dance floor.

Everywhere, the smell of weed, joints glowing a brief fiery red when inhaled by invisible owners, wrapped in the forgiving darkness.

I wondered how long I should stay, what kept me there, why I wasn't consumed with the chest-tightening panic which had gripped me earlier in the evening. But there was no crowd to fear, just a curious form of benign acceptance – mine.

'Welcome to Babyluuuun . . .'

The DJ's lips never left the mike. Eyes never opened, head moved to and fro, lost in its own internal rhythm as he disgorged his monotonous mantra.

Figures to my left. Then a voice in my ear. Cool, Carribean, chilled. 'Ya lookin'?'

I turned slowly. Another big black man. A smaller one behind, nervous eyes. With two girls, one white, one black. 'Watching,' I replied, beginning to see double.

Garlic on my face, as his hot breath caressed my cheek. 'Wan' ta take a rocket ride wid mudder nature's finest?'

I stared into his expectant eyes, creamy-brown, tinged with another life. A dealer. I wondered if . . . why not, it was worth a try. 'You know a bloke called Jimmy Smack?'

He shrugged, smiled, hadn't heard. I repeated the question, louder, my slur competing with the drowsy beat.

This time he nodded slowly, calculating something. 'What can the Doctor sort ya for, my frien'? Ya wan's rocks? I am the quarry master. Smack is no problem, if that's your thing. Blow? You wan' the best blow in town?'

I look at the black girl, stoned, half-asleep, bright-red lipstick shimmering invitingly in the gloom. I recalled Rattigan's words – 'You want to know me? You got to be me.' Who was this man? A pimp, offering one of his girls to give me a blow-job?

I shook my head. Then mumbled, 'Married man.'

The smaller, twitching friend laughed, whispered something to the Doctor, then pointed to the two girls. The blonde chewed gum, very unprovocatively.

It took a moment, but then the pimp sussed the misunderstanding, put a heavy hand on my shoulder, leant in again. 'Blow, my frien',' he repeated. 'Ganja. Best bush you c'n buy.'

'No, honest.'

He thought for a second, clearly not about to give up so

easily. Besides, he'd already seen my bulging wallet. 'My frien' wan' a little pussy, then, eh? Wan' one of the sisters to clean your cock wid her moud, eh?'

'Too pissed,' I croaked, trying to maintain whatever cool I assumed they thought I had. I was drunk, but not drunk enough to feel threatened. I made no attempt to leave, still convinced I was safer down below, that the music would drown the crowd in my head.

Dad. I'd clearly seen Dad. It was about him and me, something we'd run from, something which had . . .

'Thirty pound'll take you to paradise, my frien'.'

'Yeah, and the bloody clap clinic.'

He feigned theatrical shock. 'These are good clean girls. Fresh meat. Look at the sister, here. See how she look at you? She like you. Thirty pound and she yours.'

He had a brief conversation with the black girl. She nodded twice, looked fleetingly at me, then kissed the Doctor lazily, dead-eyed. Moved closer. Brown leather-looking jacket, short red mini, trainers. Long hair, straightened, maybe, or a wig. And full lips, full ruby-red shimmering lips . . . blood-red . . .

'Jus' enjoy!' he smiled, taking the doped girl's arm and threading it through mine. 'She know where to go.' He winked. 'All the ways, anyways.'

I fought a sudden wave of nausea, eyes searching the room, rooted to figures and faces. I watched in a trance as the pimp rooted through my wallet, swiftly passing the money to his accomplice. Somehow I took the wallet back. He smiled. The girl took my arm, led me stumbling towards a door at the back, past disconnected bodies shuffling slowly in the gloom.

'Welcome to Babyluuuun . . .'

Then up another flight of creaking steps, out into the sudden chill of the night. Still no words between us. Just a crunching, cindered courtyard and the terrifying noise of the city echoing round in sirens, screams and occasional laughter.

Yet I felt better to be in the night air, away from the sweet smoke and prying faces. I just about made out three cars parked at angles, wooden gates, and two other crumbling brick walls. The dim light of the club spilt out on to a slice of frosted ground beneath our feet.

The whore looked at me, no emotion, just a third-rate porn star's disinterested delivery. 'What's your name?'

'I don't know,' I said. 'What am I doing here?'

'Having fun.'

'Oh.'

'So what's I call you?'

'Look, I'm too drunk to . . .'

'You c'n be anyone you want to. I don' care.'

'Anyone?' A dread thought was formulating.

'Anyone.'

'How about Frank?' It was out before I knew it.

'Sure. Hi, Frank. I'm . . .' She waited, wanted me to christen her.

'Helen,' I supplied. 'Jesus, it's cold.'

'You wan' Helen to suck you off, baby? Helen soon warm you up.'

I pushed her away gently. 'You like soul music, Helen?'

'I like all music, baby. Relax. Let Helen take care of Frank fo' a while.'

She led me behind a stationary car, black and shapeless in the gloom, then pushed me firmly on to the bonnet, dropped to her knees, kissed my crotch and made a pathetic cooing sound that wouldn't convince a thirteen-year-old virgin of its authenticity.

And it was so icy-cold out there.

Another look behind me, door still fractionally ajar. I was convinced we weren't alone but was past caring. Besides, a dark inner demon told me, I wasn't there anyway – Frank was. And he wouldn't have given a stuff if a Boy Scout troop wandered by. Frank just took what he wanted. No fear. Just doing it. Sex as a trade – isn't that what he'd said?

Now she had my limp prick in her mouth, rolling it between glossy lips, looking up at me, lids half closed, too stoned to realize I was far from hard. But it was warm, wet, and I was simply too out of it myself to resist the professional tongue which had begun to speed the stiffening process.

Which is when I was suddenly consumed by a bigger desire. More pressing, gut-urgent. What in God's name was I doing? Who was being humiliated the most? Me, cock out in some dingy courtyard, or her, down on her knees, at home, ten minutes' work for my wife's hard-earned money?

A rage was growing from somewhere deep inside. She wouldn't stop. I didn't want her any more – none of them – not her, not Helen, not Frank. I just wanted me. Wanted to get the hell out of there, before I gave too much of myself to all of them. I was falling, and I had to stop it, had to get myself back on track.

I began to struggle. She read my writhing as waves of pleasure, used a free hand to work my balls, pushed her weighty head further into my lap. Looked up at me, and her eyes laughed.

'For God's sake . . .' I managed.

I did what I had to. Grabbed at her head, pulled it sideways, knocking her off balance, allowing me the space to jump from the bonnet.

She began to yell obscenities at the top of her voice. Then fell silent.

Instant fear overwhelmed me. 'Just shut up, please!' I screamed. Then, 'Are you OK? Please, answer me! Get up, come on, for Christ's sake!'

A battering on the wooden gate made me start. Then the sound I feared the most – a cluster of drunken voices.

'United! United! United!'

I felt as if my head was going to explode. The whore was coming to, anger writ large on her bloodied head. And still the fans outside . . .

'United! United! United!'

Or inside. I had no idea. The world was turning white again. I was returning . . .

. . . They'd surrounded Dad now, half a dozen or so with football shirts and scarves round their wrists, pushing him down. Then a punch, sickeningly real – knuckle on cheekbone. And Dad disappearing under a flurry of other blows, as I watched in horror, safe in a shop doorway – doing nothing . . .

'United! United! United!'

The memory left. It was night again. The whore was beginning to stand as the fans moved away from the gate, laughing, chanting as they disappeared back into the night. I had to get away, stop her, had to silence her.

What was that? Another noise, someone else moving close by? It was surely just a matter of seconds before I'd be beaten down, knifed or worse.

So I kicked her. Once. In the head. Just like they'd kicked my father, all those years ago. As I'd cowered, the son unable to assist, leaving a time bomb of guilt ticking away deep down inside. Which had now exploded.

And thank every God in heaven – silence descended again, save for the night sounds, my own rushing breath and the distant hypnotic beat of the club.

I froze, hardly daring to turn and face whoever had come to her calls. But no one rushed me. No one arrived to grind my face into the frozen cinders.

I fell to my knees beside the prone whore and threw up. It was the last I remembered of the night.

26

When I woke, I screamed.

Where the hell was I? Nothing seemed familiar. Everything was orange. I shut both eyes, feeling the numb pain of the mother of all hangovers. Then opened them again.

A ceiling. An orange ceiling. I was in bed – somewhere, somehow. I took a series of deep breaths, the sticky sweet tang of stale malt on my furred tongue. Then looked around. A bedroom, definitely. Jesus, how in God's name had I wound up here?

A noise from outside. The dull roar of some unseen machine. A door being unlocked. Footsteps coming and receding. I tried sitting up. Too painful – my whole body cried out to roll up and die right where I was.

I had a handle on the noise now. A hoover. Someone was cleaning. Next I discovered I was still fully dressed from the night before, except for my brogues which sat neatly by the side of the bed.

Somehow, I'd wound up in a hotel room. But I was too ill to care about the whys and wherefores. I groggily checked my watch. Just after eight. Must be morning. Painfully checked the tiny date dial. Definitely the morning after the night before.

The night before . . .

Brief obscene images flashed into my bruised mind.

I lay in bed for another half an hour before slowly, agonizingly rising and slipping on my shoes. Then checked my wallet. Still there. I went to the *en suite* bathroom, retched into the white porcelain, had a bright-yellow piss, then collapsed in a cold sweat back on to the bed. Death would've been such sweet relief.

But there was no comfort to be had from lying down. As my nostrils filled with sweat-excreted whisky, my thumping head played reluctant host to a feeling I half remembered and dreaded in equal measure. The last time I'd been its victim was after hitting Jemimah, when I'd experienced a mental blackout over the actual assault. I felt convinced something equally bad had happened the previous night, yet the more I struggled to conjure the facts, the more the memory seemed to rally against further investigation, just allowing tiny glimpses of a nightmare I hoped was the drink's invention, rather than reality.

In one I was running, feet pounding the frosted pavement, lungs searing from the effort. In another a woman dropped to her knees. And from somewhere close by came the screams of my father. All of it fragmented, cryptic, hideously frustrating.

I could only assume I'd stumbled upon the hotel after another of my fooball 'turns'. That the whisky had battered down the memory's defences, let loose the childhood demons, and that I'd run. Scared. Found this place and managed to secure a room, before collapsing in a drunken heap. Surely nothing else had happened?

Had it?

The answer came in a half-remembered kick. Nightmare or reality? I hardly dared consider it. But the image stayed, refusing to be filed away by a memory weary of protecting its host. It was the same girl who'd dropped to her knees, smiling. Only now she was trying to get up.

My God, what had I done?

None of it made sense. I sat up, tried to massage my neck, rub some life back into my face, telling myself over and over to start the day, leave the night behind. I had to get on, didn't have the space for anything else.

Gradually the shock on the girl's face began to fade from my mind, but my father's cries remained for many minutes.

At nine, I managed to phone Jemimah at the London office. The conversation was short, which suited me fine. I'd barely been able to dial the number for shaking fingers.

'J?'

'How are you?'

'Dicky, truth be told. Think I may have gone down with something.'

'Better not be a hangover, Adrian.'

'Feels more like flu.'

'Right.'

'You having a bad day, J? I can ring back later.'

'A bad night.'

I chanced my arm. 'Missed me?'

'We had a visitor.'

'What?'

'Listen, Adrian, I really don't want any more of your life crashing in on this family. It just isn't fair. He damn nearly scared Guy to death . . .'

'Whoa. Take a breath. Who scared him?'

'One of your lunatic bloody friends. Waiting at the back door at half past ten last night. Guy had just gone to call the cats in, when he sees this weirdo standing there.'

'Who?'

'Someone called Nick. Said you'd know him.'

'Oh, Christ!'

'You do know him, don't you?'

'Vaguely. Look, J . . .'

'It really shook us up, Adrian.'

'Sorry. Really.'

'I mean, it's all well and good for you to go gallivanting off up north, but please spare a thought for your family.'

'What did he want?'

'Have you heard a bloody word I just said?'

'Look, I'm sorry. What could I do about it?'

'Don't get stroppy on me, Adrian. I'm the one trying to sleep at night knowing there could be any number of crackpots hiding in the damn bushes.'

'He's not a crackpot, J. He's . . . well, I think he used to be a policeman.'

'You "think"?'

'I don't know him that well.'

'Well, he seems to know a lot about you. Your address for

starters. Guy couldn't sleep, it upset him so much. He spent the night in bed with me in the end.'

'Did you call the police?'

'And say what, exactly? He was gone in seconds.'

'They could've looked for fingerprints, checked the rest of the garden.'

'I couldn't.'

'Why not?'

'He was gone before I knew it. Said what he wanted to say and left.'

'Which was?'

'That he needed to talk to you. I told him you were in Manchester. He said that when you phoned, to tell you to meet him at Piccadilly Station, around one, today.'

'Today?'

'For Christ's sake, Adrian! That's all I know. It really upset us and you seem a damn sight more concerned about him than your own family.'

'I'm sorry. Really.'

'Can we expect you back later today?'

'God, I hope so, J. I've got to try and trace a journalist who might be able to shed a little light on things. After, I'll most probably head home.'

'Right.'

'Love you.'

But the line went dead before she could reciprocate.

So, Nick Moira had called in the night, seemed keen to meet with me. Why? It just got more and more entangled.

Somehow I found the energy to stand and leave the room, wandering along the short corridor until I found a creaking staircase leading down to what I presumed was the lobby and reception. Pushing the heavy fire door seemed to drain what little strength I had left, and I only just made it to the wide wooden desk.

'Listen,' I said slowly to the middle-aged female receptionist. 'I don't suppose you can tell me where the heck I am?'

She pointed to her badge – Anne Docherty, Park Hotel, Fallowfield.

'Thanks,' I said.

'Room number?' she asked, turning to a battered-looking computer monitor.

I gave her a blank look, then remembered the door key in my hand.

She punched in – sixteen. 'That's fine. You paid in full last night. Cash.'

'Do you know,' I was squinting in the glare of a fine winter's morning. 'What time I arrived?'

'Search me, love. Don't work nights. Porters have all gone home.' She looked me over. 'Good night, was it?'

'Not really.'

'Shame.'

'Did I sign for anything?'

She thrust a room reservation form under my nose. 'Can't remember a bloody thing, can you?'

My eyes struggled to focus, finally picking out a signature at the bottom of the crowded page. Which looked a little like mine. 'I'd just love to know how I got here, that's all.'

'There's plenty like you, love. Stag night, was it?'

'No . . . look, it doesn't matter. Thanks, anyway.'

'Ta-ra.'

I wandered out into a crowded street, walked around for a minute or two, then spied a black hackney cab, flagged it down. 'I'm looking for my car,' I told the driver. 'I left it in the city centre last night. A multistorey whatnot. Near the Shakespeare pub?'

We set off.

Twenty minutes later, I'd retrieved my briefcase and papers from the Cavalier, then took the same cab over to the offices of the *Manchester Evening News*. Even through the beating hangover, I was pretty sure I was still over the limit to drive there myself.

During the short journey, I had time to reflect on the previous night – what an absolute arsehole I'd been falling off the damn wagon after all this time. What had happened? What order of events had so easily conspired to have me knocking back the double malts like a seasoned drunk? Rattigan? The crowds in my head? The things I'd 'seen'? But the more I thought about it, the less I wanted to know. I'd felt crap about lying to Jemimah on the phone, but now resolved to try and accept whatever had happened as a ridiculous one-off. It was the only way to cope. I knew the folly of my ways, and wouldn't repeat the exercise.

A short time later, I was standing on weary, shaking legs in the *Evening News* offices. More details, given this time to the receptionist, then another long wait. Finally a copy of the article on Jimmy Rattigan arrived. A photocopy which cost me another six quid.

I sat and read. It told me little more than I already knew. Jimmy was a well-known character about town, sometimes did a bit of busking outside the Arndale on a fiddle. Indeed, the more I read, the more I found it difficult to pinpoint any real 'human interest' in the piece. There were one or two garbled quotes from the broken man himself – brief references to life in the East End after the war – then Karen Allison delivered what she obviously believed to be the *coup de grâce* – poor old Jimmy's dad was strung up for killing a copper before the wee mite was even born. She summed up with a predictably clichéd paragraph blaming the horrors of poverty in family life, the damning spiral of drug addiction, and there for the grace of God go us all, blah, blah, blah . . .

My stinging eyes scanned the print, but my mind was elsewhere, back with the girl, the black whore, and that kick. Surely it wasn't that hard? Yet I'd done it, assaulted her, as surely as I'd once set about my own wife. I prayed desperately that she wasn't out cold for long. Someone would have come to look for her, wouldn't they? Perhaps they didn't – too stoned to notice she was missing. Perhaps she never came round, couldn't, neck already broken by . . .

And how had I got away from that terrible cindered court-yard? Stolen a car, scaled the crumbling brick wall, walked calmly back through the club and out on to the street?

But what if I'd killed the girl? What if that very moment there were a dozen murder squad detectives crowded into the courtyard, milling round a frozen corpse?

I suddenly began to sweat. Here was I, sat calmly in a newspaper office, for Christ's sake! Perhaps at any minute there'd be a frantic rush of reporters out of reception to get the exclusive on the killing . . .

I tried to calm myself. Reread the article, pushed the doubts from my mind, convinced myself the girl was OK, most probably woke with just a bruise and a bad head. With that I felt a little better. Temporarily.

I left the building to find the nearest phone booth.

This time when I rang Karen Allison I managed to speak to her. She sounded bleary, blamed a heavy night out.

We agreed to meet at eleven, in a small Greek coffee shop near Cross Street. I was grateful for the time and space, visiting the cash machine once more, then stopping off for a fry-up and three bottles of Lucozade at a greasy café on Oxford Road. I was beginning to find my bearings a little now, familiarizing myself with the elegant layout of this steam-cleaned, sand-blasted city.

Eggs, bacon, sausage, black pudding, chips and beans, plus a steaming mug of tea, went some way to straightening me out, though I was beginning to wish I'd at least used the shower back at the hotel. My clothes stank of the night before, and I guess I did, too. Eating the greasy food took me almost half an hour, nauseous mouthful by mouthful. After, I asked the waitress about Piccadilly Station, whereupon she gave me both a sympathetic smile and comprehensive directions.

I was ten minutes early meeting Miss Allison, seating myself in the small warm café, and watching the energetic staff serve cold customers steaming hot mugs of coffee. Some came in two's or three's, idly chatting and gossiping; others wandered in with just the morning papers, immersing themselves in global news while the world passed indifferently by outside.

And it was only as I waited that the reality of my situation fell so sickeningly into place. There I was, about to delve even deeper into the past history of a man whose predilection for motiveless violence obsessed me, when just a few hours previously . . .

Because I had a slightly sharper focus on events now. Images, long-crushed memories were falling hideously neatly into place. Things which had long eluded me were staring me full in my hungover face. And no matter how much I wanted to banish them back to the protective safety of the subconscious, events had set them free, forced me to look at them, understand them in the light of a thirty-nine-year-old adult, rather than a nine-year-old boy.

What I could no longer deny, was the guilt I'd felt as I cowered and watched my father's senseless beating. Dad – my idol, my rock – had been torn down and smashed as I did nothing. And the strangest memory I now had of that time was in the first few days after, lying in bed at night, wishing, really wishing, I'd taken the same punishment, that somehow we'd gone down together, father and son, fighting to the end. I spent many nights hating my unblemished, inadequate body – to me the inescapable proof of cowardice. So I set out to re-create myself, eat myself into a new Adrian Rawlings, burying the guilt under thousands of unnecessary calories. Pathetic – but true.

In retrospect, perhaps all I needed was to be told that I'd done the right thing, that nothing I could have done would have made the slightest difference, any acts of misguided heroism might have been extremely dangerous. But no one thought to tell me. So the guilt festered, with the result that all these years later, I could only now begin to understand what drove me to rationalize random violence.

Maybe someone like Rattigan was the first to punch my dad. Perhaps I needed *him* to tell me a nine-year-old child couldn't have possibly stopped him. Perhaps I needed *him* to tell me that I couldn't have prevented myself from kicking the girl, and that anger, guilt and hatred can't be walled up indefinitely. In a cruel twist of irony, the Beast of East 16 had become my only salvation. But without a fuller understanding of what drove him to kill Helen Lewis so casually, I was no closer to self-acceptance or redemption. He still held all the keys.

Karen Allison arrived, made two phone calls on her wretched mobile before saying a word to me. I ordered a mineral water, whereupon she nodded, so I ordered another.

At which point she put the phone away. 'Adrian, right?'

My turn to nod. She was pretty, but in that hurried I-look-much-better-when-I-go-out-in-the-evening way. Long black hair had been brushed into a tight ponytail, some lipstick, minimal foundation.

The phone rang again. She frowned in apology and took the call. 'Sorry,' she said after. 'Dreadful things, aren't they?'

'Guess you need one, your line of work.'

'Can't be without it. I'll turn it off. Put the pager on.' She cut straight to the chase. 'You wanted to know about Jimmy?'

I gave her a potted history – the thesis, my interest, big brother Frank.

'Jesus,' she said. 'He never mentioned a brother.' She took out an old A5 notebook, pen poised. 'He talked about his father, obviously. But no brother. I remember, it was odd.'

'Odd?'

'The interview. He insisted we do it at his sister's place. She lives in a large house in . . .'

'Wilmslow. I was there. Yesterday.'

She gave me an odd look, trying to work me out. 'And she never mentioned a brother, either.'

'He's alive and well, I'm afraid. Frank Rattigan. But you may remember him as the Beast of East 16.'

She thought for a moment or two. 'I'm not sure.'

'About ten years back,' I added. 'He spent the best part of three days torturing an air stewardess to death.'

She snapped her fingers. 'Yeah. I'm with you. And this is Jimmy Smack's brother?'

'The very same.'

The dark eyes widened. 'Jesus, this has the makings of a real exclusive. And you say you've met this man?'

But I didn't want her this close, needed to deflect the conversation back to my own agenda. We both had information to trade. In less than a minute she'd changed from mildly interested to wholly absorbed. I had her hooked, but needed to let her dangle for as long as possible. All day, if I could. 'So it was Jimmy's idea to be interviewed at his sister's place?'

'I think it was more hers, really. He's a bit of a part-timer, our Jimmy. He sometimes pops back there during the winter if it gets too rough on the streets.' She took a sip at her mineral water. 'The impression I got was she sort of . . . looks after him. Has a room made up for him if he needs it. More or less allows him to come and go as he pleases. Bails him out of trouble with the law. Not that he's a crook, mind. More of a local eccentric, I suppose. I did a series of six of them, but Jimmy's tale was the weirdest. All the others were really rather sad, but Jimmy, well, he seemed on the streets by choice, if you like. And the sister seemed to accept this. Made it easier for him, in a way. But the whole situation was a bit strange. All the time I was sitting there, drinking tea out of bone china cups, and there was this woman, nervous as a cat on a hot tin roof, telling me how much she cared for her brother, spent a fortune putting him through private rehab. clinics, always kept a bed for him . . .'

'None of this appeared in the article.'

'She asked me not to. Begged me. Guess it might have ruined her standing in the local WI, having a junkie living part time in the neighbourhood.'

'So how come she agreed to host the interview, then?'

'She told me afterwards she hoped that if Jimmy saw the bleak truth in black and white, he might come to his senses. She was bitterly opposed at first, but Jimmy obviously still keeps in close contact. When she found out I was interested in featuring him, she more or less told him to talk to me at her place. It was her way of controlling it, I suppose. She wanted him to be seen as a victim of drug abuse rather than a local weirdo. It was like she almost mothered him in a way.'

'Strange way of showing it.'

'Listen, Adrian, smack's a pricey commodity. Risky business. It seemed obvious to me Jimmy was getting some much needed financial assistance to maintain the habit. There was simply no way he could score decent H simply by busking. An odd bottle of supermarket cider, maybe – but good gear costs dear; bad gear costs lives. There's all sorts of mixed-up shit selling itself as grade-A smack round here, but the truth is most of it's cut with all kinds of rubbish by the dealers. There's a fair proportion of addicts dying injecting God knows what into their veins. Jimmy's one of the old school, straight heroin mainliner, an endangered species up here. Most of the ex-smackheads and young kids have moved on to rocks.'

'Crack?'

She nodded, ponytail bobbing cutely. 'Instant high, terrible come-down. They freebase the stuff all over town. Police can't do damn-all about it. Black gangs armed to the gold teeth with Uzi's control the trade like an LA street war. No, good smack's hard to find. You need a lot of money and connections.'

'She's scoring for him?'

'My guess is that she stumps up the readies. God only knows who the dealer is. But it's got to have cost her thousands, he's been on it a lifetime. Tried methadone four times, apparently. I suppose she's given him up as a lost cause. Simply ensures he always has the cash to score the best quality H. Like I say, it was very weird.'

'And not a word about brother Frank?'

'I didn't know to ask. But now this has all come to light, I guess I'll be ringing her up and . . .'

'Not for another few weeks, please. I've got your number. I'll give you a call when the time's right.'

'But . . .'

'Please, Miss Allison. Hold fire. This could be a much bigger story than you know.'

Now she was really intrigued.

'The sister's husband. Younger man, name of Richard Horton. Know anything about him?'

She shrugged. 'He was there, in the background. Barely said a word, really.' She thought for a second. 'Runs a little electronics business, I think.' Consulted her notes again. 'Works from home a lot. Insisted I send a fax of the proposed article to him before publication.'

'Which you did?'

'Seemed innocent enough at the time. Chances were he was slaving away to make the money to give to Jimmy to score.'

'Who told you about Jimmy's father's execution?'

'That was Jimmy. I was trying to find a reason for his . . . unusual lifestyle. When he told me of the hanging I realized I'd really hit gold with the story. You know, a focus point.'

'And the sister, Elaine Horton? What was her view?'

'That it hadn't made a difference. Jimmy's mother had remarried shortly after, and he'd had a father figure all his childhood. Time and time again, she blamed the drugs for his predicament, not the past.'

'And did she tell you that the second husband was a family friend? Himself another policeman, closely involved with the father in running black-market activities in the East End?'

Her eyes opened wide. 'No, she didn't.' She took out a pen. 'Look, Adrian, I really want to get some of this down . . .'

'In time. Not now, please, Karen.'

'But this . . .'

'Isn't the right time. Believe me.'

'She told you all this?'

'I already knew. She couldn't really deny it.'

'From talking to this . . . brother, Frank?'

'And others.'

'So what now?'

'Jimmy. I need to find him, talk to him again.'

'You're not the only one.'

'On my own, Karen, please.'

'But I could . . .'

'Really screw things up for me.'

She smiled.

'Sorry,' I said. 'You've been kind, coming here, helping. I promise I'll let you know the moment I find out more. I just need to speak to Jimmy on my own. Then he's yours. Please, tell me where I can find him.'

She held my gaze for several seconds, before writing down several hostel addresses, and well-known haunts of Manchester's dispossessed. 'You will call, won't you?'

'Promise. Just give me a few weeks. Meantime, if you want in on any of this, see what you can dig up about Richard Horton's electronics business. I have a hunch it's not the only line of work in his life.'

'Taking it pretty seriously, aren't you, this thesis of yours?'

I stood to leave. 'It's become a good deal more than just a thesis.'

'What's it about?'

'Me, I think.'

27

So, the game began. I just hoped to God I was up to playing, and that whatever courage I had left wouldn't fail at the eleventh hour. I'd made a vague plan over my near indigestible breakfast, now was the time to make the first move.

Trying as best as I could to forget my hellish head and banish all thoughts of the night before, I waited approximately ten minutes before phoning the residence of Elaine and Richard Horton. The answerphone was on. No surprise. I wondered how long Karen Allison had waited before ringing the same number. One, maybe two minutes? A quick flick through the Filofax, then out with the mobile? Thirty seconds max. She'd struck me as a true professional – freelance journo after a fresh angle on a previously unexciting scoop. She wouldn't have waited long.

Three rings and the recorded message kicked in: 'I'm sorry. You've reached the home address of Richard and Elaine Horton. I'm sorry, there's no one . . .'

But I knew there was. Almost saw her in my mind's eye, watching the phone, listening, heart thumping, waiting to discover who was after the tarnished family silver this time . . .

I cleared my throat. 'Pick up the phone, Elaine. It's Adrian Rawlings. I can call her off, Elaine. I can send Karen Allison packing. Doesn't feel so good, does it, having the press back on your case? Only this time, she knows a little more about the family, Elaine, doesn't she? Please, pick it up, Elaine. Let's talk about this . . .'

A panicked voice cut in – hers. Thank God it wasn't her husband's. 'What have you been saying? Just leave me alone!'

'Put it this way, Elaine. I know a good deal less than you, but a good deal more than Miss Allison. But she's good at her job. It won't take her long to catch up. I didn't want to involve her, Elaine, really. And believe me, I can call her off.'

'Why are you doing this? Wasn't yesterday enough for you?'

'I just want to speak to all of you. Together. You, your husband and Jimmy. Just the four of us. Tonight. Answers. The truth. Do that for me, and I'll see Karen Allison is deflected elsewhere. It wouldn't take too much more from me before she had enough to really start digging around. Your choice, Elaine. Me – or the press.'

'Are you getting some sort of twisted kick out of this? It's blackmail, you know that, don't you? Let me tell you something, Mr Adrian-bloody-Rawlings, I'm a good deal tougher than you'll ever know. Now why don't you crawl back under whatever stone you came from and leave decent folk alone.'

I was getting nowhere. It was time to cut up a bit rough. I didn't feel too bad about it, because for all Elaine Horton's suburban sensibilities, she'd been pretty quick to have me threatened with life in a wheelchair a few weeks back. 'Fair enough. I'll just set the journalist loose with a few more facts, then, shall I, Elaine? How about I mention your husband's assignation with Frank, just days before Helen Lewis died? Remember? The green Jag police were looking for? Richard had one of those, didn't he, about ten years ago? Quite a coincidence. God only knows what the papers'd make of that. Or the police, for that matter.'

'It's all history. All dealt with and forgotten.'

'Then perhaps you should think how Jimmy's going to react when news of his brother breaks all over the papers.'

'There's no story. You're wasting your time, and mine.'

'Like I say, let's let Karen Allison decide, eh?'

'Why are you doing this? This isn't "research" – this is . . . sick.'

And I was forced to silently admit that it quite possibly was. Certainly out of character, anyway, threatening anyone, let alone an innocent woman. But then again, I'd done a lot that was out of character over the previous twenty-four hours, maybe I was simply going with the flow. 'Look, Elaine, no one else's going to know. Please, it's really important. I have to know what made Frank the man he is.'

'The devil, Mr Rawlings, made my brother. And he's done a pretty good job on you too.'

'Then let's talk about it. Tonight. No tape recorders, no press. Just the four of us. Then I go. God's honest. You never see me again. Life returns to normal.'

A long silence. 'Ring me later. I can't think . . .'

'I'll be there at six, Elaine. If you've done a runner, then I'll have no choice. I'll have to set Karen Allison on to you. She has the skills and experience to find out all I need to know. Only it won't just be me getting the answers, it'll be thousands of *Manchester Evening News* readers. It may even make the nationals.'

Another long pause, then the breakthrough. 'Just call her off. Now. Please.'

'When did she phone?'

'Minutes ago. You've no right . . .'

'OK, stay calm. My guess is she'll be over to see you in the next half-hour. I'll call her up. Divert her. Just sit tight. Don't answer the phone. I'll be along at six. And don't run out on me, Elaine. I really don't want to make life any more difficult for you. So you can forget calling up the old man and having him break my legs. Anything happens to me – Karen Allison's going to know about it.'

'What kind of a man are you?'

The question threw me. I didn't have time enough for the answer, anyway. 'See you at six.'

There was no point in checking any of the dosshouse addresses Karen Allison had given me. I reckoned that Elaine would be dispatching her drug-dealing husband to find Jimmy at that very moment, planning to take him back to Wilmslow and the three of them getting the hell out of Dodge before the cavalry arrived. Karen had virtually told me as much – that Elaine practically mothered her younger brother, she'd want him with her, away from the likes of me.

I also suspected Karen would be well on her way to Wilmslow too, equally desperate for a face-to-face with the main cast.

Time to start bluffing for real. I checked my notes for her list of contact numbers, then called her mobile.

Her voice, broken. The unmistakable sound of rushing traffic. 'Yes?'

'Karen, it's Adrian Rawlings.'

'Adrian. Hi.'

'Listen. I've found Jimmy.'

Surprise. 'What, already?'

'Second address you gave me. Listen. I've got a problem. He's out of his tree. Keeps mumbling that he'll only talk to you. Says he only trusts you with his story. I can't get any more out of him.'

'Where are you?'

Hook, line and sinker. 'Somewhere called . . .' I craned my neck for a street sign. 'Quay Street. Leads on to the Granada Studio Complex. Lots of coaches. He says he wants to go in. Listen, Karen, I can't . . . oh shit, he's wandering off again . . . hang on . . .' (Any innocent bystander would at this point have been intrigued to see me rush six paces from the phone booth, call Jimmy's name three times, then run back.)

'Adrian? What's happening?'

'He's heading towards the TV studios. Look, just get here, will you?'

'Calm down. I'll be there as quick as I can. Just stay with him. Walk him around for a bit. If he's just shot up, then he's going to crash out any second. Take him to a pub. Then ring me back. Just don't lose him.'

'All right. But I've got to go. He's . . . he's . . . I've got to . . . I'll call you!'

It was time for a drink. Tomato juice followed by a pint of orange squash, something to pick me up, continue the much needed rehydration programme. I drifted into a city centre pub, wondering if I'd visited the place at some time the previous night.

I stayed for a while, doing my best to concentrate on

the business at hand rather than what might or might not have occurred the night before, then bought some Chlorets for my dog's breath, before slowly following my breakfast waitress's directions to Piccadilly Station, wondering all the while what on earth waited for me there. I felt certain the stranger claiming to be DCI Nick Moira wouldn't show up. Not follow me all the way to Manchester, surely?

Inside the noisy station canopy a few pigeons scrapped for a leftover sandwich. The tannoy boomed in the cold impersonal space which resonated with the shudder of locomotive engines and sudden high-pitched whistles. A wino in about four overcoats somehow managed to succeed in sleeping through the cacophony, still clutching a can of Special Brew. All around, the stink of piss and burger-fat permeated every nut and bolt of the place.

I waited by a photo booth, wondering what the hell was I doing there, today of all days, with everything else I had to deal with.

A shrill whistle blast. Two pigeons flew past overhead. A baby began to cry. The huge departures board rolled and flicked its black columns of white information. Another tannoy announcement, inaudible above a departing engine's roar. I stamped both feet to beat the chill.

Then suddenly, a voice to my right. 'Follow me. Discreetly.'

I jumped, then turned to take in the departing stranger, giving him twenty yards before I followed.

The man claiming to be Nick Moira had indeed made it to Manchester.

28

And so began a bewildering game of cat and mouse, him walking ahead, glancing behind, adjusting his pace whenever I showed signs of catching up. Then, even more frustratingly, when I slowed, he slowed. I found myself becoming angry at the charade, broke into a jog to catch him – but so did he.

We must have gone some two hundred yards from the station back towards Piccadilly Square in this ridiculous fashion, when I thought enough's enough. I just wasn't in the mood for any of it, had too much else to worry about. I was beginning to pant with the unfamiliar effort, needed to sit down and reflect further on all the other factors I already had clogging up the day. I felt like a weary circus plate-spinner, leaping from one precarious cause to the next. If this one was to drop, then I wouldn't be unduly bothered, regardless of what he'd teased me with about Rattigan previously. There was only so much I could deal with, and cloak-and-dagger following games fell well outside the remit. I resolved that if he was so keen to talk to me, he'd find me.

I spied Yates's Wine Lodge up ahead and set off for the tranquillity it offered. Drawing level with the entrance, I slipped inside, made my way through the suited lunchtime crowd towards the thronging bar, ordered another pint of orange squash, then cut back to find an empty table.

A minute later he eased himself into the seat opposite, still checking over his shoulder. Whatever the reason, I had to admire his consistent style. Everything about the man seemed as nervous as the first time I'd seen him in the uni. car park. If it was an act, he deserved an Oscar for best performance as a shambling lunatic.

'Good place, good thought,' he said quickly, eyes flitting across the crowded bar.

'You scared the hell out of my family.'

He began ripping at a damp beermat, knee jerking rhythmically, pointlessly. 'Sorry about that.'

'What were you thinking of?'

'To talk to you, of course. Couldn't see you about. Eventually, the door opened. I was freezing my arse off out there, had to ask the kid where you were.'

'Why not simply knock on the door?'

He looked at me for a brief second, blinking in bewilderment. ''Cause they still watch me. Couldn't risk it.'

I said nothing, wondering just how insane he really was, what sort of excuse I could make to leave. But all the while something kept me there – someone – his mention of the damage Rattigan had done to him. Plus the fact that he'd followed me the best part of two hundred and fifty miles to meet me. It seemed only fair to give him five minutes to make his case.

'Listen,' he said quickly, voice rising. 'Count yourself lucky you've still got a family. I had one – till the Rattigan storm broke.'

I flinched, suddenly alarmed he could turn nasty at any moment. It was obvious to the coward in me that placation was the most diplomatic tactic. 'OK. Just don't shout. It makes people nervous. Me included.'

He nodded, lowered his voice. 'Too right you should be nervous, Mr Rawlings. Your phone calls to the Met looking for Williams, Shot and myself have been causing some pretty big ripples.'

'You are him, then? DCI Moira. I'm sorry, but . . .'

'Used to be. Fuck knows what I am now.' He gave me another piercing stare from behind yellowed, bloodshot eyes. 'Sometimes, I don't even feel human.'

I said nothing, allowing him to continue, almost unable to believe the shabby twitching man before me was once an able CID man who now blamed Rattigan for his downfall – as if by meeting the man he'd somehow been tainted, ruined by the Beast.

Nick Moira began decimating a new beermat. 'I still got one

or two pals in Scotland Yard. When you began putting calls through to Mile End nick, alarm bells went off. I got to hear about it. Trusted friend, I don't want him involved. Anyway, they put a trace on your calls, found you, stuck you through the computer . . .'

I was incredulous. 'Just because I'd rung a police station?'

He shook his head. 'No. Because you'd mentioned my name and Rattigan's in the same breath.' His eyes appeared to glaze over, he looked suddenly tired.

'You want a drink or anything, Nick?' I tried.

He pulled himself back. 'No, you're all right. It clouds things, does stuff to my head.' He pulled a battered tin from a pocket and began to roll a cigarette. His yellow-stained fingers shook, sending slivers of dried tobacco across the tabletop.

He lit up. 'You wanted to talk to me, Mr Rawlings. I'm here.'

'It's Adrian,' I said a little uncomfortably. He was calmer now, more impressive somehow. I was seeing him afresh, suspected that he probably might have made a good detective. The air of Upholder of the Law still hadn't entirely left him. Or maybe it was a darker, guilt-ridden realization that here was I, talking to an ex-policeman, and less than twenty-four hours previously . . .

'I heard the original interview tapes,' I continued hesitantly. 'And then after, a detective hinted that in his opinion there were a lot of unanswered questions.'

Moira simply stared back.

'That perhaps' – my feet were beginning to sweat – 'the investigation was stalled in some way.'

He smiled. 'Student, aren't you? On the way to a PhD in criminology.'

'Forensic psychiatry.'

'Don't look so worried. You're clean. It's all on the print-out. But what you've got to understand is, I need you.'

'Sorry?'

He took a deep drag, looked furtively all round, beckoned me closer. 'Rattigan did some kind of deal with the ACC. Ten years I've been paying for that.' He grew more animated, as I grew more nervous. 'You think I'm mental, don't you?'

'I don't know you that well, Nick,' I replied honestly.

'What you've got to understand, Adrian, is what's involved in all this. Rattigan's case goes a whole lot higher than you'll ever realize.'

'Sure.'

'Don't patronize me. Just listen.' He took another two quick drags on the wafer-thin cigarette. 'Your pal up at Essex was right. When they first brought Rattigan in, we reckoned there was a whole crock of shit he was covering up. Williams, Shot, myself, we all knew the bastard was bluffing, sitting on something. So we gave him the third degree. You've heard the tapes, right?'

I nodded.

'There was the business with the cash, the Jag – we had loads of options. Then, on the third day, he suddenly asks to see the Assistant Chief Constable. Insists on it, says it'll wrap the whole business up nicely. 'Course, by then, we've got virtually the whole tabloid press camped outside the nick, demanding answers. So we agree. Contact the ACC. He comes over. Five, ten minutes he spends talking to Rattigan, who comes out smiling like he's just walked out with seven score-draws on his coupon.

'Minutes later, my guv'nor's called in to see the ACC. Next we know, the case has been handed over to the shrinks. The whole team's baffled, can't really take it in. The guv'nor's as gutted as we are, but hasn't got any choice. We have to charge Rattigan with the murder without ever knowing why the fuck he did it. Simply accept he'd changed overnight from a very heavy criminal to some sort of psycho. A press conference was called, the ACC looking pleased as fucking punch, telling all the vultures how Rattigan had been charged on confession.'

'This deal you said Rattigan had . . .'

'I'm coming to that. That night, all the lads, including my guv'nor, drown our sorrows in the boozer. It's like the whole business stinks to us. Rattigan's assured of a place in a mental home instead of doing a life stretch behind bars, and that's a big fucking difference in custodial lifestyles. We figure the evil sod's got away with it.

'Anyway, during the evening, my guv'nor calls me over,

lets me know he's as confused as anybody by the ACC's orders. Then, in the same breath, more or less tells me he'd turn a blind eye if I chose to pursue matters a little further.'

'Which you did, right?'

'Too right. The whole thing was a shit-shambles. Stank of corruption.'

'And?' I was hooked, drawn in.

'I began quietly asking round, pulled in a couple of my snouts, checked with some of the hacks compiling pieces on the Beast of East 16.' Moira stubbed out what remained of the cigarette, then began rolling another. 'I started to learn a little more. Like Rattigan's dad, for instance, strung up for topping a copper. Another killer saying damn-all about motives. Then there was someone else, someone vital to it all.'

I went with instinct. 'John Templar?'

'Bang on the money. Sergeant John Templar – people's hero, rose to Chief Superintendent in time, before taking early retirement and his place as head of Mile End Council for seven years. He made a lot of very powerful friends, did John Templar.'

'The man with the hands of a hero,' I replied. 'Who also took up with Rattigan's mother.'

He lit up again. 'Did you know they have a "John Templar Memorial Suite" in Mile End Council offices? His obituary ran to nearly half a page in *The Times*. He's still held up as an exemplary officer to new recruits, even now. An example, I'm told, of just what today's freshly scrubbed young copper should be aspiring to – a community-minded hero, prepared to risk death and dispense sympathetic justice in the same goddamned breath.'

I felt the need to demonstrate a little of my own knowledge and research. 'But he was a black-market racketeer during the war, wasn't he? Him and Joseph Rattigan together.'

'And plenty more besides,' Moira added. 'Templar was as bent as they come. The more I found out about it, the more it began to slowly make some sort of sense.'

'The deal Rattigan struck?' I guessed. 'He threatened to blow the lid on Templar, have his good character besmirched by the black-market rackets?'

Moira paused for a minute, as if choosing his words with care. 'It had to be more than that, didn't it? The whole rescue act at the gas explosion more or less stuffed selling a few bits of knocked-off gear well into a cocked hat. But I had nothing else to go on. Templar was dead, so was Rattigan's mother.

'So I went back to the guv'nor. Told him I was convinced the whole business was tied up in Joseph Rattigan's silence at the trial. I mean, what made him kill the other copper? I already knew from local old lags that Scrimshaw was running the same sort of shit as Templar. Chances are the three of them were in it together. But why say nothing at the trial, when he would have known they were going to top him for committing a capital crime? The more I thought about it, the more I realized there was only one man I could ask. The guv'nor arranged for it, on the sly, for me to see Rattigan himself.'

'At Oakwood?'

He nodded, exhaling, clouding me in dirty yellow smoke. 'You ever seen his digs in there?'

'No. We meet in another room.'

'He's got it nice and cosy, I can tell you. Wallpaper, telly, radio, books, like a sodding holiday camp. Anyway, I began to wonder, didn't I?'

I rubbed my tired face. 'The deal he made, right?'

'Exactly. Not only had the ACC's lot kept him out of prison, now it looked like they were ensuring the arsehole lived the life of riley inside.'

'Jesus. Why?'

'I could only think it was to appease him. Keep him happy, shtoom. I think they were terrified that he'd find a way of leaking whatever he knew about John Templar to the outside world. And that it must have some bearing on them. So it had to be bigger than just some bent racketeering in the war, didn't it?'

'Yeah,' I replied. 'Maybe.'

'And that's the right word for it, Adrian – maybe. I never got further than Oakwood. Rattigan told me fuck-all, and by the time I got back I'd been rumbled. Someone at the nick had blown the whistle about my trip out there. The guv'nor called me in, and I was the fall guy. Bye-bye, promising career.'

'They sacked you?'

He laughed tonelessly. 'Oh, they were cleverer than that. First off, they'd obviously done a number on the guv'nor. Shit-scared, he was. Told me I had an appointment with the force's own psychiatrist, that I'd been working too hard, colleagues had started to notice a marked deterioration in my work. And all the time he's telling me, it's like our "arrangement" never existed. I walked out of his office devastated, totally confused.'

'You saw the psychiatrists?'

'Had to – or they'd sack me. Blackmail, wasn't it? I went, they said I needed time away from the job. I went bananas, played right into their bloody hands, lost it big time. I was so angry – really, really pissed off.' He put down the roll-up, began ripping at another beermat. 'Next I know I'm up before a disciplinary hearing, ACC's one of them, my report on the desk in front of him. I'm told I need some "help". That I should accept it, or leave the force. I did. They took me to a funny-farm in Kent, told my family they were worried, looking after me.'

'And you had no recourse to anything else?' I asked, stunned. 'No union rep to turn to?'

'Fuck-all.'

'It's unbelievable.'

'Tell me about it. I've lived it. They want to make you out as mad, they can. Problem is, you go a little mental fighting the injustice of it. Sort of prove them right, really. End up not knowing who the hell you are.' He started on another beermat. 'Hardest thing was the wife and kids. Only young, they were. Trooping over to Kent, listening to me ranting and raving – and, you see, that only confirmed it. I was some sort of paranoid schizo spouting a load of old bollocks. Conspiratorial delusional fantasies, they called it. Didn't matter how much noise I made, no one'd believe me. In the end, I had to do as they wanted, deny the whole thing, simply to get myself out of there. In the meantime, the wife had got scared. The force had spoken to her about my unsuitability to hold another post. I was given a few grand as a pay off. Started drinking, going downhill, usual old cobblers. Couldn't get another job with my medical history. So she left. Took the kids, fucked off.' He looked up at me, face devoid of all emotion. 'And that's me now. Ex-DCI Nick Moira – nutcase, occasional shelf-stacker, pisshead.'

I had nothing to say.

'Just be careful, Adrian. I know why you're up here. Rattigan's got a sister, ain't he? You're after the same thing I wanted – answers. Be bloody careful, there's one hell of a lot they can do.'

'I'm not sure what I want any more,' I said. 'You're frightening the life out of me.'

He looked around the crowded pub. 'Listen, if you ever met any of them – they'll tell you I'm some kind of lunatic. Surprised they haven't already.'

'No one's even mentioned you.'

'Believe me, they know what you're up to. Pals tell me things. Your records were requested by the men at the top.'

I began to share his unease. What if he was right? 'I'm just doing this as a student, Nick. I don't have any special interest in Rattigan, honest.'

He offered me a mocking smile. 'That what you're going to tell them, eh? That the best you can do? Doesn't really explain you plodding all the way up here to talk to Rattigan's relatives, does it? They'll think that demonstrates a very special interest indeed. Go home. Leave it.'

'I can't. I've set too much in motion. I'm finding out stuff all the time. You know Rattigan's brother, Jimmy? He lives up here, too. And the green Jag? Rattigan's sister's old man had one at about the same time Helen Lewis was murdered. I think maybe he's some sort of dealer. And then there's this journalist who's . . .'

Moira held up a hand. 'I don't want to know any of it. I've said what I came to say. The rest is yours. Just weigh up what you've got to lose, for God's sake.' He made to leave. 'And do me a favour.'

'Sure. I'll try.' And I meant it.

'If you find out what the deal was between Rattigan and the ACC, let the whole bloody world know. That's all. At least that way my wife and kids'll know that the old man wasn't the bumbling loony the others always said he was.'

'Sure, Nick, I'll . . .'

But before I could finish, he rose, turned and left.

29

All of which left me in a terrible quandary. Indeed, I was almost relieved when he slipped furtively out of my life. It had all been too much, too earnest – and maybe, too dangerously believable.

My mind felt like exploding from the potential permutations of Moira's tale, but I simply hadn't the time to analyse it, place it in the order of what I knew for sure and what I half suspected. It was too crazy, another league entirely from my amateur investigations. But I wished to God I'd taped his every word.

I sat for a couple of minutes, watching others, drinking, laughing, envying them their uncomplicated lives, then retired to the toilet, sat in the end cubicle, locked away from life and its assorted complications. I didn't need to go as such, just craved the feeling of shutting a door on the world, time out from the chaos. And the longer I sat reading the predictable graffiti, the happier I felt, isolated, hidden. 'Engaged' the lock announced, yet the sweet beauty was that the occupant was blissfully disengaged.

But only for a few precious moments. There was work to do.

It was nearly two – time to make another call. When was this day going to end? I shut my eyes, tried to calm myself, rerole again. More subterfuge. Second ring, she answered.

'Yes?'

'Karen, it's –'

'Adrian! Where are you? I've been . . .'

'A pub somewhere down by the canal. Look, Karen, he keeps bloody wandering off. I can't keep him much longer, for Christ's sake! Just get here!'

'Jesus wept, I've been looking all over for you! Where-abouts by the canal?'

'Look, I don't know Manchester. It's bloody difficult just keeping him with me.'

'All right, all right. The name. Give me the name of the pub.'

'Yes, of course. Hang on, then.'

And then, I simply hung up. Brilliant, for a man in my condition. I hoped I had just about bought enough time to fetch the car and drive back over to Elaine Horton's – because I had no intention of actually waiting until six. I knew full well she'd be long gone by then. Car packed, Richard Horton at the wheel, little brother Junkie Jimmy in the back. Probably head for the Lakes or something, North Wales maybe. I just couldn't see Elaine as the type to calmly sit behind net curtains waiting for our early-evening showdown. No, six o' clock was a little white lie of mine, part of the plan I'd crudely figured out over breakfast. I would arrive well before three . . . which gave me less than an hour.

I stopped at Boots for Rennies and paracetamol, hoping somewhat naively they might clear my head and settle my stomach for whatever lay ahead.

30

'You must not enter a house where there is mourning. Do
not grieve for anyone. I will no longer bless my people with
peace, or show them love or mercy. The rich and the poor
will die in this land, but no one will bury them or mourn
for them.'

Jeremiah 16, 5–7

It had been a long time since I'd felt so nervous and uneasy.

First off, I had to check the *A-Z* I'd bought in order to find
my way back to the Hortons' quiet suburban solitude. It was
raining again, dark clouds screening what remained of the
afternoon's blue sky, sending down heavy drops of polluted
filth on to the city.

Next I retrieved the car, paid a charge of nine pounds for the
parking, then set off for Wilmslow, travelling south towards
Didsbury and the M63 to Stockport, stopping and starting
at an endless stream of traffic lights struggling to cope with
mounting traffic.

The medication had done little to soothe any part of me. I
couldn't help thinking about Moira, wondering if paranoia
was infectious, then found myself checking the rear-view
mirror too often as I did so. And what about Richard Horton?
What sort of a bloke would he turn out to be? Would he go for
me, defending his wife and reputation from my unwarranted
intrusion?

An unwelcome feeling returned, familiar from the night
before, that somehow I was fated, cursed to this moment,

driving in the drizzle, uncertain, afraid, yet knowing this was the place I had to be.

Two forty-five, and I pulled up outside the Hortons'. The four-by-four parked in front of the double garage announced Richard Horton's presence. There were suitcases inside.

Nothing else for it, time to exorcize some ghosts.

I offered up a silent prayer, then pressed the doorbell. Nothing. Tried again. And again. One more time. I tried peeping through the front window. No sign of anyone inside. Perhaps, a voice told me, I should go, forget about it all, convince myself I'd tried my best, that the entire venture was little more than self-indulgent folly . . .

Footsteps. Oh, good God! Then the front door opened.

'You'd best sod off, pal. While you still have legs that work for you.'

Somehow I found my voice. 'Afternoon, Richard. How about you let me in so we can clear this up?'

'You what?' He was taller than I'd remembered, late-forties, start of a receding hairline, and a face which wore a mask of screwed-up hatred.

But to my surprise, I didn't turn and run. There was a belligerence to me, perhaps born out of weariness, years of running and hiding. I was too old to cower in shop doorways as thugs did their stuff now. The fat, frightened boy who grew into a cautious idealist was about to finally make his stand. 'I'll just ring the journalist then, shall I, Richard? Or maybe I won't have to. Christ knows, it's been a difficult enough job keeping her away from this place up till now. But she's a bright girl. Won't take her too long to realize she's been duped. She'll most likely be on her way up here now. Then we can all sit down together. Won't that be cosy?'

He made a sudden move towards me, but thankfully an arm appeared, pulled him back, just as I braced myself for a jaw-breaking impact.

'You said six!' Elaine Horton was scared. I grew in confidence.

'I lied, Ellie. Lot of it about, isn't there?'

'Just leave us alone! We're respectable people.'

I looked around, surveyed the calm, quiet avenue. 'I don't

want to make a scene, really I don't. What would the neighbours think, eh? Tell you what, let's get this over and done
with, then you can flit off to wherever you're planning
before Ms Allison arrives with a notebook full of searching
questions.'

Standoff. Silence between all three of us.

I broke it, time ticking on. 'I just want to talk to Jimmy.'

'He's not here.'

'Come on, Elaine. I know you keep a bed here for him
when he chooses to come back. And I hardly think you're
going to allow him to wander around on his own now this
storm has broken.' Then I shouted, knowing it'd cause a stir.
'Jimmy? Scored any decent smack recently?'

'Leave us be! There's nothing to say.'

'After I've spoken to your little brother.' I raised my voice
again. 'Wanna buy some heroin, Jim?'

'He's not here!'

'Prove it. I look around. If I can't find him, I'm gone. It's
a promise.'

'I haven't seen him for days. He's his own man.'

'Oh, but Richard has, Ellie. Gave him a fix just last night,
didn't you? Little trip out in the family motor. Very considerate.'

He swallowed hard, shot his older wife a crushed look,
seemed to shrink visibly before my eyes. In that split second
he wasn't such a big thug any more, and for an instant I almost
felt sorry for him. One tiny glance had spelt out something
far more illustrative. Elaine wore the trousers. Elaine was the
brains behind the operation, not Richard.

'You'd better come in.'

'Thanks. It won't take long, I promise.'

Back in the luxurious living room, I quickly glanced at the
mantelpiece, where the damning photo of the green Jag still
gathered dust. A body grunted in broken sleep on the couch.
Jimmy Rattigan, snoozing fitfully.

Elaine cleared her throat, Richard stood behind her. 'I
just don't know what you hope to achieve by all this, Mr
Rawlings.'

'Fair question. I'd be asking the same. But then again,

maybe I don't have so much to hide.' I sat down in an armchair across from the sleeping body. 'I've been lucky since I left you yesterday. I followed your husband last night, found Jimmy. Stumbled across an article in the *Evening News*, then tracked down the journalist responsible. And she told me a lot of stuff you didn't.'

'Money? Is that what it's going to take? A thousand? Two?'

'I don't need cash, Elaine.'

Richard obviously felt it was time to reassert himself. 'Listen, you nosey piece of . . . !'

'Don't!' Elaine's command, not mine.

Jimmy stirred a little. Rubbed both eyes, then saw me. I think he smiled, possibly recognized me as the mug he'd taken for a packet of fags and a drink the previous evening.

I waved. 'It's me again, Jimmy. The man who won't stop asking questions. Quite a story, isn't it? Quite a family you have here. Big brother locked up for murder, big sis ensuring you're getting the best gear on the streets, making a little bed for you at home. You must be the best-kept secret in Wilmslow.'

'Leave him alone!'

'Why didn't you mention Frank in the article, Elaine?'

'It was none of anyone's business.'

I nodded, then turned to Richard Horton. 'It was you, wasn't it?'

'What?'

'You met Frank at the fruit farm. The mystery man in the green Jag.'

I saw him flinch. A minuscule movement, but it gave the game away. Pity, in a way. I almost liked the bloke – one of nature's finest, a man who couldn't ever lie convincingly. But he gave it a shot – had to, really. 'Sod off!'

'You gave him a grand in cash. Why?'

'No way!'

'Come on, Richard. Do us all a favour. Ms Allison could turn up at any minute, then all hell's going to let loose.'

He walked to me, trembling. 'How about I do you a favour, and fucking kick the lying shit out of you?'

But I was stronger, feeling better by the second, could sense an end to it all. 'Because I'd tell the papers. And the police. That simple, really.'

Elaine intervened, her voice strained, desperate. 'Why are you doing this?' Then she sat awkwardly at her younger brother's side, shielding him.

'I think Frank had reasons for killing Helen Lewis. Precise, traceable reasons.'

'Then you're as mad as he is.'

Which caused me to smile. 'In some ways, you're right. Maybe that's why this is so important to me. Nowhere in Frank's miserable criminal record are there any concrete pointers that he was ever anything other than a bullying yobbo. Stupid assaults, fist-fights. Then, suddenly, he spends three days torturing, murdering and dismembering a woman. For "fun", he says. See what I'm saying? It doesn't connect with any other part of his record.'

She began to fidget uncomfortably. 'Like I've already told you, Frank was simply bad from day one. Nothing he's done has ever surprised me.'

'You pay for Jimmy's habit, don't you?'

She said nothing.

'Because you love him, as a sister. And that's a good thing, really.'

'What do you know about good?'

'You've spent a fortune ensuring he only gets the best dope. But I want to know what turned him on to heroin in the first place. How about I ask him myself?'

Elaine glared at me, warning me off. 'You leave him alone!'

'It was to buy drugs, wasn't it, eh? The money Richard gave Frank at the farm. He and Jimmy have been addicts for years . . .'

Then came the sleepy, croaking objection which was to turn all my misconceptions on their head

Jimmy Rattigan was with us. 'Frank – a junkie?' He began to laugh, continued for several seconds. 'Fuck's sake. You know nothing. He's never touched it, except to . . .'

Elaine – to Jimmy – 'Shut up!' Then – to me – 'His brain's gone. Rotted away. Doesn't even know what day it is. Can't believe anything he . . .'

'Go on, Jimmy,' I pressed. 'Tell me what really happened. End it for me.'

He shifted himself up on to one elbow, still giggling. 'End it? Oh, that's a good one, pal. Only it won't ever end, will it? Not for me. Never. I've got that cunt inside me for the rest of my fucking life.'

Elaine – 'There's nothing to say! Nothing to know! We're going, Jimmy. Going away!'

'Who, Jimmy?' I urged. 'Who's inside you? Frank?'

Jimmy shook his head. 'The other fucker. Me dad.'

Elaine took hold of his hand. 'That's enough, Jimmy. It's all over, now.'

'Ain't never going to be over!' he roared. 'Leastways not for me!'

Elaine began to cry. Her husband moved quickly to comfort her, but she shrugged him off, clinging to her younger brother once more.

I tried again. 'It can be over, Jimmy. You know, don't you, know all about Frank, why he killed the girl?'

'It's all bollocks.'

'Try me.'

'What for?'

There was a long silence as I struggled to find a good enough reason. 'For all of us,' I said eventually.

And so he did. Slowly, falteringly, disjointedly, gaps and vital testimony supplied by Elaine as she sat stoically through-out.

It took just over an hour, and at the end, I hugged them both. For neither was guilty of anything, except for once being children.

Even Frank was once a terrified little boy.

31

August, 1946

He didn't like Wednesdays any more. And there was no point in running, because they always found him. They knew all his hiding places, would often ask others where to find him. Every Wednesday, the same . . .

He remembered the first time, Dad taking him upstairs the night before while Mum and Ellie scrubbed pots and pans in the ever-steaming kitchen. It was early evening, still light, a perfect end to a summer's day.

'Frank,' he'd said, sitting close on the bed, arm around the yawning six-year-old boy. 'If I asked you to do something for Dad, something very, very important, would you do it for me?'

'Dunno.' He wanted to run into the tiny garden, search for his friends, maybe go round some old bomb sites, play army. He didn't like the sticky sweet smell of his dad's breath.

'Something really important, Frank. A secret thing.'

'Secret?'

'Our secret. Just you and me.'

'What about Mum? Ellie?'

The worried man shook his head. 'Just you and me.'

Frank Rattigan looked at his scuffed shoes. 'P'raps.'

'I'll get you some sweets. That'd be nice, eh?'

'Why are you crying, Dad?'

'Because . . . I'm happy. Happy that you're going to help me.'

'What kind of sweets?'

Joseph Rattigan sat a little closer to his curious son on the creaking bed. 'Gobstoppers, liquorice laces. Whatever I can. Will you help me?'

'S'pose. Do I get 'em now?'

'No. Not yet. Tomorrow afternoon.'

'But you said . . .'

'Keep your voice down. Please.'

Frank began to idly swing his legs to and fro. Sweets would be nice. Didn't get many sweets now the Germans had been beaten. Everything was pretty boring now the war was over. But Dad tried to make it better. He really loved his dad. Always coming in through the back door with a little treat under his dirty overcoat. Sometimes a ham, three tins of pineapple, extra blob of butter. Dad knew how to get 'stuff'. Other kids told him so. Their parents didn't seem to approve of Frank's dad, said he was a naughty man. But that couldn't be true, could it? Frank knew what being naughty was, and that involved breaking windows and having fun. Dad was good. Dad got them all 'stuff'.

'Listen carefully, Frank,' said Joseph, voice slightly strangulated, anxious. 'I want you to come straight home from school tomorrow. No playing with your friends. Straight home. D'you hear me?'

Frank nodded. He'd be there. Not that he had any intention of going to school – why bother? But he'd be back home at three if there were sweets about. 'Mum goes out on Wednesday afternoons.'

'That's right, son. She does. That's why this has to be our secret.'

'Doesn't she want any sweets, then?'

'No. She doesn't. Just come home as quick as you can. Promise?'

'Yeah.'

'Good boy. Not a word to anyone.'

That first Wednesday. The first time he could remember that he'd been back in the house at five past three. An empty house. Ellie out with friends, Mum visiting Granny in Forest Hill. A dark house, cool, familiar smells, soapy washing hanging from the kitchen ceiling.

He jumped from the kitchen chair as the front door opened. Two voices – Dad's and Uncle John's. His heart began to thump. Uncle John was a policeman, smacked his bottom when Dad wasn't there to tell him off. Used to frogmarch him back home, make him sit on the kitchen floor as he had tea with Mum, then take him into the dirty-brown back room and administer the punishment.

And always after, when he'd tearfully try to cuddle Mum, she'd push him away, saying how tired she was, how tired he made her, always getting into bother. Sometimes she'd ask him why he was such a naughty boy, but he had no answers. I'll try, Mum, he'd promise. I'll really, really try. That'd be nice, she'd reply. Then Uncle John wouldn't have to waste his time trying to beat some sense into you. Off you go, now. Stop crying. Few smacks never hurt anyone.

Frank shook as his dad led Sergeant John Templar into the kitchen.

''Lo, Frank.'

'Hello, Uncle John.' He looked at his dad, but couldn't meet his eyeline.

The big policeman dropped to his knees, huge oval face in the young boy's. 'Been a good boy, then?'

Frank's bottom lip began to tremble. 'I haven't . . . I never done nothin' this time! I . . .'

'Hush, Frank. Hush.' The voice was strange, quietly seductive.

Frank wanted to go to the toilet. Something felt wrong. Something . . . weird. He wanted his dad to make the man go away. He didn't want to have the policeman smack his bottom any more. Dad should do that, not Uncle John.

Joseph Rattigan sighed heavily. 'John, just . . . get it over with. She could be back any second. Please.'

'Dad?'

'Please, Frank. Just . . . go with Uncle John . . . for a minute. He's not going to hurt you. I promise. Just . . . be a good boy for him.' There was a long silence, both adults staring at the nervous youngster. 'Will you do that for me? Yes? Frank?'

'And afterwards,' John Templar added, 'Dad's got a little treat for you. You'd like a little treat, wouldn't you?'

'When's Mummy back?'

But Joseph Rattigan had his back turned, leaning his head against the cool damp wall. 'Frank. Please. Just . . .'

The policeman took his hand. Softly. Not like the other times, grabbing at a torn shirt collar. This was gentler. Like Mum used to before he started being so naughty at school and stuff. But it still didn't feel . . . right.

'Come on, Frank,' Templar coaxed. 'I'm not going to hurt you. Just a little chat. You and me. That's OK, isn't it? Eh?'

So he went with the policeman, into the dingy back room, watching as the big man pulled the heavy curtains, darkening the musty room even further.

'Come and sit down, Frank. That's good. No. No. On my lap. That's right. You're shaking, aren't you? There's no need for that. I'm not going to hurt you. What a good boy you are. And those sweets are something to look forward to, aren't they? Now then, Frank. Do you want to kiss your Uncle John? You kiss your dad, don't you? There, that wasn't so bad, was it?'

'Can I have my sweets, now?'

'You know what I am, don't you, Frank?'

'A policeman.'

'What a clever boy. Now I'll kiss you for being so smart. Oh, that was a funny one, wasn't it? On the lips. Now then, Frank, I want you to listen carefully. You know Dad sometimes comes home with little treats for the family? Nice things to eat?'

'Yes.'

'He's not really supposed to do that, Frank. It's against the law. Do you know what that means, Frank?'

'He could go to prison?'

'That's right. And you wouldn't want that, would you?'

'No.'

'No. That's right. You'd never see your dad, again, would you? That wouldn't be very nice, would it?'

'Why are you touching me there?'

'Just listen to me, Frank. I don't want to put your dad in prison. We're all friends, aren't we? And because I like you, and your mum and dad, and Ellie so much, I'm going to be a really nice policeman.'

219

'What's that thing?'

'Don't you worry about that. Just stand up for me, Frank. That's a good boy. You do know what I'm saying, don't you?'

'That you're going to be nice.'

'So you can still have a dad. Now then, look at this. That's a funny thing, isn't it? Not like yours, is it? Shall we look at yours, Frank? Tell you what, why don't I just help you off with these, eh? There. That wasn't so difficult, was it?'

'Can I have my sweets, now?'

'Do you want to hold it, Frank? It's funny, isn't it? Go on. Does it feel warm? Now, how about another kiss? That really would make me happy. Very good. Now, turn around. No, don't worry, I'm not going to smack it. I just want to . . .'

'I want me dad.'

'In a minute. Don't want to make me angry, now, do you? Now, this is a very grown-up thing to do. You're really being such a good boy. You just have to sit down again in my lap. That sounds easy, doesn't it? Keep facing the wall, don't look back. Then when it's all over, you can have some sweeties.'

'It hurts!'

'Keep looking forwards, Frank. Tell you what, how about looking at that picture on the wall? Can you see it? The one with the lady? That's a nice picture, isn't it?'

'Please stop . . .'

'Don't turn round, Frank! I'm sorry, I didn't mean to shout at you. Quiet now. Come on, Frank, just keep . . . looking at the lady. See how she smiles? She likes what we're doing. Having all this fun. Thinks you're being such a grown-up little boy, helping your dad like this. Now just . . . that's it! All right, all right . . . quiet . . . be quiet, Frank! Big boys don't cry. Look at the lady. Just look at the lady in the picture. See . . . how . . . she . . . smiles . . .'

32

Returning home to Chelmsford early that night, I was lucky not to be the cause of a major road traffic accident. Twice I almost drifted asleep at the wheel, victim of a near-fatal cocktail of hunger and exhaustion. The journey just seemed to roll on for ever – M6, Birmingham, roadworks, Spaghetti Junction, Cowley Services, A14 switchbacking its way ever eastwards . . . on and on . . . Huntingdon, M11, driving rain . . .

My tired eyes ached from the glare of oncoming traffic, whilst my mind, once so keen for the answers it now held, felt curiously numb, strangely detached from the dark, rushing world outside the car.

In just over an hour Rattigan had been demystified, explained. But there was little euphoria to show for my success in nailing the Beast, any excitement I felt quickly drained away as I watched Elaine, Richard and Jimmy drive off in the four-by-four, headed God knows where. I was left alone, a willing but shattered recipient of their buried histories. I felt abandoned, almost.

So I too, drove away, keen to outsprint Karen Allison, grateful she hadn't arrived during the last sixty minutes. I ran for home, keen for the sanctuary it offered, the welcome I hoped awaited me there.

And how I was going to change. I had it all figured out, a new beginning. No more malt, no more cynicism, no more forensic psychiatry. I was to be a phoenix rising from the ashes of my contempt, a husband and father reborn. At least, that was the plan . . .

Inevitably, one of the reasons why I felt so low was that

I couldn't banish *her* from my mind. Every few miles, the same thoughts resurfaced – What in God's name was I doing with her in the first place? Why did I even consider doing what I did? Paying for sex? I just prayed she was OK. She must have been, or I would have heard something on the local radio station. But what had led me down those dingy steps into the club in the first place? What lured me there? Rattigan – was he to blame? Or was it simply in me – I did it because I could – for 'fun'?

Sometimes, during the journey, I'd go over what Jimmy and Elaine had told me earlier that afternoon, trying to make sense of the long chain of cause and effect put into such hideous motion so many years ago. But I was too tired to take it all in, couldn't comprehend the desperation that forced a father to pimp his young son to a policeman in exchange for turning a blind eye to his best efforts to feed his family. Different times, I'd been told over and over – the aftermath of a global war, rationing. But was any of it a legitimate excuse for what happened in a back room fifty years ago?

Try as they might, even the sultry Supremes belting out their greatest hits on tape couldn't distract me from thinking about my own father. Indeed, it was almost as if the tinny sound froze me in a bygone age, when as a young boy I'd watched as a pack of thugs had beaten him senseless.

Curious how the memory worked, its editing and selection. I'd gone to Manchester in search of Rattigan, but had run smack into me. And now that I'd been revisited by the scene, other pictures from the past fought to be seen. I remembered standing outside the hospital, waiting for my mother, then walking home, desperately wanting to find something appropriate to say, but coming up with nothing, struck dumb by a blanket of suffocating guilt that I'd stood by and watched as the fists and boots had flown in.

Yet, in a curious way, things were rendered somehow explainable. I now understood the sudden transformation in my father, from keen fan to stay-at-home bore. The looks my mother sometimes gave me, almost as if I was somehow to blame for the attack. Moreover, there was another revelation, my own obsession with rationalizing random violence. I could see the bloody roots now, trace back its beginnings to the horror I felt as I watched my father fall inelegant victim to a motiveless mob.

Somehow, I made it back to the house by nine thirty, then sat slumped in the car, unable to walk inside, offended by the easy opulence which awaited me.

I waited ten minutes, glanced up and saw the front bedroom light suddenly switched off. Jemimah, warm under the duvet, exhausted from another day peddling tat to the masses. Such an easy, uncomplicated life, so different from Rattigan's past.

And perhaps that was what I found the saddest. Not the image of the young sodomized boy – but our assumption that somehow things had changed since then. That all our electronic, labour-saving technology had created a much more loving race, elevated us above food-crazed animals. We'd shut our eyes, nod respectfully, and talk about 'the bad old days', thanking our lucky stars we had an Argos in every town, a dishwasher in the kitchen.

But I had a suspicion that the bad old days were still here. Fast food only made us shit quicker. Deals like Joseph Rattigan's were still struck every day, only now the abuser had a video-camera to record the action.

Silence in the house as I entered. Juliet, still in school uniform, sat before several textbooks on the living room table, studying. Revising. Trying desperately to remember a hundred salient facts before the morning's mock-exam. She wanted to be a doctor.

My son Guy lay sprawled on the leather sofa in the lounge lit solely by the dim colourful blur of the television. Another cop drama was reflected in his thick glasses. He looked up, nervous as always, his father's son.

'Hi, Dad.'

'Guy.'

'Mum's gone to bed.'

'I know. You all right?'

'Sure.'

'Trouble at school?'

'No.'

I sat, noticing his eyes never left the flickering screen. 'A word of advice. The bigger they are, the harder they fall.'

'Right, Dad.'

'You know what I'm saying?'

'I guess.'

'Don't let anyone mess with you, Guy. They don't give up. It never stops.'

'I'm OK, Dad, really.'

'I just wanted to say that, that's all.'

'Thanks.'

'Right.' I hesitated, wanting to do something tactile, but couldn't. He visibly relaxed when I rose and left the room.

Upstairs, into the darkened bedroom. Complete heavy silence. I stood silhouetted by the hall light. 'Hi, J.'

'Hello, love. Couldn't wait up any longer, I'm so tired.'

'Not the only one.'

'Come to bed, then.'

'I stink. Need a shower.'

She yawned. 'Did you see your friend?'

Moira. 'Yeah.'

'He scared the life out of Guy.'

'He's sorry about that.'

'Are you finished with all this stuff now? Did you find what you were looking for?'

'That. And some other stuff. J?'

'What?'

'After I've showered . . . will you just hold me?'

And she did.

33

January, 1947

In the way of all 'secrets', Joseph Rattigan's 'arrangement' with Sergeant John Templar was beginning to take on water. For six months, the Wednesday-afternoon trysts had carried on with almost clockwork precision. Templar's shift system allowed him the time off after finishing his morning beat, whereupon he'd make his way round to the Rattigans', letting himself in through the back door in order to access his perverted desires waiting forlornly inside. Mary Rattigan had already left the dilapidated terrace at around one to visit her sick mother in Forest Hill, apparently unaware of the lurid games being played out on her 'wayward' son.

All went well, right up until Christmas. But by all accounts Joseph Rattigan had begun to drink more heavily, and one can only wonder at the depths his friendship with Templar must have sunk to in order that he sanction Frank's abuse. Maybe the twisted mind of the fat paeodophile was more intelligent than Joseph's, more powerful, persuasive. Maybe Templar really did have the influence to turn his informer in, deliver him to those he had shopped. Unfortunately, we'll never know, as that one vital part of Frank Rattigan's past lies rotting inside an unmarked grave within the confines of Wandsworth Jail.

Christmas '46, was among the best the Rattigans had ever enjoyed. Theirs was the only house to enjoy roast turkey with all the trimmings. Jealous, gossiping neighbours suspected Mary Rattigan had a 'thing' with Mr Dodget, local butcher. How else could she have got her hands on such a prime bird? If only they knew . . .

One Wednesday, mid-January, Elaine Rattigan, then fourteen, called home early after school and was surprised to find her father in the kitchen, drinking heavily and obviously crying. There were strange noises, too, from the back room. Frank's voice, she was sure of it, and a man, grunting. Uncle John, giving her tearaway brother another strapping?

Joseph looked up in shock as she walked through the back door. 'Ellie . . . ?'

'It's too cold to play outside, Dad. Mum said I should peel the spuds before she gets back.'

He quickly began searching through his torn overcoat, spilling pennies on to the wooden kitchen table. 'Do me a favour, love,' he announced in a loud slur. 'Pop down the baker's for a loaf.'

'Can't, Dad,' she replied, listening to the muted noise next door. It seemed to stop suddenly. Very peculiar. 'Already used the coupon for this week.'

'No, no,' Joseph insisted, marching her swiftly towards the back door. 'Knock twice at the back. Fella called Mark'll let you in. Just give him the money, he'll slip you a loaf. Go on, girl, go on.'

His bloodshot panicked eyes unnerved her. 'Was that Frank in there?'

'No.'

'Sounded like him.'

'Quickly, love, before they shut.'

'Is Uncle John beating him again? What's the little sod done this time?'

Joseph ran dirty fingers through greasy hair. 'He's . . . well, he's . . . just been bad again.' He tried a smile, felt the choking bubble claw at the back of his throat. 'You know Frank. Always needs a firm hand.'

And she did, had to share a room with her brother, listen to his disgusting lies, tales told late at night as they lay in the freezing black, dirty whispered fiction of what the good policeman, kind Uncle John was doing on Wednesday afternoons. She hated Frank, despised the lying little sod. Uncle John was a nice man, a good man, prepared to help the family, administer the punishment her own father couldn't turn his hand to. And there was nothing wrong in that, was there? Mum certainly didn't mind, Dad was out most of the time – it made sense that Uncle John, as a policeman, disciplined her brother. Not that it seemed to make any difference. If anything, his behaviour, his twisted erotic inventions got even worse. Frank was turning really bad.

Maybe Dad was to blame. Ellie was all for him handing over the punishment duties to his good friend, saw the practicalities of the arrangement, but what she disagreed with was that Dad always seemed to have a lollipop for the chastened boy afterwards. Not that the ungrateful git ever bothered eating them. Just put them in a battered shoebox under his bed. She'd counted them – twenty-seven so far, congealed, untouched. It was crazy, like Dad was condoning his behaviour, rewarding him. She didn't understand, but ultimately it was none of her business. Ellie just got on, helped her mother as much as she could, went to school, divorced herself from Frank and his behaviour. Besides, in a few years, she'd most likely marry, move out, share her room with someone she loved, someone clean. That would be nice.

Summer, the following year, Frank would have been eight at the time, truanting, getting into trouble, earning his reputation as the local tearaway. He developed a friendship with another boy from the next street, Mark Profit, two years his junior, and together the two of them would run riot around the poverty-stricken streets of the East End. One afternoon, Mathew Profit, Mark's big brother, a strapping lad of fourteen was sent by his distraught parents to find their son. He made straight for the local allotments, where an army of unemployed ex-servicemen toiled over tiny rectangles of broken ground to supplement their meagre rations with tatty cabbages, onions and potatoes.

He found the boys in one of the sheds. Frank had his penis in Mark Profit's mouth. A fight broke out, during which Mathew was beaten senseless by Frank, who never bothered even pulling his trousers up.

Later that night, John Profit, father to both boys, called

round. Elaine Rattigan remembers the terrible scene. Her father, drunk as usual, was slapped about by the irate, disgusted Mr Profit in the hallway. Her mother screamed abuse as the larger man piled into her ineffective husband, leaving him slumped and bleeding. It was all the confirmation young Ellie needed. Frank was a queer, a liar, and an evil little cheat. She asked if Frank could sleep downstairs, but her mother wouldn't hear of any of it.

'Folk say a lot of things about us behind our backs, Ellie. You'll just have to get used to that.'

'But, Mum . . .'

'Hush! None of it! There's them out there that don't know nothing. Your father does his best to get us a few extra bits and pieces. Does better than most of them. He's a good man, by the by. But these is hard times, it makes stupid folk livid. Causes their minds to invent ungodly lies. Mind you pay 'em no heed. Frank's a handful, but a good lad underneath. He'd never do nothing like that.'

'But, Mum, the stuff he tells me about Uncle John . . .'

'You just be grateful for what the good Lord provides, Ellie. Let's have no more of this.'

Which made Elaine wonder, many years later, how much her mother really knew about what went on on Wednesday afternoons, and the real cost placed on a tin of black-market pineapple chunks.

One can only wonder, too, at the rapidly developing confusion in Frank Rattigan's young mind. The initiation into the adult world of secrets and sex. The need to experiment with friends, share his forbidden knowledge gained from a policeman, approved by his father – surely it couldn't be wrong in any way?

Perhaps there was a pointer in the dusty box of uneaten lollipops Elaine Rattigan so vividly remembered. The wages of sin even a hungry little boy couldn't swallow.

Yet I'm certain Frank found some sort of incredible strength from the confusion, a rage exploding from within. How an eight-year-old boy could brutally beat a lad almost twice his age astonishes me. Yet, according to Elaine, Mathew Profit always avoided Frank from that moment on.

34

January 15th, 1949

Another wet Wednesday afternoon.

Frank Rattigan, now eight, made his way slowly back home, timing his retreat from truancy, using the back alleys, whistling quietly, spying a cat, wondering what sort of noise it would make if he . . .

Because he *could* do that – inflict pain at will. A small chunky boy, his stout frame housed a growing strength, fuelled by raw anger, growing daily in its capacity to hurt. The other boys, those his own age, kept clear, heeded the local rumours and whispered street warnings. Frank 'did' people, but never knew why it felt *so good*. Never stopped to analyse, punching one more time, experimenting with blows, choosing shots, picking targets, improving . . .

Maybe he'd see a group of them, dodging between houses, signalling the chase. He'd be after them. Instant response. Animal. No mercy. He lived for those times. Just him. Against them. The simplest of all human equations – he was 'bad'. Therefore given licence to be 'bad'. Expected, really.

So word got round. They'd sometimes plan, wait for him. A silent huddle of older boys, revved, ready. Which Frank relished. Another tear-up.

And always the same end result – Frank had a pocket-ful of useful allies, butterfly-knife, razor, snooker ball in an old sock. His chaos reigned supreme. He took on three of them once, older boys, about fifteen – and swiftly cut his way from their half-hearted effort. Eight years old, and Frank Rattigan reckoned he owned the world, took what he wanted, did as he pleased – except on Wednesday afternoons.

It was better now that his father didn't come home midweek. He told Frank he didn't need to be there, that the boy could handle it himself. Just the two of them – Frank and Uncle John, fucking in the back room. Oh, yes, Uncle John had taught him a whole new vocabulary. Weird words for what they did for food, Dad's freedom. It was like they were a team, Frank mused. Dad got the treats, he payed the price. Not that it cost much. And it felt great to be taken into such confidence by grown-ups. None of the other kids knew how to get ham.

Five past three, Frank had been waiting for nine minutes, trying to relax, like Uncle John taught him. There were all sorts of tricks, secret tips. A dab of grease, the slight shift of ageing thighs under young buttocks . . . Just look at the lady . . . Don't look at me! It was the only time Uncle John seemed to get angry these days, and Frank well remembered the damage inflicted by the big policeman's temper. But he didn't get strapped any more, Uncle John's methods had changed. Now they kissed, tongues colliding in a drizzle of spittle, smothered moans in the darkened back room.

Yet, all the while, somewhere further back, in a recess hidden deep inside Frank's mind, something screamed . . . and screamed . . . and screamed.

But it wasn't a problem. Frank crushed the primitive objection – by crushing others.

Ten past. The back door opened. Laughter outside. Frank's bowels loosened a little, the screaming started . . .

There were two of them this time. Uncle John and a younger man, staring at him. The smell of stale drink mingled with the kitchen's own noxious odour of the ever-boiling black-market ham. A sweet piggy, clinging damp, lined the cold walls.

Frank stood, unsure. He looked to Sergeant Templar for an explanation. No games that afternoon? No grown-up business next door?

Templar turned to the younger man, swaying slightly. 'See what I mean? Regular little chicken, ain't he?'

The other nodded eagerly. 'Perfect.'

Templar began caressing Frank's cheek. 'This is my friend, Frank. He's called John, too. I want you to be nice to him.'

'Hello, Frank,' PC Scrimshaw added. 'Your Uncle John's told me all about you. What a good boy you are.'

Something was wrong. Frank began to object. The screaming grew louder . . .

Elaine Rattigan also felt sick that afternoon. Violently sick. Unfortunately for her, the stomach-churning incident occurred as she tried to fit an old lady for a pair of winter boots at Tilly's Shoes. Mr Compton, manager, tried his best to calm the horrified customer, but it was obvious to Elaine that her career prospects lay in the same vomity ruins as the thick heap of sick on the shop floor. Stuff it. She hated the job anyway, and finding another wouldn't be too difficult. She was sixteen, attractive, willing to work hard.

She walked home, suddenly elated in post-nauseous relief. No more feet. No more bunions, sweaty socks, blackened toenails, blistered heels poking through torn stockings . . . she was beginning to feel sick again. And, oh God, it was a bloody Wednesday afternoon! Can't go home to bed . . . don't want to lie there, listening to . . .

Because deep inside, at sixteen, she knew. Couldn't swallow the ham, cheese and bacon Dad brought home. Couldn't meet his eye. When was this goddamned rationing going to end? How much longer did the world have to wait for food? The war ended four years ago – yet still they queued – still Dad did his 'deals' – still Uncle John 'disciplined' her brother.

She couldn't pinpoint when the awful truth first started to dawn. Maybe it had its dreadful beginnings in her own encounters with local lads. Nature had ensured Elaine Rattigan was a sought-after sixteen-year-old, leading her trembling into a secret world of snatched kisses and frantic adolescent fumbling. And it was here, in freezing back alleys, that Frank's lurid descriptions of the aroused male member concurred exactly with the hot straining organs she held in her own hand. Everything was as he'd described, the smell of spurting semen, looks on their faces, pressure of their hands on her budding breasts at orgasm. Just like Frank had said, exact testimony to the truth and confusion lying in the congealing box of lollipops under his bed.

Secrets, secrets, secrets . . . Children could never keep them. Frank had confided in her, not realizing how his revelations would appal. But it was too much to face. She wouldn't believe it of her own father. Couldn't be true. Not Uncle John. He just . . . disciplined the boy, her errant brother. And for God's sake, the whole neighbourhood knew what bad news the little basket was. Couldn't be true . . . couldn't . . . couldn't . . .

Bide your time, Ellie, she told herself. Another couple of years, three at the most, then marriage, ticket out, away from the madness. Think of Mum, the pain it would cause her. Think of Mum . . .

And above all else, stay away Wednesday afternoons. Frank's bad. Deserves his punishment. Two more years, three at the most . . .

But the nausea wouldn't subside. She weakened with every step, had to lie down, feel the reassuring warmth of her own bed.

Two minutes later she walked in the back door, tiptoeing, praying for silence. But she heard them. Moaning from the back room. The obscene slap of flesh on flesh. Grunts, groans, muttered perversities . . . and somewhere in the cheap ecstasy she heard Frank, his voice louder than the others.

She continued past the back-room door, relief flooding in as she reached the stairs. Then ascended, step by step, away from . . .

Others?

There was another voice, shrill, competing with Uncle John's and her bad brother. Younger. More urgent.

Just get up the stairs, Ellie, she told herself. Climb into bed. Pull the blanket over your head, block it out. You're ill, not hearing right. Mind's playing tricks. Get some sleep. Ignore it, it'll go away . . .

Some time later she woke from half-sleep, jolted by a commotion downstairs. Another shout, abuse, repeated. Dad!

He's home! She pulled the coarse blanket tighter over her head, curled into a crying ball, trying in vain to block it out.

More voices as Uncle John shouted back. Then the stranger began to swear, too. Frank cried. Furniture began scraping. A loud crash. Uncle John said something indistinct. Her father swore back. Another crash. A moan. More shouts. Then the back door slammed shut.

Silence.

Ellie strained to hear beyond her own pounding heartbeat. A minute passed before she threw the suffocating blanket off and listened to the distant sobs. Dad?

She waited another five minutes before walking downstairs. The sobbing increased as she hesitated by the back-room door. Then opened it.

Dad and Frank lay in each other's arms and she watched in silence as he covered the side of his naked son's unforgiving face in kisses.

'Sorry,' he said, over and over, lip cut, bleeding. 'I'm so sorry.'

Frank saw his sister, just stared right back, face a blank.

She closed the door.

Nine hours later, Joseph Rattigan was arrested for the murder of PC John Scrimshaw. During his trial, he would refuse both to take the stand, and to give any substantial reason why he killed the upstanding young policeman.

He was convicted of a drunken assault, and paid the ultimate price. Court commentators at the time were baffled at Rattigan's reluctance to offer any form of defence that might have saved him from the inevitable death sentence.

'Whatever circumstances prevailed on that January night,' wrote one. 'Joseph Rattigan took his secret to the grave. However, I would suggest that it is better for our emerging society to remember the loss of a law-abiding officer, than the petty motives of a murdering felon.'

35

(Edited transcript of interview recorded with Jimmy Rattigan, Elaine and Richard Horton – Manchester, October, '97.)

(Thirty-three minutes.)

A.R.: But you knew, didn't you, Ellie? Knew what was happening in the back room?

ELAINE: It was just so sick. What if Mum found out? How could I tell her, after what had happened to Dad? She was already destroyed. They wouldn't even let us bury him.

A.R.: And you never once talked to her about Wednesday afternoons?

ELAINE: (long pause): I think perhaps . . . she already knew. Maybe it was simply better for her to be out, away from whatever was going on. You have to remember, we weren't the only ones cutting deals. The whole of the East End was at it, scraping around for extras, buying in on the black market. But we were doing better than most. We had a joint of meat most weeks, fresh fruit . . . oh God! . . .

A.R.: And Templar? After your father was hung?

ELAINE: He began making overtures towards Mum. She clung on. Considered herself lucky, I suppose. Or perhaps she no longer cared. She'd loved and lost. Maybe she thought she deserved Uncle John. Christ, I don't know.

I suppose that deep down I was just glad he didn't . . . play any games with me. You know? Can you understand that? I was terrified he'd . . . start on me.

A.R.: But he kept seeing Frank?

234

ELAINE: People like that don't change, do they? He had a way, a manner of using his importance. Threatening us with imaginary power. And we were only kids, knew nothing. Except that the police could take your parents away and . . .

A.R.: But it didn't just stop with Frank, did it?

JIMMY: He soon tired of darling Frankie. Started losing his boyhood looks, see? Dad liked 'em young. I remember . . .

ELAINE: Jimmy, don't. Please. Don't.

JIMMY: How much longer can we sit on this, eh? How much longer are you going to play at being Mum, keeping me off me head, so's I won't bring it all up? Eh?

You left me with him. You knew what he'd done to Frank, and you went and left me with him. I hated you for that.

ELAINE: Oh, and God, haven't I paid the price since then? Richard and I, we've done everything for you. Richard's nearly lost his business three times sorting you your . . . stuff. How much longer are you going to make me suffer for something that happened years ago?

A.R.: How old were you, Jimmy? When it first started?

JIMMY: Couldn't tell you, pal. Fuck knows. Tell you one thing though . . . (begins to chuckle) . . . Dad used to make Frank shave all his pubes off. I guess he would have been about fifteen at the time. Big young lad he was, though, I can tell you. Hard as nails. But in that room . . . when Dad took us in there . . . it was as if all the power left his body. He just collapsed, sort of. And Dad, well, he'd make Frank speak in this high-pitched sort of kid's voice. His was breaking at the time, and Dad obviously didn't find it a turn-on. Not that he used to fuck Frank that much any more. He had me now, didn't he?

ELAINE: Jimmy, you don't have to . . .

JIMMY: I remember Frank would be kneeling at Dad's feet, holding me hands. 'Look at the lady, Jimmy,' he'd say, as I'd be sat on Dad's lap, facing the wall. We had this picture, see. Sort of Spanish lady effort my real dad had nicked from somewhere. Long black hair, red carnation by her ear, huge eyelashes, cleavage. 'Look at the lady,' he'd say. And Dad'd be underneath doing whatever . . .

ELAINE: I'm just so sorry, Jimmy. I . . .

JIMMY: Know what I used to think? Frank cared more'n you did. At least he used to hang around for me. After you and him had left home. Meet me from school, try and walk me home or something. Big, flash geezer he was by this time, all sharp suits and dolly birds.

But I hated him. Every fuckin' ounce of the two-faced cunt. He weren't no hard man. 'Cause he couldn't deal with my dad, couldn't face him out. The only human being on earth who ever deserved a fraction of Frank's violence – and he got away with it, never got so much as a slap. So he took it out on any poor sod who came his way.

I reckon that's Frank's only regret. That he never topped me dad. I know it's mine.

A.R.: When . . . did the abuse stop?

JIMMY: When I was about seven or eight, I suppose. He was getting old. Libido was dropping, I don't know. He used to beat me instead, then make me tell Mum I was a filthy liar, that everything I said was a lie, all sorts of weird stuff.

Then, about that time, Mum tells me about . . . my biological father. She gets all these articles out, photos of him, and it's like my whole world collapses. Too young, see? Too young to be told. But I guess she thought I was going the same way Frank was – a nut-job. Reckon she wanted to scare the shit out of me or something.

But it was too much for a kid to take on board. I mean, I'd known Templar wasn't my real father, that weren't no family secret. But whenever I asked about him, they all told me he'd gone away. No one had ever mentioned the murder, or the hanging. Not Frank, not Ellie, no one. Too ashamed, I guess. Or protecting me in some way, perhaps. I'd heard stuff, of course, bits of horror stories from local kids about someone in the family being strung up. But that was just kids. We was all at it, winding each other up. I never paid none of it no attention. I had a mum and a dad, and was vaguely aware he weren't the same father to Frank and Ellie. Never thought no more about it, really, till that day.

A.R.: It must have come as quite a shock.

JIMMY: All I know for sure is when I sat there, pouring over this stuff, with Mum crying and pointing at pictures of him, I'd never felt so alone in my life.

See, up till then, there was always a chance he'd come knocking at the door one day. I'd sort of imagined it, my private fantasy. Stupid, really. But I was only a kid. And suddenly it wasn't going to happen any more. He was dead.

A.R.: After your mother told you – did you talk to Frank and Ellie about it?

JIMMY: Couldn't.

A.R.: But surely, after all that time thinking . . .

JIMMY: I didn't want to hear it from anyone else. Would've confirmed it, you see? I had to block it out, pretend the conversation had never happened, forget the face staring out of the old newspaper. It was easier to pick up the fantasy again, race to the front door at every knock, praying one day he'd be there for me.

Strange, ain't it, how we cope with stuff we just can't handle?

A.R.: And during all this time, you never once told your mother about Templar's abuse?

JIMMY: Would have been just as pointless. Dad had got her convinced I was a liar. So I bided my time, went with it. Dad kept on getting promoted, we moved to a bigger house. Eventually I grew too big for him to bend over his knee.

And the worst part was that all the flaming neighbours worshipped the bastard. Local hero, my dad was. Chief Superintendent John Templar. Pillar of the fucking community. Joke, ain't it?

A.R.: And when you left home?

JIMMY: Took my chances on the streets. Made a few bob.

Have to thank the old man for that. Given me a skill, you see? Got to fifteen, mid-sixties it must've been, and I was selling my arse for a living.

A.R.: And did you see much of Frank?

JIMMY (laughs): Never really set eyes on the mad prick. Hated him. Whole of the East End's saying what a tough bloke Frank was, but I knew he'd had it the same as me. Fucked up the arse from the year dot.

I became one of them . . . what d'you call 'em? . . . rent boys, I suppose. Trading it in for a bed, food, booze, any shit'd make me forget. Drugs was an easy way out. Some of the wogs were starting a line in blow, home-grown grass. I went for it. Sort of spiralled from there.

ELAINE: Jimmy, that's enough talk for now.

JIMMY: Please, Ellie, it's time, eh? All these years we've never really talked about what that fat shit done to us. And I couldn't give a toss if Mum knew or not. She's gone, dead.

But here we all are. Just about scraping by. Doing time for his crimes. I was a kid, for Christ's sake!

I want help. Counselling. I ain't stupid. The smack's gonna kill me, sis. But I can't kick the bastard till I've sorted the past. I can't. And you can't carry on sorting all me gear for me. Fuck's sake, you ain't no dealers. Look what happened to the hostess . . .

ELAINE: Jimmy . . . No! Not now!

A.R.: Helen Lewis?

JIMMY: Poor kid died for me – my habit.

ELAINE: Frank butchered her. It was nothing to do with you. Nothing!

(Long silence.)

JIMMY (begins to laugh): Talking of Frank, listen to this. 'Bout seventeen, I was. Selling my tail, getting high. Car pulls up one night as I wiggles down Elephant and Castle. Flash, it was, Daimler or something. Anyway, window rolls down.

Heavy-looking geezer asks me how much for an all-nighter up West. Apparently he'd got a mate who'd just done a stretch and needed some boy-fun. We drive up to Holland Park somewhere. I had about three joints in the car. Stoned as a dozen Keith Richards, I was.

When we arrive, the motor slinks off. It's like a palace in there, only there's all these heavy-looking types pissed up, lying around the place, few birds, coke on the table. I'm thinking, shit – do I really want to be here? – when suddenly, I'm sent upstairs to 'do the business'.

The room's dark. Pitch-black. I can't see nobody. I'm beginning to panic, reckon I've been well set up, when suddenly I hear this familiar voice. 'Get undressed,' it says. 'Don't look at me. Come over here. Sit on my lap and look at the lady.'

A.R.: Frank?

JIMMY: Large as life. Couldn't think straight. Felt as if me whole head was going to explode. And all the time he's telling me to . . . do stuff, you know. Just couldn't handle it, couldn't face it. Turned the light on. Saw him, sitting in this fuckin' armchair, bollock-naked and . . . just couldn't handle it.

A.R.: What happened?

JIMMY: We just . . . looked at each other. He was half shocked, half . . . I don't know . . . sort of dead. I went downstairs. Split as soon as I could.

He got done for turning over a nigger-dealer that night. Real damage, nearly killed the bloke. Got three fuckin' years. Dad died while he was inside. It was the only time I ever saw him again. A great time. Revenge – sitting there across from him, telling him his Uncle John, my Dad, had passed away peacefully in his sleep.

God had done it, you see? Finally rid the world of me dad. Not big hard Frank. God got bored of waiting. Gave him a well-deserved heart attack.

And you know what the biggest joke is? They give the evil shit a ceremonial burial. Full poxy honours deal. Loads of coppers all dolled up in their finest, spouting off about what a top bloke good old John Templar had been.

I came up north. Found Ellie.

She looks after me, now.

Frank's no one. I'm sorry he did for the girl. Really sorry. And maybe that's my fault. Fuck – I don't know. But he could have ended it for me – he could have knifed that dirty fucking father I had. But he never.

All he did was hold my hands.

A.R.: Richard . . . I need to ask you something. It's important.

HORTON: Christ, haven't you asked enough?

A.R.: You're a good man. A better bloke than I am. Much better, believe me.

HORTON: We've answered your questions. It's time you were leaving.

A.R.: You marry Ellie, and Jimmy comes too, doesn't he? But you accept him, take him in, because you love your wife. It's wonderful. I couldn't do it. True love.

HORTON: Fine. Finished now? Only we have to leave. You've set a bloody journalist on to us, remember? Walked into our lives, turned them upside down . . .

A.R.: The money you gave Frank that day at the fruit farm in Suffolk. That was for drugs, wasn't it?

HORTON: I'm asking you to leave – politely.

A.R.: Why give Frank all that money? A grand?

HORTON: It's none of your business. Now . . .

A.R.: I know it was your car – the green Jag. Has to be drugs, doesn't it? I mean, you're the man who keeps Jimmy supplied with grade-A heroin.

ELAINE: We were having a problem . . .

HORTON: Ellie! . . . No!

ELAINE (sighing): Maybe Jimmy's right, love. Maybe it's time we all faced up to this.

HORTON: I don't believe you're saying this! Now . . . after all this time? He's just a bloody student, for Christ's sake!

ELAINE: But it never goes away, does it? It's all still fresh as yesterday. (Long pause.)

We'd been having problems with our regular guy. The police had arrested him, and finding another reputable dealer was nigh on impossible. Jimmy was getting withdrawals and we were forced . . . well, Richard was forced, to try and score whatever he could, wherever. It was hopeless. We're not drug dealers, Mr Rawlings. Our contact was inside, we were in big trouble.

I'd always tried to control Jimmy's habit, only feeding him quality. Richard had 'a friend of a friend' who was a chemist, said he could ensure the heroin he sold us wasn't laced.

Richard set about finding a different dealer. Imagine that? A respectable businessman touring the streets for a damn drug dealer? I'm sorry, love, so, so sorry. None of it's your fault. None of it. (Begins to cry.) Anyway, there was nothing doing. We were out of our depth. Then we got word from one of the chemist's friends that he was still in business, albeit by proxy from a cell in Strangeways.

We were desperate. We had Jimmy practically prisoner in the house, ranting and raving. It got so bad, we had to hide all the knives, tie him to his bed. And we couldn't call a doctor, because we were so frightened it'd all come out – everything.

Anyway, Richard finally got word that one of the chemist's former girlfriends was bringing some heroin back from Hamburg later that week.

A.R.: Helen Lewis?

ELAINE: But even then, we were too terrified to go to London and collect it. What if it was a trap, and there would be a gang waiting to mug us for the money?

A.R.: So you got Frank to check it out?

ELAINE: He used to ring when he could, checking on Jimmy, sending odd bits of cash every now and then. A fiver one month, tenner the next. Pathetic, but I suppose it was all he could manage, what with him being on the streets. A sort of thought-that-counts thing, as if he almost cared in a way.

Anyway, he said he'd collect the gear for us. Told us where to find him. Stephen went to the farm and gave him the money.

And that was it. That was all we ever did, Mr Rawlings.

A.R.: And then?

HORTON: Then what? I can't believe you're asking us that! Jesus Christ, you've met the fucking man! He upped and off with the money, then went totally off his fucking head! First we hear of it is that the psychotic bastard's been arrested for murder!

ELAINE: Please, love. Calm down. It's all right.

A few days later a package arrived in the post. The stupid sod had mailed the drugs to us, done his bit. It sounds so completely heartless, but I was just so glad to finally get Jimmy high again, end the withdrawals.

Pretty soon after, we heard what he'd done, read it in the papers. We just couldn't believe it, it was just ghastly. We didn't know what to do, just sat and waited for the knock on the door. It never came. Frank hadn't told the police about our involvement. The weeks went on. The closest it came was when we heard on the news that they were hunting for a green Jaguar. We had it scrapped.

Then, the trial. Still nothing. Frank was . . . you know . . . confirmed as insane . . . we were in the clear. Richard had managed to find a new dealer. Local chap. That's some irony, isn't it, Mr Rawlings? All the trouble we went to, and the perfect supplier was less than four streets away. Respectable house, too. Just goes to show, you never can tell, eh?

But even to this day . . . I still hate to think of what Frank did to that girl. What we started. I simply can't stand to wonder about it, how she suffered like that. But I do. A lot of the time, I'm afraid.

Believe me, Mr Rawlings, it still haunts me every goddamned day.

36

Disinfectant. Pine Fresh. Dettol, maybe.

Floor polish, rubber soles squeaking on its brilliant, unyielding surface, heralding my anxious arrival.

And music, piped from God knows where . . .

RECREATION SIX – again. The two of us outside – me carrying her, under wraps. My briefcase was searched, then my body, for the third time in as many minutes, a familiar routine of rough hands frisking intimate places.

And behind the door, he waited . . .

It was the Monday after the trip to Manchester. During the weekend, I'd tried to blend back into the family with shopping trips to Tesco's, meals out and a trip to the cinema. But I simply couldn't relax – Monday beckoned, and my last scheduled meeting with Rattigan was never far from my mind.

Two forty-five, and I walked into the room. Rattigan acknowledged me with a slight smile. I quickly put the cigarettes on the table, then briefcase and my silent guest on the floor behind. I sat in the usual bucket-seat, watching Millar from the corner of one eye. He gave nothing away.

Rattigan reached for the cigarettes. I placed the micro-cassette between us. He smiled again. I took two deep breaths. Somewhere close, someone screamed. Then silence. It was up to me to start it.

'Afternoon, Frank.'

'Apparently.'

'It wasn't a question.'

'Makes a change.' The puffy lips curled in momentary sarcasm, glistening in the cold, bare room.

'Slight change in the routine today, Frank.'

'How . . . exciting.'

'Just my questions to answer.'

'Can't wait.' He lit up, exhaling venomously towards Millar. Then said to him, 'Can't wait, can we, eh?'

'So,' I said, taking another deep breath in order that I might get my thoughts in order. 'Perhaps I should start by telling you I've been away.'

'Not got much of a fucking suntan.'

'Wasn't a holiday, Frank. I went to Manchester.'

No reaction from the buggered-boy Beast.

'I went to see your sister.'

He began to applaud, slowly, menacingly.

'Had to, really, didn't I? After your insistence that she knew nothing. Too strong, wasn't it?'

He waited a few beats. Rubbed his leathery nose. 'You've changed.'

'A lot's changed.'

'Ellie talks a lot of shit. Got herself hitched up there with some toy boy, lives in a big, posh house, bored out of her mind most days. Invents stuff. S'how she's always been.'

'And Jimmy?'

A slight twitch of the jaw. Another deep drag. 'Jimmy's fucked up.'

'Runs in the family, does it? I mean, your father was hardly . . . average, was he?'

'He was a mug.'

'And Uncle John? John Templar?'

'Some toerag my whore mother took up with.'

I nodded, mentally timing the pause. 'So how did it feel, Frank? You and Templar?'

Millar's eyes darted between both players.

Rattigan shrugged, passed the buck back to me.

'He used to rape you, didn't he? He had a hold on your father. You were used as a human bargaining chip. He sodomized you every week while your mother was away seeing relatives.'

A wicked smile. 'Had a fall up there, did you? Bang your head, fat-boy?'

'Ellie told me, Frank. She knew.'

'Then she strung you a line, didn't she?'

'Must have been hard,' I said. 'Especially when Templar turned his attentions on young Jimmy. You do remember that, don't you, Frank? Jimmy certainly does. The whole experience turned him into a useless junkie. Ellie does her best to look after him now. But you know all that, don't you? Know how Jimmy Smack needs his fix to run from the past. You've even tried to help once or twice, haven't you, eh? Sorting some grade-A for your little brother.'

'This is better than fucking *Jackanory*! They led you a right little dance, didn't they?'

'They're sorting it out, Frank. Or trying to. Not that it's going to be easy . . .'

'You're breaking my heart.'

'Maybe the real tragedy about your case is that it needn't have happened. But history placed you there, created those needs, the bizarre arrangements made by your dad and Templar in order to . . .'

A second twitch of the jaw. Rattigan stubbed out his cigarette. 'Know what I think, you deluded little wanker? I reckon you should spend a bit more time in here. Sort your mind out. You've got too many filthy fantasies locked away in there.'

'You were buggered from an early age. So was your brother. What was it you used to do, while Templar raped him? Hold his hands. You – the East End hard man, local wide boy, street-fighting Frank Rattigan – why did you have to do that, Frank? Hold his hands? Is that the only way he'd sit still as . . .'

Rattigan – to Millar – 'I ain't going to listen to this crap all day!' He stood.

Millar. 'Sit down and shut it!'

A long silence. He wavered. Then slowly turned to me, smiled, blew me a kiss, took a bow, sat, then lit up again. 'Shit. I'm having fun here. Go on, entertain me.'

'Everyone failed you, didn't they, Frank?'

'If you insist.' Sniggering.

'Nowadays, maybe there'd be social workers who'd look into your case. Perhaps the school would alert the authorities. But back then, the world didn't have time for one badly behaved boy, it was too busy trying to right itself after the war.'

'Fucking history lesson an' all, is it?'

'And the grown-ups were so cunning, weren't they, Frank? Pushing all that responsibility on to you.'

His tone changed, darker, lower. He pointed a fat finger, stabbing at each word. 'People have died for saying less than you did.'

'Like Helen Lewis, Frank? But I doubt she had the chance to say anything.'

'Expert now, are you? Expert on death?'

'I know enough to suspect that it could never be purely "fun", Frank. Bit of a buzz at the time, oh yeah. Nice coarsing adrenaline rush. But it doesn't last. Not three days. Other stuff starts getting in the way. Remorse, for instance. Helen Lewis's death was never "fun". It was inevitable – a necessity. She was the past which didn't care, the face which wouldn't love you. Right?'

Rattigan's top lip began to curl. A metallic edge lined the voice. 'Listen to the shit you spout. I loved every fucking minute of doing the tart. Sometimes, late at night, I think about it, replay the best bits. Sweet fucking dreams, fat-boy.'

'I've heard it all before, Frank. The psycho act. But the point is, you aren't one. You're just some poor sap who went a little bit berserk. End of story. Forty years ago they would have hung you like your dad. Like father, like son. Losers, both.'

He leant back, chair creaking under his weight. 'Won't work, you know.'

'What's that?'

'This . . . goading thing. Trying to make me suddenly get all angry and confess.'

'Confess to what?'

'Reckon you're a right smug little bastard, don't you?'

'All that anger. Everyone you hit. They were all him, weren't they? Different guises of the one man – John Templar. You beat them because you were too afraid of him. Know what your brother says?'

'Couldn't give a shit.'

'He says that'll be your one regret. That you didn't have it in you to finish him off. That you bottled it.'

'Jimmy's brain is porridge.'

'Remember the last time you saw him?'

'Can't say I do.'

'He visited you in prison. Just after Templar died. It was about the time you decided to "go solo", quit the gangs, become a tramp.'

'Finished?'

'Why? You going to threaten to kill me again? Or my family, perhaps? Rape my wife and kids? It doesn't scare me any more, Frank. Because you don't. Prison-face or not, all I see is that little boy, trousers down, waiting for . . .'

'You're a very sick man.'

I shook my head, holding his glare, diffusing it, forcing it from my eyes. 'I couldn't work it out, Frank. And Christ, it really bugged me. Why the sudden turnaround? Then I realized. It was shame, wasn't it? Your own shame that you never had the guts to kill Templar, not even beat him up, or even aim one punch at his perverted face.'

'I ain't bottled from nobody! Ever!'

'It was because you *loved* him, wasn't it?'

'Fuck off!'

'He showed you kindness, didn't he? He cuddled you, whispered stuff, stroked your hair, caressed you, gave you sweets. I bet he made you tell him, didn't he? Tell me you love me, Frank. That what he said? Was it? And you did, didn't you? Little boy lost, hated by everyone. Except this man. The man you shared a grown-up secret with. The man you loved all his life until he died.'

'Bullshit!'

'He gave you the only bit of affection you had. But it was better than nothing, wasn't it? And that bit of you that knew it was wrong, grew to hate, fanatically hate everyone and everything. It grew because you grew. You changed, from boy to young man, lost your allure. Templar didn't want you so much. There was a new pretender to Templar's love – little Jimmy. That must have hurt, Frank.'

A sudden explosion of violence. A fist crashed down on to the table. 'He never fucking raped me!'

Millar tensed

'Ellie and Jimmy, they told me what happened. Shared a

room with her, didn't you, Frank? Late-night chats. Boasting, weren't you? Does strange things, young love, awakens all sorts of feelings. Had to tell someone, didn't you? That was Ellie, wasn't it?'

'She knows fuck-all.'

'Templar'd sit there, wouldn't he? In the gloom. Trousers down, ready. You'd kiss for a while, then you'd have to straddle his lap . . .'

'No!'

'Facing away, facing the wall. Facing the "lady". Remember the lady, Frank? The smiling señorita? Do you know why he made you do that, Frank? Because he couldn't stand to see your lovesick young face as he took you. He didn't want you to "love" him. He just wanted to use you, as *he* wished – not as you wanted. So he faced you away, simple as that.'

'No! He . . .'

'Loved you? I don't think so, Frank. He used you. And all the time, you had to look at the lady – denied his affection. Pretty as a picture? Your words, remember?'

'We're all flies.'

'Yeah, flies . . . buzz . . . buzz. Eating shit every day. So what? Change the record. You aren't mad. Or bad. The act doesn't work any more, Frank. You're just . . . sad. The little boy who never loved again.'

'Just don't get it, do you? Who's the saddest, eh? You with your filthy little theories, or me – laughing at every fucker who thinks they know?'

It was time to bring her in. I reached behind me, lifting her gently on to the table. Eighteen inches square, wrapped in brown paper. 'Talked a lot about "fun", haven't we, Frank? I thought it was about time I had some.' My fingers started on the top edge, shaking slightly as they found the end of the parcel tape. 'Brought along a visitor. Old friend of yours. All the way from Manchester.'

'So fucking what?'

The first piece of tape came off. 'Jimmy didn't have quite the regard that you had for Templar. Maybe the magic didn't work so well. Perhaps it had a lot to do with the fact that he had to call him "Dad". Must have been very traumatic. Having to keep it all a secret from Mum.'

Rattigan's piggy eyes were locked on to the package.

I started on the next strip of dark-grey tape, along the left-hand vertical edge. 'After your "whore" mother died, Ellie and Jimmy went through the house. Big place, it was; Templar had done well for himself. Ellie sold it, then auctioned all the stuff inside, used the money to help finance Jimmy's drug habit. But there was one thing Jimmy wouldn't sell. A reminder of the past he needed in order to keep his hate for you alive – the big brother who held his hands. Any guesses?'

'Get on with it, fat-boy. I'm getting fucking bored of the Perry Mason impression.'

I began peeling back the right-hand strip. 'He took it to his room in Ellie's house. Put it up on the wall. Kind of a therapy thing, I suppose. Needed it to confirm what had actually happened. He gave it to me, when he learned I was coming to see you. Sort of an early Christmas present. Kind of him, don't you think?' I began to work the last strip away from the paper.

'He ain't on my list.'

'You used to meet Jimmy from school, sometimes, didn't you? Take him back home, offer him up to your former lover as some sort of . . . present. That's how it was, wasn't it? Anything to please Templar.'

The final strip was off. I began unwrapping her, revealing the worn blank back, two pins, cotton stretched between. She lay face down.

'So,' I said brightly. 'Still denying it?'

'Every filthy word.'

'Fine. Then perhaps it's time to say "*Hola*" to an old friend.'

I lifted the picture from the desk, revealing her inch by inch, watching as Rattigan's pupils dilated in utter horror. Full face, I held her eighteen inches from his, confronting him with a red carnation, long black hair and the timeless smile which had forced him from the only man he had ever loved.

Rattigan exploded.

Millar was over in a second, pushing the panic button as Rattigan lunged for the picture. An alarm shrilled. Millar had an arm round Rattigan's throat. Saliva foamed from the Beast of

East 16, his face screwed into a painful comedy of raw anger. He swung for me, but I jumped back, still holding the Spanish lady.

'Look at the lady, Frank!' I said, unable to contain myself. 'See how she smiles!'

The door opened. Two more orderlies burst in to assist Millar, sitting on thrashing legs, kicking, injecting, swearing, bruising, containing.

Moments later, I sat back down, strangely empowered by the violence, glad to be the cause rather than the recipient. Rattigan was reseated, closely guarded, eyes already beginning to glaze from the tranquillizer.

I reached into my briefcase, brought out a page from Rattigan's file. A picture of a long-dead Welsh air hostess named Helen Lewis. Then silently placed it on the table, next to the smiling fifty-year-old señorita.

Someone had switched off the alarm. Silence descended again. Just heavy breathing. Then gradually everyone in the room looked at the astonishing resemblance between both pictures.

'Snap,' I said simply.

Rattigan's doped eyes met mine.

'You met Richard Horton at the fruit farm,' I said calmly. 'They couldn't find decent heroin for Jimmy, but they'd been given a name, a London address. You told them you would handle it. You set off. Horton had given you a time when Helen Lewis was due back at the house. The flight was delayed that day. I've checked with the airline. She was five hours late. You made your way to the house, then broke in.'

Rattigan's eyes began to close, lids descending, rooted to the two pictures. He shook his head several times, then turned back to me, finally began to falteringly tell it as it happened. 'Just wanted to help Jimmy get his gear. Horton had a big yellow streak, didn't have the bottle for it. Reckoned he'd be turned over. I said I'd collect. Drugs – shit, aren't they? I went. She weren't in. Waited for ever. Cold outside . . . so bloody cold. So I broke in . . . easy . . . just sat and waited.'

'But then you saw her picture, didn't you, Frank? Saw her in her uniform. That smile. That "look".'

He nodded.

'And as you sat waiting, you began to hate her, didn't you? A complete stranger you'd never even met. Simply because she looked exactly like the picture on the back wall all those years ago. The picture Templar made you stare at, the picture which denied you his love.'

Rattigan began to mumble, fighting sleep. 'Bitch deserved every fucking minute of it.'

'You never tortured her for money, did you, Frank? Or the drugs?'

'I got my own back. She had to pay.'

'But it was never "for fun", was it?'

'No. For me.'

'And afterwards, you found the heroin.'

'Small package in her flight bag. Posted it off to Ellie some time the next day. Then came back and minced the girl up. Terrible fucking job, that was.' He looked up, piggy eyes momentarily begging some sort of understanding. 'I couldn't help myself. All these feelings . . . Then when the filth arrived, I'd had a chance to think it over. Reckoned maybe they'd shit themselves if I started shooting off about . . . me Uncle John. It was all I had. Couldn't bear the thought of more prison.'

'So you struck a deal with the ACC?'

'Had to. Only chance, really. He went white as a sheet when I told him I'd run my mouth off in court about John fucking Templar and his thing with kids. They bought it. Guess they didn't want the papers telling the world what a filthy piece of shit their big "hands of a hero" copper was, even though the bastard was already six feet under.' He looked at me, struggling to focus. 'Guess that's how it is with reputations, eh? Earn yourself a good one, and the whole fucking world rallies round covering your dead arse. Different if you're labelled scum, though. I ended up here. Sort of worked out, until now.'

'I'm sorry, Frank,' I heard myself saying.

'You ain't sorry, fat-boy. Don't know the meaning of the word. Don't know . . .'

Then the last words I heard him say before he drifted into unconsciousness.

'We're . . . all . . . flies.'

37

Thirty minutes later, I found myself sitting in Neil Allen's office one final time. Slumped, exhausted, empty. Strange faces offered the occasional empty congratulation. Documents were proffered for me to sign, confidentiality agreements. I wearily put pen to paper, longing to be gone, to be home.

I refused a glass of wine.

When we were alone, Dr Allen sat down beside me, eyes fixed on his own glass of cheap white. 'Curiously flat feeling, isn't it?' he said eventually.

'Could say that,' I replied.

'I have this theory,' he went on. 'That our entire profession is peopled by men and women who invest too much time looking into the motives of others, rather than stopping to analyse themselves. A classic blocking tactic – unravel the mysterious workings of a really insane mind, and you never need ponder the darker workings of your own.'

'Maybe.'

'I've seen it over and over. Students, professors, nurses – all equally convinced they have an inside line on another's madness. Each seeks to rationalize the psychosis, normalize it, as they become totally absorbed in another human being. And then after, their own demons return. Until they stumble upon another unfortunate individual with his or her mental mess to be untangled.' He took a sip of wine. 'What will you do now? Now you've "solved" Rattigan?'

'Go home and sleep.'

'And after?'

'Sleep some more.'

He smiled. 'But eventually, you'll bore of the relaxation, Adrian. Something will drive you back to criminology. The thesis will be finished, awards bestowed. You'll bow to the lure of more mental puzzles, believe me.'

'Who knows?' I replied.

'I do.'

'What will happen to him?'

'Rattigan?'

'Now that he's most probably in the wrong place for the crime he committed?'

'Nothing.'

'Nothing?'

'He'll stay here, regardless of your discoveries. The state pays us handsomely to keep him here, whether he's a true sociopath or not. And between you and I, I'd rather have Rattigan in my care than someone else with a genuine psychosis.'

'Better the Beast you know, right?'

'Infinitely. And I dare say he'll be offered a new counselling programme, should he decide to take it. Child abuse, victim therapy, that sort of thing.'

'You know he'll never agree.'

'We can but try.'

'He'll most likely die here, won't he?'

'Who can say?' Allen finished his wine, stood, made for his desk. 'Now, if you'll excuse me, Adrian . . .'

I couldn't let him go before I'd asked one final thing. 'Why did you let me take the picture in to Rattigan this afternoon? Especially after the ticking-off you gave me when I showed him the magazines. Remember, no visual aids without prior clearance?'

He thought for a second. 'Because I had faith.'

'In me?'

He studied me carefully. 'I suspect you had a lot more invested in this than you'd be prepared to admit. Your dogged tenacity proved it in my mind. The research, trip to Manchester, all of it pointed to a man with an agenda, rather than a student after bolstering up his PhD. Then again' – he paused and smiled. I was almost beginning to like the man – 'I'm probably totally wrong.'

I flushed a little, stood. 'Dr Allen,' I asked awkwardly. 'I was listening to something on the radio the other day, and I wondered if you could help me with it?'

'Help you?'

'It was a news item,' I quickly pressed on. 'Apparently a group of football fans had set about someone after a game. They gave him quite a beating. Anyway, when the police finally managed to get to the guy, they found someone cowering close by. It was his son – who'd seen everything.'

'Well?'

'I just wondered . . . I mean, in your professional opinion, is that kid going to have a lot of problems later in life?'

'Why are you asking me?'

'Because it was one of those things you hear that just wouldn't go away. I just kept thinking of the boy, watching his father being set upon. Then wondering how the experience would change him. If at all.'

Allen shrugged. 'I really can't say. I don't know enough about the circumstances. Do you?'

'What?'

'Know any more about this boy? His father?'

'No.'

'Sure?'

'Absolutely.'

'And this "news item" – it's left you now, has it?'

'I think so.'

'Good.' He held out a hand. 'There are three billion people on this planet, Adrian. And a million different reasons why each of them does any one of a thousand things every day.'

I shook his hand.

He held it in his for a second. 'Just don't expect to make sense of any one of them – ever. Especially yourself.' He showed me to the door which led to the corridor which finally connected back to the outside world.

'Thanks,' I said simply.

'Enjoy your rest,' he replied, then closed the door.

I returned home, joined 'normality'. Ate, washed up, showered, shared the sofa with Jemimah as we watched television.

'It's finished,' I said, moving closer, feeling the warmth of her shoulder against mine.

'Good.'

We fell silent as the *Nine o' Clock News* began. Then the weather news, regional round-up.

'I don't know that I'm cut out for forensic psychiatry,' I said later, yawning.

She turned to me. 'Why the sudden change of heart?'

'I don't think I need it any more.'

A frown appeared. '"Need" it? Jesus, Adrian, it's a bloody career, not an addiction. You've studied for years to get this close, and now you're backing out?'

'Hell, it's been a long day, that's all.' I kissed her.

A familiar theme tune began – BBC's *Crimewatch*, all drums and whistles.

She disentangled herself gently. 'More bloody crime. It's just cheap TV, that's all. I'm turning in.'

'Yeah, but you'd love it if it had ad-breaks.'

'Don't be too long.'

But as she left the room, my world, my dreams of a new beginning, collapsed. I wasn't alone. Another smiling woman caught my eye from the television screen, beaming two-dimensionally, taking me back to a nightmare I'd tried hard to forget – a cindered car park in Manchester just four nights previously.

An unseen presenter's voice filled the room. '. . . sometime last Thursday night. Simone's body, however, wasn't discovered until Saturday morning hidden between a parked car and a wall at the back of the club she was thought to have used for picking up customers. Manchester Police tell us she died from severe head injuries . . .'

It was her. No mistake. And dead? The woman was dead? But that meant . . . oh, good God . . . please, no . . .

'. . . investigating officers are looking for a white male, around forty, to help with their . . .'

I scrabbled for the remote, dropping it twice in my haste to shut the damned thing off – shut it out of my life.

I'd killed her!

I sat stock-still in the warm silence of the room, both palms sweating, head light and dizzy. It couldn't be, surely? But I'd seen the photograph with my own eyes. Her face – brown skin, ruby-red lips, the same ones which had . . . just moments before I'd . . .

I never made it to bed that night. Went and checked on Jemimah, assured her I was OK, just suddenly interested in a late film which had just started. She took it well, turned over, settled herself for the night ahead. Minutes later, when I returned to switch off the bedside light, I was greeted by the innocent sound of deep sleep.

I checked too, on the children. Standing in their separate doorways, studying every inch of their young faces, lit by the landing light behind.

Then I sat downstairs in quiet darkness, planning what to do, what would be for the best. I couldn't stay where I was, not in the house. I had to get away, find some space to make sense of what I'd done – what I'd become.

I agonized for over an hour, before finally, silently, packing some clothes, papers, briefcase, and slipping out of the front door.

I cried as I drove away. But I can't remember who for.

38

In less than an hour, I stood on the brown earth cliffs of the east coast under an icy night sky, willing myself to jump. What was it Rattigan had said – make the leap?

The tide was turning, literally, way below my feet. The water seemed almost calmed, idly slopping as its black weight began slowly following the lunar pull of a new day.

I wished I'd left a note for Jemimah, a few scrambled words of explanation. But what would it have struggled to say? What words could go even halfway towards explaining what I'd done? Yet it tore deeply to think of her, still sleeping, unaware.

And inevitably, the longer I stood, the less likely it was I was going to end it. Suicide requires a desperate courage which had already failed me. Yet how could I go on? How long would it be before someone recognized the police description? Before I was charged, sentenced, for murder?

Perhaps the most crushing blow was the stupid bloody manner of it. A brief drunken kick. The girl and I must have both got very unlucky.

Yet according to the programme, she'd sustained severe head injuries then been dumped behind a car. Did I do all that too? I just recalled the one push, one kick. But then again, the loss of memory at the vital moment was chillingly familiar. Even to this day, I still can't actually remember hitting Jemimah – but I know I did, just can't find the mental replay.

And now I stood alongside Rattigan as a murderer in my own right. But it was worse, so much worse than that. Rattigan's crime was explainable; I was the fool who'd rationalized his madness – then gone and killed myself, for no real motive, no real reasons. I had none of Rattigan's abusive excuses. Adrian Rawlings had wanted for nothing, ever. Yet he'd still descended to the depths, got drunk and killed.

A psychiatrist might well suggest that I'd always had it coming, that the whisky only released an anger I'd spent a lifetime repressing, and that subconsciously, I needed to drink, in order to exorcize my own 'beast'. He'd most probably pour over my childhood, searching for telltale clues, just as I'd done with Rattigan. But his search would turn up nothing more extraordinary than a nine-year-old boy who once saw his dad get walloped by a few thugs way back when. Not motive enough, in my book.

However much I loathed Rattigan for what he'd done to Helen Lewis, I'd done worse – which made me worse than him.

And I wasn't going to live with that.

I slept in the car, then rang Jemimah early next morning, did my best to explain that I needed some time away. It was one of the hardest calls of my life. She was confused, upset, and I had no answers to give. Not then, anyway.

And so began seven weeks living as a fugitive – these last seven weeks, as I've been attempting to put the whole dread business down on paper.

I found myself a bedsit, less than a mile from the sea. The room stinks of old tobacco, but it's too cold to open any windows. I write most days, only ever leaving to buy another pad, more provisions. And yes – the occasional bottle of malt, there seems little point in denying myself its anaesthetic benefits now.

Something drives me on – perhaps it's Nick Moira and my last glimpse of him as I promised to tell all regarding Rattigan's 'deal' with the ACC. I had no idea how paranoid the man really was, or how much of his tale to believe in, but certain things appeared to make sense. Rattigan had more or less admitted to brokering the deal to ensure an easier sentence. And that the name John Templar had certainly opened the cushier doors of Oakwood for him.

I still have the photocopied article entitled 'Hands of a Hero!' detailing Templar's manual heroics at the gas explosion. Strange, when I look at the grainy photograph of the blistered hands, to imagine the other, secret atrocities they were also involved in. For just as they dug one terrified family out from the ruins, they buried another one completely.

I have no idea if Nick Moira is really being watched lest he blow the whistle on what little he knew about John Templar. But it's obvious he believes he is, and that his life has been tragically wasted as a result of his beliefs. So who am I to quibble? Maybe Templar went on to become part of some secret order procuring children for their gratification. Perhaps Rattigan's court confession would have lit the touch paper that set about exposing a whole can of rotten worms, people with interests and positions too powerful to risk exposure. Who then had Nick Moira removed from his post and sectioned in a mental home.

Obviously, I can't try and track the ex-policeman down again as I'm now wanted for murder myself. I'll never know the answers, and in that respect maybe Neil Allen was right – however hard we look, we'll never ever really know any of anyone's business.

Each night I lie awake wondering how much closer the police have got to me, how much longer I can survive like this. I'm trying as best as I can to vary any ATM transactions, but it wouldn't take them long to discover what area I'm in, then begin closing the net.

And I know I'd never last in prison. Don't have the 'face' for it – Rattigan told me as much. Sometimes I wonder what he'd make of me now, his pet fat-boy, a killer on the run. I'm sure he'd smile one more time for me if he knew.

I've written three times to Jemimah, trying to reassure her, desperate she doesn't have me listed as a missing person. I doubt it would take the authorities too long to put the pieces together, compare dates of my trip to Manchester, trace postmarks, interview landlords in the area . . .

God knows how many times I've begun the journey back to Chelmsford, desperate to park opposite the kids' schools, just for a glimpse of them. But I always come to in time, turn back. I have to finish this first – and thank Christ it's nearly done.

I've thought long and hard about the next step, and think it's for the best. I don't see how Jemimah and the kids would cope any other way. For Christmas this year, I'll be giving them all something that's long overdue.

A fresh start.

I conclude by saying that I am deeply sorry and ashamed for what I've done. I can only hope that this journal may provide a few answers to those who seek them, an explanation to my dear and beloved family, and a warning to those foolish enough to follow in my footsteps.

My need to understand brought me no power, no joy, no knowledge. Except that finally, we must all answer to our own gods – and beasts – as they sit in judgement upon our lives.

There – it's over.

It's time to make the leap.

AFTERWORD

The preceding manuscript was posted to me on the 23rd of December, 1997, from a post office in Frinton, Essex.

It isn't unusual in my line of work to be sent long and detailed documents which may contain items of potentially newsworthy interest; however, to receive one of this length was completely exceptional.

Intrigued, I sat down to read it on Boxing Day evening, finishing in the small hours of the next day. I was stunned and horrified in equal measure, well remembering the worried, starkly ashen-faced man who had given me such a runaround one October Thursday just ten weeks previously.

My first thoughts were to contact the university records office for Adrian's address. I was desperately worried for him. However, I had to wait until after the New Year before tracing and speaking to Jemimah at the Broomfield Road address.

The family was in mourning. Adrian's body had been discovered on the 29th of December, 1997, in the bedsit where he compiled the journal. A verdict of suicide caused by a lethal cocktail of alcohol and barbituates was recorded by the coroner's office.

Understandably, the whole family was quite shattered by grief, but I felt it was my duty to pass the manuscript on to Jemimah, certain it was what Adrian would have wanted. With her eventual permission, I began the process of verifying claims made within the journal.

I began by collecting, then examining, all of Adrian's notes and address books taken from the Frinton bedsit by Essex Police. There were tapes too, of the six sessions with Rattigan transcribed in the manuscript. However, despite repeated attempts to locate the tape purportedly made at the Hortons' house it has never come to light.

Next I contacted the lesser players in the drama, and can confirm that Mrs Bhaku at the ILEA, Mr Eric Saunders, retired headmaster, and Martin Bellamy – solicitor originally representing Rattigan at his Old Bailey trial – all remembered Adrian's meetings with them. When shown sections of the journal concerning their involvement, each agreed that the truth had been correctly set down, conversations recorded more or less exactly as they'd happened. As, indeed, did I.

It's a strange feeling to read another's impression of oneself as I had done. But I'm forced to admit Adrian got it just about right with me, too.

However, others seemed less keen to speak to me. I put through a total of nine calls to 'DI Russell' at Essex Police Headquarters, telling the switchboard operator the precise nature of my enquiry. To this day, I've never received any communication from him, either written or verbal. I'll keep on trying.

Next I began researches into John Templar. Once again, it's all as Adrian described it. There is an opulent suite named after him in Mile End Council offices. A portrait, too, in the grand chamber, a man resplendent in police dress uniform, hands on his lap holding ironed white gloves. It was particularly difficult to reconcile the painted lap with Jimmy Smack's tale of what had also happened there.

I was told by council officials that Templar was indeed a genuine hero who'd won the hearts of his local community. He'd had many friends, raised thousands for charity and was also a prominent Mason. Nobody seemed to have a bad word to say about him.

Except, it seemed, Jimmy Smack.

I made finding him a priority. Indeed, without the transcribed micro-tape detailing allegations made against Templar, it became vital that I talk to Jimmy and the Hortons.

They'd vanished. Both the house in Wilmslow and Richard Horton's small electronics business are currently up for sale, with estate agents refusing to divulge the vendor's current whereabouts.

The trail grew progressively colder. Attempts to locate the man described as Nick Moira proved equally frustrating. While Metropolitan Police confirm an officer of the same name was in their employ during the Rattigan investigation, he left the force a short time afterwards suffering from a stress-related illness. The Met told me they had no idea where he currently resided.

Next, I contacted the executive at Oakwood asking to see Dr Allen and even Rattigan himself. Both meetings were denied. But in response to a letter detailing certain questions arising from the journal, regarding the unsuitability of improperly structured student training programmes – and the potentially dangerous and tragic circumstances arising from them – Dr Allen did reply in March, 1998.

The letter expressed remorse on behalf of the hospital for Adrian's death, but then went on:

'However, as I haven't seen a copy of the journal you refer to, I can only stress that this hospital has for the last seven years enjoyed a close relationship with both staff and postgraduate students at Essex University. It would be both negligent and complacent to suggest that Adrian's dealings with his subject were in any way exceptional – or could have had some bearing upon his untimely demise.

'As an established journalist, I hope you appreciate that such dangerous and ill-informed speculation could result in the future suspension of training programmes such as ours, with the result that trainees are denied access to valuable work experience.

'To answer another of your questions – any mention Adrian may have made about a similar instance regarding the suicide of another female student during training at another institution is, to my knowledge, completely untrue. I know of no such case.

'However, our own internal Home Office enquiry into this sad and tragic affair did reveal that perhaps Adrian Rawlings's own mental state needed more careful analysis before we accepted him on to our student training programme. But to state so publicly would be unwise in the current climate.'

Investigations at the Home Office proved just as frustrating, bringing denials of any future plans for the review of any operations carried out in high security mental institutions.

To this day, Jemimah feels terrible guilt for letting her husband slip away so easily. But as she tearfully explained, she agreed to his telephone requests for space, because he always ended by swearing to her that, 'It'll all be sorted out for the best at Christmas.'

She trusted in him, but now hates herself for doing so.

After much deliberation, we decided to contact Manchester CID regarding Adrian's alleged murder of prostitute Simone Andrews. It was an extraordinarily courageous gesture by a woman still in mourning.

I'd followed what small developments there'd been, mostly reported in the *Manchester Evening News*. The case was still unsolved, despite the public appeal for information regarding a man who matched Adrian's description.

Police had established from witnesses at the Babylonia basement nightclub on Booth Street, Manchester, that Simone did indeed leave the club with a white, middle-aged man who was clearly thought to be much the worse for wear from drink. Simone reportedly even had to lead her drunken partner outside, much to the amusement of other witnesses. It was the last sighting of the well-known local prostitute.

Friends went to look for her after twenty or thirty minutes, but found no trace of either Simone or the man. They assumed she'd made another arrangement with him, perhaps gone back to a hotel. The door from the cindered back yard to the street was left slightly open. Police were later to discover that the padlock had been forced, a clue perhaps as to how Adrian left the courtyard without going back through the club.

It is a measure of Jemimah's strength as a woman that she allowed her dead husband to be considered as chief suspect. When witnesses were shown photographs of Adrian, they confirmed he was the man Simone had taken outside.

However, without key witnesses to the attack itself, Greater Manchester Police have been forced to label the murder as still 'Unsolved', regardless of Adrian's confession.

And there the trail ends. Too many of the key players are

either dead or unwilling to talk. Make what you will of the latters' silence, but for me the major question has to be the whereabouts of the tape Adrian made of the final damning conversation held in the Hortons' house that Thursday afternoon. Without it, I am unable to verify any of Elaine and Jimmy's past involvement with John Templar, or the precise details of the alleged drug deal which led to the murder of Helen Lewis.

We simply have to take Adrian's final written words for that – and as a man who was honest enough to admit to casual murder himself, I know who I believe.

Jemimah Rawlings has since moved from Chelmsford to start a new life elsewhere. We've become friends, and sometimes when I'm working nearby, I'll drop in and see the family. Occasionally, when the children are in bed, and we settle down to chat over another bottle of wine, she'll wander over to the music centre and put on a C D. A misty look will cloud her eyes.

It's always Aretha Franklin.

Karen Allison.
May, 1998.